A SEASON IN THE WEST

Also by
Piers Paul Read

Novels

GAME IN HEAVEN WITH TUSSY MARX
THE JUNKERS
MONK DAWSON
THE PROFESSOR'S DAUGHTER
THE UPSTART
POLONAISE
A MARRIED MAN
THE VILLA GOLITSYN
THE FREE FRENCHMAN

Nonfiction

ALIVE: THE STORY OF THE ANDES SURVIVORS
THE TRAIN ROBBERS

A Season in the West

Piers Paul Read

Random House   New York

All rights reserved under International and Pan-American Copy-
right Conventions. Published in the United States by Random
House, Inc., New York. Originally published in England by Martin
Secker & Warburg Limited in 1988.

Library of Congress Cataloging-in-Publication Data
Read, Piers Paul
   A season in the west.
   I. Title.
PR6068.E25S43 1988   823′.914   88-29682
ISBN 0-394-57530-X

Manufactured in the United States of America

First American Edition

A SEASON IN THE WEST

ONE

The news that Josef Birek had escaped from Czechoslovakia reached London at the end of April. He had walked into Austria from Jugoslavia but once in Vienna had asked to go to England. His British admirers went to work at once to make the necessary arrangements. They were all exhilarated to know that he was free – particularly Laura Morton, who had first translated his work.

Laura was one of those lovely fresh-faced English women who are still to be seen among the Arabs and Iranians in Kensington and Knightsbridge, popping into Harrods or Peter Jones or picking up their children from private nursery schools. Her husband, Francis, worked in the City as the husbands of such women often do, but her headscarf and tweed skirt suggested that her heart was really in the country.

Yet there was more to Laura Morton than this conventional appearance suggested. The very fact that she spoke Czech and had a degree in Slavonic studies shows how tradition and eccentricity are sometimes mixed together in English county families. Her father, Sir John Brook, had been a celebrated explorer who had financed his own expeditions to Borneo, Patagonia and Sinkiang. Such far-away places are familiar now – one has only to buy a ticket to get to them – but the stories of his journeys which were published to great acclaim had led Laura to admire him even more than a daughter usually admires her Papa. When she was ten years old her father had promised, in an offhand manner, that one day he would take her to China on the trans-Siberian express. 'But you'll have to learn Russian, old girl, because I'll count on you to order the tea.'

At the genteel boarding-school where Laura was sent for her education no one could teach Russian but the art teacher was a Czech painter who had fled from Prague in 1948 when the Communists came to power. He was persuaded to give Laura lessons in his language, and knowing something so unusual had won her a place at Oxford. There she had pursued Slavonic studies, and had even learnt some Russian – enough, certainly, to order tea on the trans-Siberian railway – but she never went to China with her father because he died before she took her degree.

When she left Oxford she married Francis Morton and it was not until her two older children were at boarding-school that Laura found her life empty and looked for something to do. It was her husband, Francis, who reminded her of her knowledge of Czech, which, although it had grown rusty over the years, was still there and could be polished up if anyone could make use of it. Originally he had been reluctant to see his wife take a job but he changed his mind, and so offered her services to the Comenius Foundation, where he was Chairman of the Trustees.

The Comenius Foundation had been created in 1968 to help those who had fled from Czechoslovakia after the Russian invasion. Later it had extended its work to help the dissidents who stayed behind. It was financed by voluntary donations – either from individuals or corporations like Louards, Francis's merchant bank – and much of the money went on a magazine called *Outrage* which published the works of dissident writers in English translation. This was not just an artistic enterprise: it had been established over and over again that the better known a writer was in the West, the less likely he was to be harassed and persecuted behind the Iron Curtain. To establish the reputation of a young writer like Birek was the best way to protect him in his own country.

A second function of the Foundation was to help those dissidents who managed to escape to the West. There were not only complicated formalities to be gone through to get a visa with the right of abode; there were also difficult adjustments to be made to life in a free society. After growing up in a socialist system, most were unprepared for the rigours of a market economy. It was often difficult to find ways for them to earn their living. Many spoke only Czech, and even those who spoke English sometimes discovered that their academic or technical qualifications were not recognized in Britain and so could not find work to match their talents.

At first there had been some resistance to giving Laura Morton a job at the Foundation. A bored banker's wife, it was thought, could not have the dedication or the discretion required. But not only was her husband Chairman of the Trustees, he was also a friend of the director. Laura was therefore taken on as a translator at the Foundation's offices in Bayswater; and once the doubters had met her, all their objections disappeared because she was not only modest but attractive, and she got down most cheerfully to the menial chores of copy-editing manuscripts or correcting proofs.

The real surprise came, however, when she turned in her first translation of a samizdat story which had been smuggled out of Czechoslovakia. The story itself was not outstanding, but she had rendered it in a sturdy prose which suited its style and made a change from the somewhat erratic English of the émigré Czechs who usually did the translation. Clearly she had worked hard on it and she continued to work hard on anything she was given, sitting at her desk and chewing her pen while several of her colleagues wasted their time bickering, intriguing and making cups of coffee.

Someone once said, rather cynically, that if the work she translated had not been by dissidents it would not have been published at all. In their more honest moments, most of those who supported the Comenius Foundation would have acknowledged that the quality of the stories and the essays in *Outrage* was not exceptional, and that few could be expected to read them for pleasure alone. That did not diminish their confidence in their cause, because the official writing was no better, but it did mean that *Outrage* had a modest circulation, and that few of those who bought it actually read the material it contained.

Only Laura read every issue with a grave concentration, not just because she felt that she should, but because it opened her eyes to a world quite different to the one she had known until then. If she had read much before she might not have been so struck by, say, Kutchek's novella *Winter*; but a love of literature was considered suspect in her social set so until she came to work for the Foundation she had read nothing more demanding than the novels of

9

John Le Carré and the occasional winner of the Booker Prize. By translating, however, she was forced to enter the detailed working of each author's mind; and slowly all she had learned while she had been studying for her degree about fictional form, or the rhythms of the Slav languages, came back to her; and she would let drop remarks like 'Clearly influenced by Čapek' or 'So many of these younger writers try to imitate Kundera'.

Her confidence grew with her experience, and by the time she had worked for the Comenius Foundation for eighteen months the director, Andrew MacDonald, who was also the editor of *Outrage*, came to trust her to select some of the work that he published. Whenever a new batch of samizdat writing arrived in the office, she shared with Miroslav Maier the task of deciding what was good and what was bad. Invariably she went out of her way to see something in everything because there was a poignancy about the physical appearance of these underground publications – the elaborate binding of the carbon copies of typescripts – which undermined her critical judgement. When every little office in England had a photocopying machine, the Czechs could make only four or five copies at a time, and for an edition of a hundred they had to type out a novel twenty-five times.

Perhaps for this reason many of the manuscripts were not long. The first work of Josef Birek, for example, was only five pages – a little story of great elegance and innocence about an adolescent boy who comes to realize that his mother has a lover. This Laura translated together with a poem by Birek about snowflakes which came from a collection of poets from Prague in the next bunch or samizdat publications.

It cannot be said that Laura discovered Birek – he was first published by an émigré journal in Munich – but she was the first to translate him into English, initially in *Outrage*, then in an anthology of Czech stories which was published in London by the Harvill Press. She also wrote an article about Birek which was published in *Encounter* and so was considered, among the English at any rate, the greatest authority on his work.

She heard the news of his defection from Miroslav Maier, a colleague at the Foundation – an émigré from '68 who was in awe of

Laura Morton because she was rich and beautiful and he was poor and seedy. In the office he was obsequious; in his fantasy he was bold, and behind his drooping eyelids he subjected the modest Englishwoman to all the erotic indignities that his Slav imagination could devise.

On that cold damp evening in April it was Maier who was telephoned from Vienna and told in Czech that Birek was free and wanted to come to England. Laura, in the same overheated room, could only half hear and half understand what was said. She picked up the name 'Birek' but assumed that Maier was discussing a new work. It was past five: she could not finish the work she was doing that day. She looked out of the window into Pembridge Square, saw that it was raining and wished that she had brought her car, which she did from time to time, even though she lived close by.

These thoughts ran through her mind as she saw Maier look at her while he was jabbering in Czech, and finally, when he put down the telephone, say to her in English: 'Did you gather what they were saying?'

'No.'

'Birek is in Vienna.'

Her face flushed with surprise. 'You mean he is free?'

'As a bird.'

'How?'

Maier shrugged his shoulders and told all he knew – that Birek had been allowed to go to Jugoslavia and had merely strolled across the border into Austria. 'He wants to come to England,' he said as he crossed towards the door to tell the others. 'Apparently he speaks excellent English.'

Laura should have gone with him: she would have to know, after all, what preparations would have to be made for his arrival in England; but the news that he was coming had somehow disturbed her as if she had been told that the hero of a favourite novel was coming to lunch the next day. With Birek safely and heroically behind the Iron Curtain, and with his real identity veiled by his various attractive heroes, she had allowed herself to imagine what he might be like, and in her fantasy go beyond strict curiosity into one or two little imaginary encounters which contrasted in their innocence with the depraved daydreams of her colleague Miroslav

11

Maier, but which embarrassed her all the same because she was a married woman and Birek was almost certainly at least ten years younger than she was.

It was true that she did not look as old as thirty-nine. Few who met her for the first time could believe that she had a son of seventeen at Eton and a daughter of fifteen at North Foreland Lodge as well as a younger child at home. Her figure remained slim, and her face almost free from lines and wrinkles.

How did she do it? The old vicar of Risley, where the Mortons had their country home, put it down to her innocence. Certainly those wide ingenuous eyes went with her girlish figure; but what the vicar did not know was that Laura's blonde hair was streaked every month by an amusing Italian called Paolo; or that twice a week Laura went to see a Mr Bruce who had a private gymnasium off Kensington High Street where actresses and models went to keep their figures trim. Nor could he have imagined the many different lotions and unctions which crowded together on Laura's dressing-table – Japanese washing grains, oatmeal moisturizing cream, eye-lid lotion, neck-gel, and so on.

A more cynical admirer, Charlie Eldon, ascribed her youthfulness to her immaturity. Her best friend, Madge, thought that it came from having so many servants to do the drudgery while Madge's husband Ben put it down to the two weeks' skiing at the beginning of March when everyone in London had given up hope that the sun would ever shine again. Yet these advantages which came to Laura as the wife of a merchant banker did not exclude those moral qualities recognized by the vicar of Risley. Laura was pretty but she was not vain. Her care of her body was methodical rather than conceited, as if the prudence and thrift of her banking husband which led him to take care of their houses in London and Wiltshire had influenced her to preserve her body as an asset without ever intending to cash it in. She never consciously considered that she preserved her attractiveness to attract a member of the opposite sex: it was more to earn the esteem of other women.

The news of Birek's defection, carried by Miroslav Maier into the different rooms of the rambling flat which served as the offices of the Comenius Foundation, caused a flurry among the five or six East Europeans and English slavophiles who happened to be there that evening, and at once further calls were made to Vienna, Munich, the *Daily Telegraph* and the Home Office, all to ensure that the news was true, and that if it was it should receive some attention: for while the Foundation was modest, almost anonymous, about its own activities it was not without ideological passions; and it was always good if the public was reminded that even in the era of *glasnost* and détente there was no freedom of expression in the socialist states of the Soviet Empire.

All that, however, had nothing to do with Laura, and since it was now almost six she slipped out and walked home on the wet pavement of the quieter streets behind Notting Hill Gate. She liked to be home in time to read a story to her six-year-old daughter Lucy before she went to bed; and on this occasion, as she closed the door of the house and propped her umbrella against the wall so that its drips would fall on the doormat, she could hear from the splashes and squeals that came down the stairwell into the large hall that Lucy was still in the bath. She put down her leather briefcase, hung up her coat, and went up to watch the pink little body of her youngest child in the final stages of its ablutions.

The nanny, Gail, sat squarely on a chair by the bath with a towel on her knee. She was a heavy, spotty girl from Burnley in Lancashire who felt as little affection for Laura as Laura felt for her. When Laura appeared at the door she greeted her in only a most cursory way and Lucy too, who resented her mother's absence at work during the week, hardly smiled when she saw her but continued the game she was playing with an empty bubble-bath bottle. When Gail, who had plans to go up to a wine bar in Covent Garden that evening with the neighbour's nanny Tracy, told Lucy to give up her game and got her out of the bath onto her knee, Laura retreated from the nursery bathroom and went down the stairs again to her own room.

There she took off her shoes and lay back on her bed to read the *Evening Standard* until Lucy, with brushed hair, brushed teeth and wearing a dressing-gown, came to demand her bed-time story. Gail had by now gone to her room to smarten up for her night out, and for the last moment of her daughter's day Laura herself was in charge. She read her a Babar book, kissed her good night and turned off the light; then retreated once again to her own quarters to take a bath.

The toes of her tights were still damp and cold from the walk on the wet pavement but in the tub, with the scalding water up to her chin, her body became as pink as her face. Little globules of scented oil floated on the surface. She sighed and looked up at the ceiling.

The bathroom around her was as handsome as the woman it served. The bath itself was a heavy old cast-iron tub with lion's claw feet and beautiful, neo-Victorian taps. On the wall there were five bright prints in the style of Matisse by a friend – a woman – who held exhibitions in a little local gallery. The bath and the basin were surrounded by pretty blue Provençal tiles; and there were two elegant bowls to hold the toothpaste, pincers, dental floss, nail brushes, razor blades, Alka-Seltzer, mascara and all those other things which accumulate in a bathroom.

This bathroom was next to her bedroom, so when she now heard a door open Laura knew that her husband had returned. She heard his footsteps cross the bedroom as he went to put his briefcase next to his chest-of-drawers; she heard the bed springs squeak as he sat down to change his shoes for a pair of shabby moccasins; then the floorboards creak as he crossed to the wardrobe to hang up his jacket and thread his tie into a piece of curtain-wire nailed to the inside of the wardrobe door. A few more creaks – he was back at his chest-of-drawers to take out a jumper which he now put on. All these movements she could not see but she knew were taking place because the creaks and the pauses confirmed her husband's unchanging routine.

In a moment, as she expected, the door to the bathroom opened and Francis Morton came in – directing, as usual, the kind of cursory glance at his wife's poached nudity that is normal after eighteen years of marriage.

'So . . .' he said, as he always did, sitting down on her towel on the chair beside the bath.

'So,' she repeated, as she always did, and she sighed, because even though those habits of his like putting on a jersey when he was just about to take a bath still irritated her she could no longer be bothered to show it.

Francis Morton was now forty-five but he looked a good ten years older than his wife. This was partly from exhaustion, partly from an affected *gravitas* which he used to keep others at a distance.

He was still considered handsome and had once been thought funny but as he had grown older his humour had become increasingly wry until finally it had disappeared altogether. To look at now, with his thinning hair, stooping figure and a stomach which spilled over his belt, he looked so much like a man who works in the City that no one could think that he could ever have been anything other than one of those old-fashioned buffers who had got his job through family connections.

This impression was false. He had once been lean and ambitious, winning a scholarship from Eton to Balliol and then a first-class degree in Philosophy, Politics and Economics. His father had been a barrister who specialized in libel and Francis too had read for the Bar, meaning to pass from the law into politics and do some good for the human race. All this he had abandoned when he had married because the money Laura brought as a dowry had made him feel that he must make more or be labelled, in his own mind, as a man who lived off his wife. He had therefore gone into banking, growing over the years into the role he had chosen so that now, as Laura rose to get out of the bath, he stood and held out her towel with the languid gesture of a bored patrician.

There had been a time when he would have stepped into the same water, but now he loathed the slimy feel of the scented oil which Laura had added for the sake of her skin. Thus while she sat wrapped in the towel on the chair he had vacated he pulled up the plug to let the water out of the bath. He went back into the bedroom to remove, along with his other clothes, the jersey he had just put on, then returned to the bathroom, ran a new bath, and immersed himself in the clean water.

'Who's baby-sitting?' he asked Laura.

'The Atkins' *au pair.*'

'What time is she coming?'

'The usual sort of time.'

He sighed and she frowned because she knew what that sigh signified. The couple who had asked them out were more her friends than his and they moved in a circle which thought it bourgeois to dine before half-past nine. Francis, who at one time had been amused by the company of journalists and writers, now returned from work hungry and tired. The idea that he could not eat for another two or three hours, and that he would have to make conversation until midnight, led him into a mood of despair which could only be dispelled by a glass of whisky.

It was one of Laura's unspoken – indeed unacknowledged – complaints against her husband that the sociable man she had married had become a recluse – or, if not a recluse, someone who no longer enjoyed dining out or going to those crowded, noisy parties where you sit with a plate balanced on your knee. He had lost any curiosity about meeting new people, seeing new plays or going to the latest film that Hollywood had to offer. He liked to spend his evenings watching television. Only an early supper with old friends who served good wine could take him out of his house again with any enthusiasm.

He conformed, all the same, to social convention – entertaining and being entertained at the kind of candle-lit dinner party which takes place behind the shutters and curtains in the Georgian and Victorian houses of the West End of London. He kept all the engagements that were made by Laura on his behalf, and since it was down in her diary that they were to dine that night with those friends who ate late, he knew that he had time to linger in his bath. When the water began to get cold, he got out and, swathed in a towel, went into his bedroom. He switched on the portable television which stood on a chest-of-drawers and then lay down on the bed to watch the Channel Four news. Laura, too, dressed in a speckled blue and white skirt and a blue cashmere jersey, half sat on the bed and half watched the television as she filed her nails with an emery board.

This was unusual – she normally showed little interest in current affairs – and as if to justify what she was doing she said, casually, during an advertisement for paint: 'Did you hear that Birek is in Vienna?'

'Birek?'

'You know – the Czech writer, the one I translate.'

'Is he? In Vienna? Why?'

'He's defected.'

Francis did not take his eyes off the television. 'How did he get out?'

'By Jugoslavia.'

Francis nodded. The bulletin began again and they both watched and listened – Francis for the City news, Laura to see if Birek's defection would be mentioned. It was not. The news came to an end and Francis quickly switched off the television before the 'comment' which, when he saw it, usually put him in a rage.

Like most bankers, Francis Morton was a Conservative, but while most of his friends only looked to that party to further their material interests, Francis had inherited from his parents a zealous belief in Conservative ideals. Free enterprise, to him, was an extension of the free will given to man by his Creator; and the ideologies which opposed it, whether socialist or communist, were simply schemes by the envious for legalized theft.

It was no coincidence, to him, that Marxists were also atheists, and that the socialists in local government championed the cause of the sexually degenerate. To him God was on one side and the Devil on the other, and this clear equation of moral and political certainties was what led him to support the work of the Comenius Foundation. In conversation, too, he was always ready to challenge the socialistic assumptions of his more liberal friends, but as time passed he had come to realize that most of them did not want to discuss serious issues on social occasions. He therefore learned to hide his thoughts behind an affable smile and as a result, once it was established that he was not going to 'bore on about the Lefties', he became a popular guest at dinner parties – together, of course, with his pretty wife.

That night they had no further to go than Ladbroke Road – a ten-minute walk from the house – but since it was still wet, and Laura was wearing one of her best pairs of shoes, they drove there in the Mercedes. When they arrived their hostess was still cutting up aubergines for their supper. Francis drank more whisky to summon up the strength to talk to people to whom he felt he had nothing to say and when, eventually, they sat down to eat he found that his appetite had left him.

He was placed next to a woman to whom he had been talking for an hour already. They had already covered exercise, dieting and their children's education. Now she tried plays and novels but since Francis was not much of a consumer of culture they did not get far with that. They moved on by way of a documentary that her husband had made for the BBC to the question of unemployment. Here Francis was on surer ground and he rambled on for some time about the level of benefit in relation to the market value of unskilled labour. He could see that he was boring her but then she had bored him about her children. He drank more wine as if that would make him more amusing but it only made him drowsy and long to go back to his huge Heal's bed.

It was twenty to one before they got home: they had been the first of the guests to leave. While Francis paid off the baby-sitter, Laura went upstairs. She was still excited by the news about Birek which had made her the centre of attention at her end of the table. She tried to chat to Francis as she stood in the bathroom removing her mascara with cotton wool but Francis as soon as he was in his pyjamas climbed into bed and fell asleep.

TWO

The next morning, at the Comenius Foundation, plans were made for Birek's reception. Contacts in the Home Office let it be known that a visa would be issued without difficulty, and a sympathetic hearing given to his application for political asylum. A room was reserved in a modest hotel quite close to the Foundation's offices in Pembridge Square and a guest list drawn up for the party that would be given to greet him.

At first this was to be held in the offices of the Foundation, where other receptions of this kind had been given, with journalists and émigrés draining hired glasses of tepid white wine. On this occasion, however, Laura Morton diffidently suggested that the party should be held at her house on Lansdowne Square – and since even those at the Foundation who had not seen it knew that it was extremely grand, they all agreed at once that it would be more welcoming for Birek to be greeted in someone's home.

When Laura and Francis had first married, they had lived in a small house in Chelsea, bought largely with the money Laura had inherited from her father. The birth of her second child, however, made that house too small and they began to look for a larger one. Francis, who had read an article by an actuary which said that every time you move house you lose a year of your life, was determined to buy something large enough not just for a second child but possibly a third as well, and with the space and facilities to entertain in the style that would be appropriate should he ever rise to become Chairman of Louards Bank.

First of all they had to decide upon an area, because London in the early 1970s was in a state of flux when the traditional territories of the English upper classes had been colonized by Arabs, diplomats and rich Americans. As a result it was no longer possible, and therefore no longer fashionable, to live in Mayfair or Belgravia, and even Knightsbridge and South Kensington were thought by some to be too foreign.

Pushed out by the tribes of prosperous immigrants, the indigenous English middle classes had moved north to Islington or west to Hammersmith, displacing in their turn the tribes of poor immigrants – the Irish, Africans, Asians and West Indians – who in turn moved further west like the Goths before the Huns.

Francis and Laura Morton did not see themselves at that time as members of a migratory tribe, or part of a social phenomenon. They wanted to move to a pleasant house in an agreeable part of London from which Francis could travel conveniently to the City on a week-day and Laura equally conveniently leave London on a Friday evening to visit her mother in Wiltshire.

All this pointed to that part of London which some call Notting Hill and others Holland Park according to whether one wants to claim the slightly raffish and Bohemian connotation of the former, or the plummy, respectable and leafy association of the latter. Francis had said to Laura: 'Why not look in Holland Park?' whereas Laura had said to her friend Madge: 'We're looking in Notting Hill.'

Houses in that part of London were already expensive but

happily the Mortons had plenty of money. First of all their house in Chelsea could be sold for a good sum: then Laura had been told by her trustees that thanks to their skilful investments (by which they meant the general rise in the value of stocks and shares) she could count on them for sixty or seventy thousand pounds. Over and above that, Francis was by then so highly prized by Louards that he could raise a mortgage of any sum he chose at a nominal rate of interest.

There were, near Holland Park, some particularly pleasant semi-detached houses built in the middle of the nineteenth century which were large, secluded and had gardens which opened out onto communal gardens – small private parks reserved for those who lived in the houses which enclosed them. Francis decided that one of these must be his but none was for sale. He therefore noted the addresses of the most choice, found the names of their owners from the electoral register, and wrote to each from his office at Louards offering to buy the freehold.

Some were not answered; others were, with abuse; but three received courteous replies from owners who appeared astonished that their houses were worth so much money. A widow in particular had thought herself shackled to a large, run-down house on Lansdowne Square. She had always dreamed of moving to a bungalow in Bristol, and now she saw her chance. She invited the Mortons to look her house over, and once they had seen it allowed them to send a surveyor. His report suggested a reduced offer but that still seemed a huge sum to the widow. She accepted. Contracts were exchanged, and three months later the Mortons took possession.

The year which followed had been a turmoil of architects, builders and ingratiating tradesmen. Laura, who was not even thirty at the time, was at first a little embarrassed that they had taken on such an imposing residence: she was afraid that some of her friends might think it pretentious, and it was only when it became clear that it inspired envy, not derision, that she began to enjoy doing it up.

Here, however, she faced an awkward dilemma. Could she trust her own taste? When they had bought the little house in Chelsea they had chosen everything themselves – the wallpaper, the curtains, the doorknobs. She had even sewn some cushion covers and Francis had papered three of the bedrooms.

How long ago that seemed now, when Francis was too busy at Louards to give anything but the most cursory commands and Laura too preoccupied with her baby to concentrate on colour schemes and matching fabrics. Moreover the house was so grand, and the rooms so imposing, that any mistake she made would be glaring; yet she so well remembered the scorn of some of her friends for those who hired professionals to decorate their homes. Her friend Madge, in particular, always said that it was a confession of no taste or imagination.

Madge had been a fellow student at Oxford, and although their lives had taken different directions since their graduation, they continued to be friends in later life. Indeed it was because Madge was almost her opposite – the other side of the coin, as it were, to the landed Brooks and the banking Mortons – that her friendship was so important to Laura. Madge was an intellectual – that is to say she lectured on English Literature at the South Thames Polytechnic – and her husband Ben was a journalist who worked for the BBC. They both read the *Guardian* and always voted Labour – even at the election during the miners' strike: it was to Madge that Laura had said that the new house was in Notting Hill.

From fear of Madge Laura began the dreary business of going off to Peter Jones to look at snippets and samples for wallpaper, pelmets and loose covers. Then she heard from another friend that there was a woman who, since her divorce, had done some decorating on the side. In terror lest Madge should somehow be listening in on a crossed line, she rang this Eva Burroughs and the two met for lunch. Eva was enormously friendly and helpful: she longed to see the house in Lansdowne Square, and when she did, after lunch, she was full of enthusiasm and bright ideas. 'Oh this must be a dazzling yellow,' she said of the hall; 'and this, what? A misty red, like underdone beef?'

'Oh would you help me?' asked Laura.

'Of course,' said Eva. 'It's how I make my living now.'

The slightly steely look in Eva's eye which went with this remark led Laura to clear her throat and say: 'Of course, your fee . . .'

'Oh, no fee, dear. I simply get everything at trade and charge you full price. You don't have to pay me a thing.'

Which was a wonderful solution because it meant that when Madge heard about Eva and asked Laura: 'But you don't *pay* her, do you?' Laura could answer with the truth, not a lie. 'Pay her? No, of course not. She's just giving me a hand.'

Whether the percentage incited Eva Burroughs, or whether she had naturally grandiose tastes, the result of her advice was a sumptuousness and an expense which was not quite what Laura had had in mind. Francis, however, always went for the grand solution. For example, he sided with Eva on the question of a dining-room. Laura had wanted to have an open-plan kitchen and dining-room on the ground floor, with french windows leading to steps down into the garden. The basement could be converted into a separate flat. Eva, however, insisted that the fashion for entertaining in one's kitchen had passed; that a man in Francis's position – or in the position he would one day hold – should have a separate dining-room in which to entertain important customers of the bank.

Francis was persuaded and voted with Eva, and Laura went along without making too much fuss. Secretly she liked the idea of perhaps, on occasions, getting someone in to help with the cooking. Her objection to a dining-room came chiefly from her fear of Madge. She dreaded her saying: 'You don't mean that you're hiring a cook!' and indeed when Madge did see the architect's drawings showing a drawing-room and a library on the ground floor, with a kitchen and a dining-room below, she put on a phoney, hoity-toity voice and said: 'Oh, I see. A drawing-room! And a library! How *very* grand!'

Laura had blushed scarlet, and could think of nothing to say; but it is curious how quickly scorn melts beneath the warmth of candelabra, and how even Madge, when she first came to dinner with the Mortons in Lansdowne Square, wore a long dress from Laura Ashley – a shop which had tactfully grown grander as its clientèle had become middle-aged.

For a large party of the sort Laura envisaged to welcome Josef Birek, Laura would open up the double-doors between the drawing-room and the library to create one huge room running from the front to the back of the house. In the library she would place three or four card tables with gold chairs and white table-cloths. Two maids and a butler could be borrowed from Louards for the occasion. In this way she could seat sixteen people upstairs while downstairs in the dining-room, with every leaf in their table, she could seat sixteen more. Since she planned to invite fifty or sixty guests, clearly some would have to sit on the sofa or on the stairs with their plates balanced on their knees.

The budget from the Foundation for receptions of this kind was so meagre that they were never able to drink anything but the most mediocre white wine. Knowing how Francis loathed bad wine, and how ashamed he would be to serve it to anyone he knew, Laura cleverly invited some of his most fastidious friends and then left the whole question of drink to him: which meant, inevitably, a foray into his cellars for two or three cases of good champagne.

The food, of course, was her responsibility but here again there was a jolly girl, a freelance chef, who cooked the directors' lunches at Louards. She came up with some delightful ideas like glazed ham, plover's eggs and Chinese pastry parcels filled with prawns which raised the fare above the usual level of cold quiche and pasta salad.

Birek's flight from Vienna was expected at three in the afternoon, and despite all the preparations that had to be made at Lansdowne Square, Laura was able to join the small delegation from the Comenius Foundation which went out to Heathrow to meet him – Andrew MacDonald, the director, Miroslav Maier, the Czech émigré who worked in the same room as Laura, and Laura herself. MacDonald held in his hand a copy of *Outrage* in which one of Birek's stories had been published: it was not known whether Birek had ever seen a copy of the magazine, but his name was prominent on the cover so it seemed a sensible way to help him recognize his hosts.

Passengers stumbled out of the customs hall as if it was the bottom of a helter-skelter – some bewildered after a long flight across half the world, others already alert for whatever business they had to do in London. Laura's heart sank a number of times as single men who might have been her Czech slipped out from behind the screen which veiled the territory of H.M. Customs and Excise. So many of them looked dull and decrepit, and she suddenly became alarmed that this young man whom she felt she knew well after translating so much of his work might turn out to be tedious or ugly. She found herself saying to herself, as she studied the arriving passengers, 'I hope that's not him', and dreading that the eye of some dumpy youth pushing his luggage on a trolley would light up with recognition as it fell upon *Outrage*.

Then she saw a young man with a round face hesitate in bewilderment, and she said out loud: 'That's him,' not as a hope or a guess but as a statement of fact.

MacDonald stepped forward to greet him. 'Mr Birek?' he asked in English, then added in Czech: 'We're from the Comenius Foundation.'

The young man looked surprised, and glanced furtively around him before replying, in a tentative tone: 'Mr MacDonald?'

Andrew MacDonald shook his hand. 'Welcome to Britain,' he said, and then Maier stepped forward to take a photograph of the two men shaking hands.

MacDonald introduced the others; then the party turned and walked towards the Terminal Two car park. 'You cannot imagine,' said Birek in slow but excellent English, 'how often I have dreamed of setting foot in England.'

'I am afraid that Heathrow Airport is not as moving as the white cliffs of Dover,' said MacDonald in his wry Scottish voice.

'All airports are the same,' said Maier.

'Oh no,' said Birek, 'here is freedom.' He filled his lungs with the air-conditioned air and said again: 'Here is freedom.'

MacDonald had taken Birek's modest suitcase and was swinging it as they walked along. Laura, walking a few paces behind the two men, noticed not just the tattiness of the suitcase but also the scruffiness of his clothes – khaki anorak, shabby jeans, grubby sneakers – and all at once the horrible thought came to her that perhaps he would have no suit for the reception that evening.

It was only when she was seated behind Birek in MacDonald's Ford Sierra that she forgot about Birek's clothes and noticed again the fine head which had made her so sure when she had first seen him that he was indeed the young dissident writer. From behind, of course, she could not see his eyes and nose but his ears were small and delicate, almost like those of a girl, and he had a slender neck which reminded Laura of her own seventeen-year-old son.

Of course Birek was older than Johnny Morton, but as he talked to MacDonald in the front of the car Laura could sense what she had described in her critical essay as 'the poetic certainty of his unabashed naïvety'. He was astonished by everything he saw from the black taxis to the red buses. The first pub drew a cry of excitement and led him to twist around as they passed. This gave Laura a chance to see his face – his straight nose, blue eyes and high Slav cheekbones.

'I would love to go to a pub,' he said.

'You shall,' said MacDonald.

'Tonight?' he asked.

'Why not,' said MacDonald.

Laura blushed.

'You've forgotten the party,' said Miroslav Maier.

'Of course.' MacDonald turned to Birek. 'We're giving a party this evening to welcome you to London.'

'Ah. That's very kind.'

'Laura, here, is having it in her house.'

Birek turned again and for the first time looked into Laura's eyes. 'In your home? A party?'

'Yes, that is, if you'd like to come.'

'Of course I'd like to come. To celebrate my freedom, yes?' And suddenly a wide cheerful smile came onto his face which because it was directed at her made Laura smile too.

They took him straight to his hotel, the Alwyn, which was in Inverness Terrace off the Bayswater Road and was the best that the Foundation felt it could afford. To Laura it was drab and dingy – modern, functional, anonymous – but she had learned to her horror how much it cost and she wished there was some way of conveying this to Birek so that he would not feel that he was getting shabby treatment.

She need not have worried. When Andrew, who accompanied him to his room, returned to the lobby he told them how delighted Birek had seemed to have a bath with a plug and a room with a colour television. 'I had to show him how to use the taps,' he said. 'They were the new-fangled sort with joy-stick controls.'

The officers of the Comenius Foundation now dispersed to meet again later that evening at Lansdowne Square. Laura rushed home to see how the preparations had progressed, and was reassured to see the jolly girl unloading the glazed hams and other dishes from a small green Honda van. The two ladies from Louards were also there, preparing the tables, and Laura could see that there was nothing for her to do. She therefore retreated to her bedroom and lay down on her bed to rest.

She thought about Birek – how young and vulnerable he had seemed. She already knew, of course, from his writing that he was a man of extraordinary innocence and sensitivity: she remembered one touching story about a boy who idolizes nature but then, when he lies in bed with a broken leg, watches a spider eat a fly it has caught in its web; and later, from the window, a cat pounces on a bird which has been singing in a tree.

The same confusion about the two faces of nature – the innocence and the cruelty – was found in the story about the boy who discovers that his mother has a lover, returning home unexpectedly from school to hear grunts of carnal pleasure from her room. He feels angry and his mother, when she comes from her room, looks ashamed: yet why should he feel angry? And why should she feel ashamed? The story did not resolve these questions: Birek's talent was to pose questions and leave them lingering in the reader's mind.

Laura wondered to herself, as she lay on her bed, to what extent Birek's stories were based on his own experience. If so, then his mother was clearly a considerable figure – vigorous, handsome, strong. No father ever appeared in his stories: no girl friends either. There was one story she remembered about a seventeen-year-old girl who persuades the son of a corrupt official in some provincial town in Slovakia to act as her pimp with his father. It ends as the boy realizes that perhaps he loves the girl, and that possibly she loves him, but that both are irretrievably corrupted by the black-market materialism of their Communist society. That was the closest any of his heroes ever came to a love affair of his own.

It was a story of this kind, of course, which made Birek un-publishable in Prague, but it was interesting that it implicitly criticized the corruption of the Marxist ideals, not necessarily the ideals themselves: and Laura wondered, as she rested, whether Birek was a socialist or not, and whether he had left a girl friend behind in Czechoslovakia; and what this strong mother of his had felt about his defection; and who his father was; and what friends he had left behind. She realized that she had a thousand things to ask him, and she wondered how long it would be before she could trespass upon those personal things which really interested her.

At five one of the ladies from Louards brought her a cup of tea on a tray with two slices of buttered toast and pot of jam. Laura was delighted because although she had a nanny, a daily and the girl who came and cooked on special occasions, she had no permanent servants to provide little luxuries of that kind. She therefore sat back once again on her bed, drinking her tea, eating her toast, and thinking now about the party.

The chief problem, she knew, would be mixing the guests – on the one hand the supporters of the Comenius Foundation and on the other those friends she had asked to add a little glamour. They were not from what the Czechs might call the intelligentsia and she was afraid that Birek might judge her by them. She sighed. In London one's friends in middle age are mostly people one has known for a long time and went on seeing from habit when the reason for liking them was long since forgotten. Most of the men would be Francis's friends from Eton and Oxford who now worked in the City; most of the women would be their wives. There would be a barrister and a journalist among them, but they hardly counted as intellectuals since the barrister specialized in company law and the journalist wrote only about financial affairs. Indeed among the Mortons' friends the term 'intellectual' was one of abuse – usually abbreviated to 'inty' and used to denigrate anyone who talked about anything other than wine, tennis, adultery or plans for the summer holidays.

Laura liked them because they amused her – joking in the jargon of their particular set. She also sensed that many of the men admired her, which is always good for a woman's morale. When she had started to work for the Foundation she had had to endure their teasing as a 'born again inty' and a 'dissident bore', and there were times when she regarded them all as insufferably superficial, but they were good-looking, well dressed and had the confidence to enjoy themselves at a party.

In contrast the guest-list of the Comenius Foundation contained the names of the same old Slavonic academics and literary cold-warriors who by studying Eastern Europe for so long seemed to have absorbed its drabness into their own appearance. They were stilted, seedy and dull – poorer, of course, than the Mortons' banking friends, and so dressed in dingy clothes, but not so poor that they could not afford to wash their hair before a party or put on a clean shirt.

Of course Birek, if he had come to the West with only the clothes on his back, and had not had the time or the money to acquire a wardrobe in Vienna, might feel more at ease with these dingy Slavophiles than with the bankers and their wives, but Laura did not imagine that Birek would remain for long in the anorak and jeans in which he had passed through Customs. He was too distinctive in appearance not to wear distinctive clothes, and involuntarily she began to dress him in an elegant Italian double-breasted suit or a jacket of blue corduroy.

At half-past five Lucy returned with Gail and after jumping up and down for a while on her mother's bed was taken up for a bath. Laura, annoyed at having been caught napping by the nanny, went down to see if everything was prepared; and found once again that the food, the flowers, the silver, the glass and the plates were all where they should be and the staff busy with the finishing touches. The champagne was on ice and the butler had arrived from Louards: he offered a glass to Laura but she declined it with a pretty smile, saying she would drink one later.

At six Madge rang to ask what time she was expected and to inquire, obliquely, what she should wear because Madge who was socially self-conscious would not want to be under-dressed among the Mortons' grand friends. Laura knew this quite well, but in her mind she had counted on Madge and Ben to form a bridge between the two groups – the snobbish City people and the gauche Slavophiles invited by the Foundation. She rather hoped that Ben might come in a blouson and Madge not in jeans but in one of her sensible skirts. She therefore said: 'Oh come around eight, or a little after', which was unusually early; and then added: 'It's not at all grand – just some people to meet this Czech writer'; but as she replaced the receiver she blushed because she saw all around her the vases of flowers, the white table-cloths and silver candlesticks, and realized that by Madge's standards the evening would be very grand indeed.

At seven Francis returned and went straight to the cellar to make sure that the butler had taken out the right wine. The two men talked for a while about the best method to serve it, and at what point in the evening to offer claret instead of champagne. It was an amicable, technical conversation: Francis seemed concerned only to get the right liquid down the right gullet. There was no sign that he anticipated any enjoyment from the evening which lay ahead.

They bathed; they changed – Francis into a dark suit, Laura into a silk dress by Cardin which Francis had bought for her when they were last in Paris. They came down the stairs, looking an embodiment of happiness and prosperity – a couple that would have done credit to any soap opera or television commercial.

Andrew MacDonald, who was the nominal host, arrived at eight. He was followed ten minutes later by the first guests – the representative from the Czech department of the British Council with his wife. After them came Miroslav Maier wearing a bow-tie, and tagging behind him the plain plump wife whom he had brought with him from Czechoslovakia in '68. One of the ladies from Louards let them in; the other took their coats, and the butler stood in the hall holding a tray upon which were glasses filled with champagne, orange juice, whisky and Perrier water.

Laura, Francis and Andrew MacDonald stood in the drawing-room to receive the guests as they came in; but it was apparent from the start that this first batch were overawed by the elegance of the occasion. It was not just the three servants in the hall, but also the beautiful eighteenth-century furniture, most of which Laura had inherited from her aunt (the sister of the explorer), who had in turn inherited it from her godmother who had lived in Paris at the turn of the century.

This furniture which had come fortuitously to the Mortons was now of great value, and gave the impression that they were even richer than they were. On top of this there were the pictures, some of which Laura had inherited, but others of which had been bought by Francis, who had a good eye for the Edwardian paintings which were just then coming into fashion. He had bought them cheaply in the 1970s but now, with the art market glutted by restless money, they too had gone up in value; and even those guests who were not familiar with the price fetched at recent sales in Christie's or Sotheby's could tell from the way they were hung that they were certainly not to be sneezed at: all of which added to their awe, and left them shifting from foot to foot and making awkward conversation.

Francis behaved like a robot which has been programmed to be hospitable – talking in an affable manner which, while it was in no way condescending, lacked sincerity. This artificiality exacerbated the awkwardness of these early guests, and irritated Laura, who saw through her husband's pose; but then she herself found it hard to take an interest in the man from the British Council, let alone his wife, and she began to feel that her party was doomed to be a fiasco. Two or three more couples – all guests of the Foundation – came filing in with dull clothes and dull faces, and stood awkwardly holding their glasses as if waiting for someone to make a speech.

Then Birek arrived, escorted by one of her colleagues from the Foundation, and Laura's spirits rose because all at once there was a focus to her party, and the whole thing seemed worth while. She immediately took charge of him and led him around the drawing-room, introducing him to the different guests, some of whom greeted him in Czech and some in English, but all of whom were visibly delighted not just because a writer had escaped to the West but because all that awkward waiting was over.

And Laura's spirits continued to rise because Birek, although he wore a horrible pale blue suit, showed an indifference to both his appearance and his surroundings which immediately made everyone else feel less self-conscious. His face and his voice expressed only enthusiasm and excitement, and he greeted his admirers with the panache of a prince.

At half-past eight Madge and Ben arrived – Madge in a sensible skirt and blouse. As they handed their coats to the lady from Louards another couple came in behind them – the first of the Mortons' smarter friends. Madge thought at first, with a certain smugness, that the wife was overdressed, but then as she entered the drawing-room and was greeted by Laura she saw that she was wearing her elegant Cardin dress. As they embraced Madge's eye looked over her shoulder and saw at once, with the genius of intuition, just how Laura had made use of her to put the drab guests at their ease. Worse still, now that it was fashionably late, the fashionable friends started to arrive behind her – loud, elegant and determined to have a good time despite the presence of all the dreary foreigners and pretentious intellectuals.

Here again it was Birek who saved the day because while most of these friends of the Mortons had no more interest in a Czech dissident than in a Buddhist schismatic, he was fascinated by them – questioning them about their lives with a wide-eyed interest as if he had just been admitted to a human zoo. He flattered the bankers and the stockbrokers by showing a particular interest in the City. 'In our socialist republic, you see,' he told a stockbroker called Chalmers, 'economic speculation is a crime.'

'Then I dare say, if I lived there, I wouldn't have a job.'

'You would certainly have a job because no one is allowed to be unemployed.'

'I'm not sure I'm qualified to do much else,' said Chalmers with a self-deprecating laugh.

'Everyone is qualified to shovel coal or sweep the streets,' said Birek. 'That is the kind of work some of my friends were obliged to do – though they were qualified as scientists, philosophers or critics.'

Chalmers blanched – which is to say that his usually ruddy face became merely pink – at the thought of such menial labour. 'It must be hell on earth,' he said.

'It is,' said Birek, 'but perhaps not in the way you imagine . . .'

'In what way, then?' asked Chalmers.

'No one who believes in the truth,' said Birek, 'minds suffering for the truth, and to labour with one's hands cannot compromise the spirit, whereas to teach or to write or to practise a profession demands a constant compromise with the truth – a constant bartering between one's conscience and the demands of the regime.'

They were eating at a table in the library, the candlelight falling on the white table-cloth and the silver forks and spoons.

'You mean you have to toe the Party line?'

'The Party line, precisely. But what is so debilitating, so *spiritually* debilitating, is that no one believes in the Party line, least of all those who are charged with enforcing it. At least in the past, at the time of the Inquisition for example, or in the early days of the Russian Revolution, those who imposed an ideology believed in it, but in Czechoslovakia, since 1968, no one believes in Marxism or Leninism, and so what they impose upon us is what they themselves know to be a lie.'

'Intolerable,' said Chalmers.

'And here?' asked Birek, his brow wrinkled with an expression of earnest curiosity. 'Here, is there an ideology of liberty, or no ideology at all?'

Chalmers looked baffled. 'I hadn't really thought,' he said, turning towards Laura for help.

'A bit of both,' she said.

Charlie Eldon, a financial journalist, who of the Mortons' friends was the least afraid of serious conversation, put down his fork and said: 'It is very much a bit of both, because we have Marxists, Leninists and Trotskyists who even have some political power, at a local level, and give us a taste of a totalitarian regime.'

'Yes, I have read about that in the *Economist*,' said Birek.

'You could read the *Economist* in Prague?' asked Eldon.

'In the British Council library, yes.'

'That is allowed?'

'They do not arrest you as you come out, but your name would be noted and if you had a position of any responsibility you would certainly lose it.'

'And where did you learn English?' asked Eva Burroughs, who was sitting at the same table.

'You know, for the first few years at school I learned Russian, and only Russian, but then, after 1968, my mother and my father divorced. I lived with my mother and she decided that I should learn English.'

'Did she teach you?'

'No. But there was, in the same block of flats, an old lady – the widow of a colonel in the Austro-Hungarian army – who had had an English governess as a child. She spoke excellent English, and it was she who taught me, every afternoon after school.'

Laura, remembering Birek's story 'The Lesson' about an old lady who gave piano lessons in a small flat surrounded with mementoes of a grander past, could suddenly visualize the stairs of the old block of flats where Birek must have lived as a child. 'She had a large clock, did she not,' she said to Birek with a smile, 'which would hardly fit on the mantel, and every time you went there you were afraid that it would fall and smash on the fender?'

Birek blushed and laughed. 'That's right.'

'And the carpet was rolled up at the edges because it was too large for the room?'

'Yes.'

'And in the kitchen there were still five or six old plates and saucers with the coat-of-arms of her dead husband?'

'Quite correct,' said Birek.

'Do you know this old woman?' asked Chalmers.

'I feel I know her,' said Laura.

'A writer has no secrets from his translator,' said Birek.

'On the contrary,' said Laura. 'The translator only knows what the author choses to reveal, but what little she knows only makes her want to know more.'

'Often biographies of writers,' said Charlie Eldon in his mildly mocking tone of voice, 'are more entertaining than the work of the writers themselves.'

Laura blushed and glanced at Birek to see if he seemed offended by what Eldon had said, but Birek only seemed puzzled.

'Who do you mean?' he asked.

'More people have read Painter than Proust,' said Eldon.

'Who's Proust?' asked Chalmers.

'Only because of the scandal,' said Laura, ignoring the stockbroker.

'Then I would disappoint a biographer,' said Birek, 'for the only scandal in my life is that I have deserted the proletariat.'

The evening which had started so slowly became by ten a great success. The champagne which the butler from Louards pressed upon the guests loosened the inhibitions of the dull Slavophiles and dulled the disdain of the snobs. The guests at the different

33

tables began to laugh, shout, tease and flirt in the way which makes a hostess, in retrospect, feel that things have gone well.

It also helped that Josef Birek, the guest of honour, more than filled his role as a star. By ten – when the tide turned – Laura felt ashamed that she had been embarrassed by his sky blue suit because his presence made his costume seem by the way. He was tall and, once one became used to his slightly Asiatic features, undoubtedly handsome; but above all it was his ingenuous charm which won over those who had come to meet him.

For coffee Laura encouraged her guests to move around, and she herself took Birek to a different table to meet Madge and her husband Ben. Madge, thanks to the champagne, had forgiven Laura for the dirty trick she had played on her and engaged Birek in an earnest conversation about life in Czechoslovakia. Ben, who was drunk, half-listened but took nothing in; until suddenly he lurched forward and said to Birek: 'I think you were bloody lucky, back there, and I don't think you realize how bloody lucky you were.'

Birek laughed: he needed no knowledge of English *mœurs* to recognize a man who was tight. 'In what way lucky?' he asked.

'No rat race, for one thing, and no bloody plutocrats smoking their fat cigars.' He waved his hand in the direction of a group of the Mortons' banking friends, two of whom were puffing Havanas.

Birek laughed. 'There you are quite wrong,' he said. 'Thanks to our fraternal relations with Cuba, cigars are relatively inexpensive.'

'Well here they cost a bloody fortune,' said Ben, 'a fiver apiece, and to let it go up in smoke like that is an insult to the unemployed.'

'Oh do shut up, Ben,' said Madge, not because she disagreed with him but because his tone was uncouth.

'Why should I shut up?' retorted her husband. 'He wants to know, doesn't he, what it's really like in this country . . . what our so-called freedom really means to people who can't get a job, or, if they can, don't earn enough to pay for a roof over their heads.'

'I am sure there are such people,' said Birek with a patient smile. 'I am sure there are great inequalities, and much suffering, but isn't that the price of freedom?'

'Those who have the freedom don't pay the price.'

'But surely,' said Birek, 'the freedom, even of the few, releases an energy and an inventiveness which leads in turn to a prosperity which benefits even the poorest citizen?'

'Tell that to your unemployed steel worker!'

'He may not perceive it,' said Birek, 'because no one, hit by a misfortune, can see beyond it. But, I should have thought, his conditions here, as an unemployed steel worker, are even on a material level superior to an employed steel worker in a socialist state; and spiritually the two have no comparison because in his leisure – in what he reads in the newspapers, or watches on television – he is the beneficiary of all the ferment which arises in a free society.'

'The *Sun*,' sneered Ben, 'and *Blankety-Blank*?'

Birek turned to Laura in puzzlement. 'The sun?'

'A newspaper – rather a vulgar newspaper. And *Blankety-Blank* is a silly television game.'

'Ah.' He nodded. 'Well, I dare say they are not good, but at least anyone is free to read or watch such things, or to turn to something else.'

'They may be free to do so, but they don't.'

'Just as men are free to love God,' said Birek, 'and they don't. But you cannot force them to love God, and you cannot force them to love Mozart and Shakespeare, because the essence of man – what distinguishes him from beasts – is surely his free will.'

The theological turn to the conversation confused Ben's befuddled mind. He was not used to God coming up in conversation: nor, for that matter, was Laura Morton.

'Are you religious?' she asked Birek, as if the thought had not occurred to her before.

'I am a Catholic,' he said. 'Many of us are.' Then he added, as if to justify himself: 'The Church is now the main opposition to the regime.'

'I shouldn't have thought there'd be much to choose between them,' said Ben. 'Priests and commissars have always seemed to me to be birds of the same feather.'

Birek smiled. 'Yes, you are quite right. In many ways they are. The Communists, like the Nazis, learned a lot from the Jesuits and the Inquisition.'

'Then how can you be a Catholic?' asked Madge.

'Because for all its faults, which I acknowledge, I believe that the Church teaches what is the truth.'

Laura frowned. There was a danger that all this talk about religion would spoil the atmosphere of her party. 'I suppose people are Catholics in Czechoslovakia,' she said, 'in the same way that we're Church of England here.'

'Speak for yourself,' said Ben.

Laura blushed. 'We may not go to church in London,' she said, 'but we always do at Risley.'

'Bloody superstition,' said Ben.

'For God's sake, shut up,' said Madge under her breath.

Laura decided that it was time to take Birek to another table.

Watching them, as they crossed the room, was the financial journalist Charlie Eldon who had detached himself from the conversation to remain at table smoking a cigarette. Facing him across the table was Eva Burroughs, who now leaned forward and with the familiarity of a past lover said: 'You're not being very sociable.'

He turned and put out his cigarette. 'You're quite right. I must go and talk to some of those Central Europeans.'

'Stay here for a minute and talk to me.'

'Have we anything to say?' He smiled as he said this as if to reassure her that he meant it as a joke.

'I'd like to know what you think of the guest of honour,' said Eva.

Eldon shrugged. 'I don't know his writing. I'm sure he's very talented.'

'Good-looking, wouldn't you say?' She said this with a slight sneer.

'He seems a little gauche.'

'Some people might find that endearing.'

'Do you?'

She smiled. 'I was thinking, rather, of our hostess.'

Eldon frowned. 'She's excited by the drama, that's all. In a week or two she'll see through him.' And with that he stood up and abandoning his discarded mistress crossed the room to join Laura and Birek, who were standing by the fire with a publisher called Pritchard.

'Ah, Charlie,' said Laura with a particularly sweet smile, 'come and talk to Josef.' She turned to Birek. 'Charlie is one of our very best friends. He also knows the literary world. If you liked, he could introduce you to some writers.'

'I should like that very much,' said Birek.

'Then I shall arrange it,' said Charlie.

'Just now we're asking Gerald for some professional advice,' said Laura, turning back to Pritchard, the publisher. 'What do you think he should do?' she asked.

'Have you entered into any contracts yet?' Pritchard asked Birek.

Birek shook his head. 'No'.

'You write stories, don't you?'

'Yes.'

'They're very difficult to sell.'

'Of course. I know.'

'We have much better luck with novels. You don't have a novel up your sleeve?'

'I came away,' said Birek blushing, 'with a novel almost completed.'

'That is exciting,' said Laura, who remained standing at his side.

'We would be very interested in that,' said Pritchard. 'Perhaps you could look at it, Laura, and send us in a report?'

'I'll certainly look at it, if Josef will let me,' she said, smiling at the young Czech, 'but I shall also find him an agent. I know how stingy you are with your advances.'

Pritchard laughed. 'We'll do our best. The young man will need money.' He turned to Birek. 'Have you thought, yet, of how you are going to earn your living?'

Birek shrugged his shoulders. 'As far as I can, with my pen, but if not perhaps I could be a school caretaker as I was in Prague.'

'I'm sure we can find you something better than that,' said Laura.

'I am used to living modestly,' said Birek just as another of the guests who was in the Foreign Office came up and asked to be introduced.

'Of course,' said Laura in answer to Birek's last remark. Then she took the newcomer by the hand to present him. 'Josef, this is a cousin of my husband's, Hamish Green. He was once in Prague in the embassy.'

The two men bowed to one another but Green did not step forward to shake Birek's hand. 'I'm afraid I never learned your language as well as I should have done,' he said.

'How long were you there?'

'Three years.'

'Not long enough.'

'Oh, it might have been if I'd had a Czech girl friend, but given the situation that wasn't on.'

'Particularly,' said Laura, 'since you'd got an English wife.'

Green laughed, then suddenly looked at Birek with a sharp, professional eye. 'Your name is familiar,' he said.

'I hope you've read his stories,' said Laura.

'I haven't as yet, I'm afraid. No there's another Birek – Jaroslav Birek. Is he related?'

Birek blushed. 'Yes,' he said. 'Jaroslav Birek is my father.'

'Really?' said Green. 'That's very interesting. I wonder if they realize this at the Home Office.'

'What difference does it make who his father is?' asked Laura.

'Oh, none as such, but Jaroslav Birek . . .'

'My father,' said Josef, 'is a Communist – in fact he is a member of the government – but since he divorced my mother I have hardly seen him. He has played no role in my life.'

This mention of his father brought the first frown onto the face of Josef Birek. Laura noticed and suddenly understood how his stories had shown such familiarity with the privileged way of life of the Party leaders. For a moment her mind whirled with that rearrangement of thoughts and impressions which sometimes leads to a reassessment of what one thinks of someone, but the fact that the Communist father had been disowned by the son's frown saved him from any guilt by association: indeed his rejection of a system in which he could undoubtedly have done well added to the heroism of his escape. She therefore smiled on him with a greater benevolence and led him on to meet more of her friends.

It grew late. Francis, with an ill-concealed moroseness, began to wish that the guests would go home, but saw, in the eager way in which they stretched out their arms as the butler passed with a bottle, that most were determined to stay as late as they could. He therefore went to the kitchen to tell the butler that he should now pass around fruit juice instead of champagne. Slowly, after this, the guests grew sober and as they grew sober they realized that they were tired. The Greens left first, then the Pritchards, then Mac-Donald took Birek back to his hotel. The banking friends stayed later, hoping for a time on their own, but Miroslav Maier stayed stubbornly on trying to enrapture Chalmers' wife with Czech charm. When the Chalmers left, the Maiers followed, then Eva Burroughs and finally, after a quick quiet chat with his hostess, Charlie Eldon and the couple from the British Council.

The late hour – it was half-past one – made Laura happy because it suggested that her party had been a success. While the dedicated ladies from Louards cleared up the empty glasses, she sat back on one of the three deep sofas and sighed while Francis shifted from foot to foot, impatient to get to bed.

'Well?' she asked. 'What did you think?'

'It went well.'

'It did, didn't it, considering how different they all were.'

Francis edged towards the door.

'What did you think of Birek?' she asked.

'He spoke English very well.'

'Yes.' Her lips smiled: her brow frowned. 'But didn't you think he seemed young?'

'Surely he is young?'

'I know, but somehow he seemed younger than he is.'

Francis reached the door. 'The Iron Curtain protects them,' he said, 'from many of the things which make us grow old.' He then went into the hall to pay off the servants while Laura mused on the sofa.

THREE

Charlie Eldon, who was the last to leave the Mortons' party, had been in love with Laura for two or three years. He had first seen her one morning on Lansdowne Square when going to interview an American economist who was staying with the Mortons as he passed through London. As Charlie approached the front door Laura returned from a game of tennis. She was flushed and moist after her exertions and imagined quite wrongly that she was not looking her best. Charlie introduced himself: she smiled and reached for the key in the pocket of her track-suit. Then she got muddled with her racket and the tin of balls so Charlie took the key and let them both in.

She went upstairs while Charlie interviewed the economist. It was a difficult assignment, because while talking about the Federal Deficit and the fluctuating value of the dollar his mind was on the woman whom he had met a moment before. He knew without doubt that it was love at first sight – he had considerable experience of love at first sight – and wondered whether his feelings were affected by knowing who she was. He had already heard of the beautiful Laura Morton and it was in the hope of perhaps meeting her that he had asked to interview Professor Hochheimer in her house on Lansdowne Square.

He was disappointed that coffee and biscuits were brought by the Portuguese daily. The mistress of the house did not reappear before the time came for him to leave; nor did she come to the party which the publishers gave for Professor Hochheimer's book. He knew, all the same, that in due course he would meet her again and was determined that when he did he would be prepared. He found out all he could about Francis Morton and his role at Louards from the files at the *Financial Times*, then learned about Laura's family through directories like Debrett's *Peerage and Baronetage* and *Who Was Who*. He even went so far as to read three of her father's books which he found in the London Library.

There were mixed opinions in London about whether Charlie Eldon was nice or not. The key to his character was his education at a minor public school. It is these anomalous institutions, not the coal mines or the trade unions, which provide England with its anarchists and revolutionaries, because they subscribe to a system in which a man's place in society is defined by his education yet by their own mediocrity condemn their pupils to a position of irremedial inferiority. Some, of course, grow up to ignore the snobbery of English life but others like Charlie continue to dread that question: 'Where did you go to school?'

He also preferred not to be asked about his family. His father was a businessman in the Midlands – the managing director of a company making bathroom fixtures. Charlie despised him and though he loved his mother he was ashamed of her because she was neurotic, flamboyant and Irish. He found everything about his parents' life in Northampton dull, banal and mediocre. He had escaped in his adolescence into French and Russian novels where he had imagined himself, like Julien Sorel, the lover of aristocratic women. He hoped that they existed in the England of the Welfare State but knew they were not to be found in Northampton. At the age of eighteen he took his destiny into his own hands and to the astonishment of his teachers won a scholarship to Cambridge. There he worked hard – not just at economics but at cultivating those fellow undergraduates who might be useful to him in later life.

He realized that money too was a prerequisite to the kind of life he had in mind. If he had made better connections, he might have gone into the City. As it was, after Cambridge he went to Harvard for a year and then returned to a job in London on the *Financial Times*. He hoped that as a financial journalist he could study the world of money and see how best it was to be made. There seemed time enough to make his fortune; but there is never as much time as young men assume and ten years later Charlie was still a journalist writing about takeovers, rights issues, interest rates and the money supply.

He was paid well enough to lead a comfortable bachelor life – eating in restaurants or at the Garrick Club, buying tickets for the theatre and opera, and travelling when he felt like it to Paris or New York. With no wife or children, there was no need to pay school fees or a household allowance. The only standing orders to his current account were for the mortgage and rates on his flat in Paddington, and this was more like the digs of a student than the home of a middle-aged man.

His hobby was women, particularly married women with rich husbands who were amused by the Bohemian confusion of his flat but never wanted to move in. Like Balzac he thought it silly to pay for a mistress, a newspaper or a country house because someone else would always provide them for him. He was bored by the silliness of young girls but became skilled at sniffing out the discontent of married women. He liked to see them struggle with their conscience and then benefit when they succumbed, as they usually did, to the passions pent up by their past frustration.

The uneasy husbands who had heard of his affairs with everyone's wife but their own could never understand why Charlie met with such success. He had blue eyes, a kind smile and a deep avuncular voice but his face was too heavy to be handsome and his cheeks were marked with the scars of acne in his adolescence. He was also beginning to go bald; he smoked a lot; and his eyes became bloodshot when he had been drinking.

He had other qualities, however, which they overlooked – a strong hairy body which had a certain animal attraction in itself, together with an easy way of talking with women which came from his mother's Irish blood. Had it been known that Charlie was half-Irish, then his conversational skills might have been dismissed as blarney, but because of his English name and public school accent it was never suspected, so with the tinker's twinkle in his eye he was free to play havoc with the hearts of discontented wives.

Laura, at the time when Charlie met her, did not consider that she was discontented. She had everything to make a woman happy – a town house, a country house and a husband who was successful, steady and rich. Her son was at Eton, her daughter at North Foreland Lodge and her third child Lucy safely down for the Manners Academy in Holland Park. They mixed with equally fortunate people who were either rich, good-looking, amusing, well connected or well known. None of those qualities sufficed in itself to give a permanent place in their set, but the Mortons were assured of one both by Francis's standing in the City and Laura's connection to several well established families at the core of the English upper class.

One should always beware, however, of worldly contentment. C. G. Jung once treated a couple for severe neurosis brought on by nothing but the perfection of their life. The same danger threatened the Mortons. The first inkling that all might not be well came with Laura's obsession with diet. It was not that she thought that she was too fat, but that inadvertently over the years she had been poisoning her husband and children. Suddenly Francis, who liked bacon and egg for breakfast, and a sizzling joint for his Sunday lunch, found everything poached – eggs, chickens, even beef. Rules were then imposed with a fanatic ferocity more rigorous than those of any Muslim or Jew. Butter was forbidden: so too was salt. The fish pie at Risley on a Friday evening became wild rice kedgeree, and the thick creamy milk that the children had poured on to their porridge in the country was replaced by a thin whitewash from a blue-topped bottle. Instead of the soft white loaf from the local baker there appeared brittle brown bread, studded with steel-hard grains which scratched their gums and chipped their teeth.

Worse still, Laura began to watch what Francis drank. She never openly criticized him but would read aloud from articles in the papers about heart disease, exercise and incipient alcoholism. When he got back from work in the evening, and went to pour himself a glass of whisky, Laura would happen to be there, avoiding his eye so that he could not say that she was watching him, but watching him all the same. When he offered her a glass of wine at supper, she would accept one but no more, and then look with anguish as the plates were cleared away at the bottle he emptied on his own.

The second sign of trouble came when Laura casually mentioned that she wanted to find a job. This happened when they were sitting at breakfast at Risley in the delightful kitchen with its bright blue Aga and Welsh dresser. The sun shone in from the garden; the nanny and the baby had disappeared; and Francis, wearing a dressing-gown, was sipping his second cup of coffee while reading the weekend supplement of the *Financial Times*.

Laura had finished both her herbal tea and the *Daily Mail*, and sat in silence studying her husband. Francis felt her eyes upon him and assumed that she wanted to read the gardening column in the paper he was reading. Determined not to give it up until he had finished reading it himself he hid behind the pink paper and so did not notice her slight blush as she said: 'I thought I might take a job.'

Francis remained hidden behind the paper. 'What kind of job?'

'I don't know. I hadn't thought. Something part-time, perhaps.'

Francis frowned. He felt an instinctive aversion to the idea of a working wife but realized, at the same time, that even if he had been in the habit of having things out with Laura, he might not have been able to distil a reasoned argument from his fermenting prejudices. To him working women were either emasculating lesbian viragos or, more pertinent in Laura's case, women who were bored by marriage and family life.

He did not consciously consider that Laura was looking for a lover but there was in him an instinct common to many men of his kind to keep his wife in the harem of his own home with a nanny, a daily and a child to stand guard over their virtue like eunuchs in the court of the Sultan. He was also a man of property who felt that in marrying a pretty wife he had bought an object of beauty for his exclusive enjoyment, and at the same time had engaged a manager whose energies would be devoted to his home affairs.

He knew, however, that such sentiments were out of fashion and so hardly dared express them to himself, let alone to Laura. Nor was either of them accustomed to saying what they thought on matters of such a serious nature. It offended against the stoic ethos of their class to plead one's own interest or insist upon one's own point of view. He therefore suppressed the expostulations which had been on the tip of his tongue and in a deadpan way made an oblique and apparently disinterested objection.

'There's the baby,' he said, as if Laura might have forgotten that she had recently given birth to a third child.

There was a long pause during which complementary prejudices and frustrations swirled around in Laura's mind – the egoism of husbands, the tyranny of men – at the end of which she said: 'I know.'

There was now another pause as if Francis had been distracted from their conversation by something he was reading in his paper: then the dialogue continued at the same slow pace.

'In a few months she'll be walking,' said Francis.

'Gail's pretty good.'

'It's not the same.'

'Others manage.'

'What about Johnny and Belinda?'

'They're at school.'

'There are the holidays.'

'You get holidays from a job.'

'Three weeks a year.'

'I could make some arrangement.'

After this came another of the longer pauses, with Laura waiting for a rejoinder which never came. Eventually she said, with a trace of coldness in her voice: 'You'd rather I didn't?' and at the same time rose to clear the cups and plates from the table.

'It's up to you,' said Francis, at last putting down the paper.

'I won't if you think I shouldn't.'

He stood. 'Let's wait and see,' he said as he shuffled in his slippers towards the door.

It was while waiting to see that Laura met Charlie Eldon for the second time. She was placed next to him at dinner at someone else's house, and knowing nothing about him expected nothing from him. Since he was not obviously handsome, nor well known for anything in particular, she was prepared at worst to be bored and at best to be amused in the two or three hours that she was trapped at his side. If she had been less innocent she might have noticed his quick glance at her honey-coloured shoulders and the swelling of her bosom at the bodice of her dress; but she did not notice, or noticed unconsciously, or noticed only enough to be pleased that the trouble she had taken to look pleasant had been remarked upon and admired.

What she did notice, as soon as she talked to him, was that he was not from the same set as Francis and his friends. He was too attentive, too deliberate and spoke too well, like those Indian Maharajas who went to Oxford. However he had her laughing in twenty minutes, and throughout the evening she never felt inclined to turn to the man on her right. She did not notice, or noticed only unconsciously, or noticed only enough to accept it as a formality, that interspersed with the observations that made her laugh were

45

subtle, casual questions about her own life as if he was trawling it to discover a pretext for seeing her again. He asked her, for example, about her childhood and in describing it she let out that her father had been an explorer.

'What was your maiden name?'

'Brook.'

'Was your father Sir John Brook?'

'Yes. Why? Did you know him?'

'No, but I remember reading *The Plains of Patagonia* when I was at school.'

She blushed. So many of Francis's friends from the City had never heard of her father and never read books. 'I'm so glad you liked it,' she said modestly as if she herself was the author.

'And *Ambling in Alma Ata*. I thought that was charming. He had a wonderful way of making everything he went through sound such fun. Do you remember, in the one about Borneo, what was it called?'

'*Jungle Joyride.*'

'That's right. Walking waist-deep through swamps, with leeches sticking to his skin, and laughing it off in that wonderful boyish prose.'

'You remember them frightfully well.'

'I suppose it was the age at which I read them. Are they still in print? I'd love to try them again.'

'There's some talk of reissuing one or two in paperback, but nothing has come of it as yet.'

'I'll try a second-hand bookshop.'

'If you can't find them, I can always lend them to you.'

'That would be very kind.'

They talked a little longer about the explorer. 'I wonder what made him become an explorer,' Charlie asked.

'His father was often abroad. I think he thought it was the thing to do.'

'What did his father do?'

'He was in the navy.'

'Was he the admiral?'

'Yes.'

'Sir Edward Brook?'

'That's right.'

'Only last week I noticed that picture of him in the National Portrait Gallery, but I never associated him with your father.'

'I didn't realize that there was a portrait of him there.'

'It's a rather fine painting by one of those underrated Victorian portraitists.'

'I must go and see it.'

'Why don't I take you there?'

'Oh, don't bother, honestly . . .'

'You'll need someone to guide you past all those kings and queens. And we could have lunch before, and you could bring along a copy of one of your father's books.'

'Well, all right, if you like.'

'Would your husband object?'

'No. Why should he?'

If Laura had known more about Charlie Eldon, or about Charlie Eldon's reputation, she would have understood why her husband might object; but London is a large enough city for a woman to find herself next to a relative stranger in this way, and even if she had been forewarned that Eldon was known to have had affairs with married women, it would not have alarmed her because she did not find him particularly attractive and did not see herself as the sort of woman who had love affairs with other men.

It was not that all her friends were chaste. Quite the contrary, there had been several scandals in their circle. A number of her contemporaries from Oxford were already divorced and others, though they remained together, had long-standing liaisons with other people's husbands or wives. There were one or two well-known seducers who went from one woman to another, setting a time clock at the start of an affair to run for three months and no more; and a few *femmes fatales* whose husbands' complaisance extended to befriending their lovers and acknowledging their children as their own.

To Laura these profligates were like actors hired to play a sequence of vignettes for the benefit of gossip among her friends. It never occurred to her that she might mount the stage and act in some drama herself. Nor did it occur to her that Francis, with his greying hair and saggy stomach, would ever betray her. She loved him with the affection that a girl might feel for an old Labrador who snoozes comfortably in front of the fire. Their conjugal encounters were as decorous and infrequent as she took them to be among those friends who like the Mortons had been married for nearly twenty years.

What, in her innocence, she could not comprehend is that it is the man in just such a condition who is most vulnerable to the wiles of a desperate single woman. There were many who would willingly overlook sagging stomach and greying hair for a roof over their head and a joint account. Thus Eva Burroughs, in straitened circumstances after an ugly divorce, built upon the alliance she had formed with Francis over the decoration of the dining-room, and when the moment came made it perfectly plain that if he wanted her she was his.

They had met for lunch to discuss the budget for Lansdowne Square in which Laura had shown no interest, and had gone back afterwards to her little house in Fulham to look at some samples from Colefax and Fowler; but though she had laid them out on her double bed, and had nonchalantly left undone a button at the top of her blouse, the only longing felt by Francis was to be back in his chair at Louards bank where he was accustomed, after lunch, to spend twenty minutes on the bridge problem in *The Times*.

It was not that it did not cross his mind that a short and discreet liaison would bring pleasures of a certain kind; but in the balance against the delights of Eva's favours were such practical considerations as the distance from Fulham to the City; the bad conscience it would provoke; and the demands already made on his spare time by visits to Christie's and Sotheby's for bargains among the works of art at auction, or cheap sales of bin ends.

Against factors as weighty as these, the lascivious Eva proved as light as her morals on the scales of his conscience. Francis left her house in Fulham with a bottle-green paper for the library as his only irrevocable commitment; and since the main cause of infidelity among women is the bad example of their husbands, this decision by Francis Morton that the game was not worth the candle did more than anything else to preserve the innocence of Laura.

It was this innocence which saved Laura from suspecting that she had been the object of his research in *Debrett* and *Who Was Who*, or that he did not remember her father's books from his childhood but had found them in the London Library. Had she known that he had gone to such trouble she would have despised him for being so devious, and would have refused his invitation to meet for lunch. In her innocence, however, she accepted when he telephoned a few days later: after all, she had nothing else to do and was always looking for an excuse to escape from Gail and wear some of her smarter clothes.

They met in a restaurant in Covent Garden. Charlie seemed to have been there before, or had a natural authority over waiters. He questioned them about the 'specials' which they announced in the American way, and directed Laura to choose what he thought would be best that day. She was happy to let him order – it went with his kind and confident manner – and wondered as she nibbled her bread-stick what Madge would think if she happened to walk in. Lunches were accepted in her circle as an innocent way to see a member of the opposite sex – certainly Francis had raised no objection when she had told him about this date – yet she herself was always suspicious if she saw a friend lunching with someone else's husband.

She watched him as they waited for their food. His rough complexion was more noticeable by the light of day but a man's appearance is only a small part of his appeal: it matters more to a woman who he is than what he looks like – or so they say. And since he had asked her out to lunch Laura had done some modest research on her own. Francis had described him as 'a clever journalist'; Ben, Madge's husband, as 'brilliant but to the right of Genghis Khan'. When his name came up in the company of Eva Burroughs she had frowned and said disparagingly: 'Oh, he's certainly very charming but not to be trusted.'

Laura gave Charlie the copy of *Jungle Joyride* that she had promised to lend him, and they then went on to talk about her father and mother. With the gentle, coaxing manner of a psychoanalyst Charlie asked her about her feelings for her parents, which no one had ever asked before. It had never occurred to her that she might have disliked her mother, but now that he put the question she realized that she had always felt a certain rivalry, even contempt. 'You know she was obsessed with social trivialities,

49

and was really rather snobbish, whereas Daddy's mind was always on exploring.'

'But surely he only went exploring when he was young?'

'Yes, the war put a stop to it and afterwards, I think, he felt he should stay at home because of us. But he went on exploring through writing books.'

'Did he ever take you abroad?'

'No. We were going to go to China but he thought we should wait until I had finished at Oxford and before I did he died.'

'That must have been sad.'

'Yes. Especially because we never made that journey across Siberia. I would have loved it and I think he would have loved it too.'

'Was he a happy man?'

'He was rather melancholy in his last years. The last two or three books had horrible reviews – really scornful of what they called his "*Boy's Own*" style.'

'They were envious.'

'I know. People like Daddy belonged to another era. They've been replaced by academics and specialists who like to show off their diplomas in anthropology by scoffing at books by an amateur.'

'It came with all the new universities in the Wilson years.'

'It was all political, too,' said Laura. 'They envied people like Daddy having the money to go off around the world.'

Charlie took her back through her childhood, and since she had so rarely thought about it before this unbottled a flood of memories and anxieties which he listened to with extraordinary patience. She told him stories about her family which she had never told anyone before, and even said things about her marriage which were almost indiscreet. It was only when they were drinking coffee that she realized that she had not been talking to herself. She looked anxiously at Charlie Eldon, as if his expression would reveal whether she had made a fool of herself or not, but he was opening a sachet of sugar as if there had been nothing unusual in what she had had to say.

When they went out into the street, and walked towards the National Portrait Gallery in Trafalgar Square, she felt a little vulnerable and embarrassed, as if she had just put her clothes back on after visiting her gynaecologist. She hoped she could trust him not to repeat some of the things she had said. She glanced at him as they walked along to try and see in his eyes whether he had gained any power through her indiscretion, but he chatted and smiled in the same easygoing way like an uncle taking his niece out from school.

They found the portrait of her grandfather, Admiral Sir Edward Brook, and studied it in silence for a while.

'He looks rather severe,' said Laura eventually.

'England ruled the world when he was the First Sea Lord. He was responsible for keeping the peace.'

'I don't think his home life was very happy – not to judge from what Daddy told me.'

'That was the price they paid for running an empire,' said Charlie as they continued through the gallery. 'Their children were neglected, which made them unsatisfactory parents in their turn. On the other hand we've managed a miracle of continuity, when you consider it. What nation in history has shed its empire with so little upheaval at home?'

Laura had not studied history, and so could not answer, but she did not feel that Charlie was trying to show off his knowledge or show up her limitations. He treated the question as a rhetorical one, and continued to hold forth in an easygoing way in his deep bass voice until they came back to the entrance to the gallery.

'I must go,' she said, 'to fetch Lucy from school.'

'And I must take a bus to Fleet Street.'

'Thank you for lunch.'

'Thank you for the book.'

'You must come and have dinner.'

'I'd love to.'

FOUR

If Laura and Charlie Eldon now met more frequently, it was not because he courted her. Rather she pursued him because he had one quality which made him exceptionally attractive to a woman in Laura's position: he was single. All over London, for some demographic reason that no one could explain, there was a surfeit of unattached women in their late thirties and early forties who had either never married or who had played their cards badly in a divorce – leaving a husband for a lover only to find that the lover stayed with his wife.

Since the most sympathetic witnesses to their misfortunes were invariably their smugly married girl friends, there was always the need to invite these forlorn spinsters to dinner parties or country house weekends: but it was a devil of a job to match them with suitable men of the same age. Laura, for example, had Eva Burroughs on her conscience: they had dined with her twice at her cramped house in Fulham but had not asked her back for want of an extra man. Now, however, there was Charlie, and only three days after their lunch in Covent Garden Laura asked him to dine at her house in Lansdowne Square.

It went very well. Certainly Eva and Charlie had met before, but they talked to one another for long enough to make Laura feel that putting them together had been a success. She was also delighted to see that Francis appeared to like Charlie: it was rare for him to talk much to people he did not already know, but Charlie as a financial journalist was up to date on all the gossip in the City. Indeed if Laura felt any dissatisfaction as the last of the guests left at the end of the evening, it was that Charlie Eldon had hardly talked to her.

She therefore suggested to Francis that they should ask him down to Risley. This was a little hazardous, since they had known him for so short a time. It is one thing to spend an evening with a relative stranger; another to have him for a whole weekend. There was also a tacit agreement between the Mortons that each should be able to blackball any guest the other proposed without having to give a reason. She therefore explained once again that they would need an extra man. When Francis asked her who the matching spinster was to be, she blushed and said that she had not yet decided. This did not matter to Francis, who was happy to have a man who knew so much more than he did about the latest twist in the Guinness affair.

His question, however, disconcerted Laura because the friend who after Eva was most on her conscience happened to be exceptionally pretty; and without knowing exactly why she began to rack her brain for a lame duck who was plain. She could not, at that moment, think of one and finally left it too late. Charlie had no matching spinster but there were two other couples as well as neighbours for both Saturday supper and Sunday lunch.

The weekend went as well as the dinner, largely because Charlie was such an agreeable guest. He was always ready for a walk or a game of tennis; he was helpful in the kitchen; he was appreciative of Laura's cooking; and listened intelligently to Francis's talk about wine. He did not push himself forward; he was almost shy; yet made everyone laugh from time to time. Both the wives, when they wrote to thank Laura, made a point of saying how nice he was.

Within two months of meeting him, Laura without noticing it had come to depend upon Charlie Eldon not just to make up her numbers but to put her in a good mood. So subtle was the way in which he flattered her that she did not realize what it was that made her feel so confident in his presence: nor did she suspect that he fed her the lines which made her feel so witty. Most important of all, Charlie had plenty of spare time. The problem, for a woman like Laura, was how to fill her day. It was not that she was ever idle: there were endless errands to run for Francis and Lucy, and the older children when they were home, as well as shopping expeditions for her own attire which were not, perhaps, always as necessary as they seemed. Yet somehow the triviality of all these little tasks only emphasized the vacuum of an empty day. What was the point, after all, of buying an elegant dress if there was no occasion on which to wear it? She had lunch with Madge from time to time, but now Madge had a job making programmes for Radio Four and when Laura telephoned to suggest meeting she always sounded patronizingly busy.

For this reason, whenever Charlie asked her out to lunch, she was quick to accept. She was sufficiently ingenuous not to make some coquettish pretence that her life was filled with other engagements. With the same simplicity she told him how handy it was that he did not have to go back to an office straight after lunch; they would go to a gallery together, or take a walk in the park, which neatly filled in the time until Lucy had to be fetched from school.

She realized, of course, that Charlie might have other ideas about how to fill this empty hour in the early afternoon; but she felt safe because however much she liked him, she still did not find him attractive. She assumed that he sensed this, and when they talked on occasions about the love affairs of people they knew she made a point of saying how much she disapproved. She had always told herself that she would bail out if things got tricky and in the early days of their friendship had determined never to find herself alone with Charlie in the same room.

One day, however, after lunch at a restaurant in Bayswater Charlie suggested, since it was a lovely day, a walk across Kensington Gardens to the Albert Hall, where he could catch a bus to Fleet Street and Laura to Notting Hill. She agreed and they set off towards the park. Then Charlie remembered that he had left his copy at his flat so they walked back together to fetch it.

It is difficult to say whether Laura knew what she was doing. She talked, certainly, as if it was the most natural thing in the world to go back with a friend to collect an article from his flat; but perhaps the words came a little breathlessly from her lips, and perhaps her pulse, had it been taken, would have beaten rather faster than usual.

They climbed the stairs. She entered the untidy studio and smelt cigarette smoke on the curtains but her nose did not wrinkle in disgust. Rather she looked around with a childlike curiosity and made such remarks as: 'So this is where you live!' to which Charlie replied, as he opened a drawer of his desk: 'You can see now why I can't ask you to dinner.'

'You could if you wanted to,' she said with a smile. 'It's quite a big room. You could seat eight people round that table.'

'I can't cook.'

'I'm sure you have friends who can.' In saying this she tossed her head back in a gesture of clumsy flirtation.

'Not at the moment,' said Charlie, taking his article from the drawer and coming towards her, ostensibly to lead her back to the door.

She did not move and so the arm he held out to guide her came to rest around her waist. They stood face to face; then Charlie kissed her, and for a moment she let him, but then she jumped back, her face white, her body trembling, and without a word left the flat and ran down the stairs.

He followed her and for a while they walked in silence towards the Bayswater Road. It was only when they had reached Kensington Gardens that Charlie said that he loved her.

Before he had got very far into his declaration, Laura interrupted him. 'Please don't.'

'What?'

'Talk like that.'

'It's difficult not to say something . . . after what happened just now.'

She blushed. 'I would really be grateful if we could pretend it didn't happen.'

'Why?"

'I love my husband.'

'Can't you love me as well?'

She went on walking. 'I like you very much but I really don't think I love you.'

'You wanted me to kiss you.'

'I most certainly did not.'

'Are you sorry I did?'

She blushed. 'You promised you'd pretend it hadn't happened.'

'I didn't promise.'

'Then promise.'

'I can't.'

'Why not?'

'It meant too much to me.'

'If you loved me, you would.'

'If I loved you I would pretend that I didn't love you?'

'Yes.'

'Only a woman could think up a formula like that.'

'If you want to go on seeing me, then you must promise.'

'I'll promise I'll try if you'll meet me for lunch on Monday.'

'Not where we had lunch today!'

He laughed and named a restaurant at a safe distance from his flat. She agreed that she would be there and for the rest of their walk across Kensington Gardens they talked about other things. When they parted Charlie leaned forward to kiss her on the lips but at the last moment she jerked her head aside to present her cheek beneath the ear.

Charlie now took his bus to Fleet Street well pleased with the progress he had made. He had crossed the Rubicon and had started his march on Rome. There were battles to be fought – the war was not yet won – but from the way things had gone that afternoon he had little doubt of his final triumph.

His chief weakness, he knew, was in himself. He was aghast at the lame way in which he had delivered his lines that afternoon like a bored actor playing Romeo before an empty theatre in a provincial city. Only a woman as naïve as Laura would not have noticed his lack of conviction when he said he loved her. How moving he would have been if he had used the honest language of lust, or the poetry inspired by those depravities with which he longed to enslave the banker's wife.

He knew, however, that love was the password which would let him through her defences. The kiss that afternoon had confirmed what in all modesty he had suspected – that Laura did not find him particularly attractive. She had not collapsed in his arms. Her body had not abandoned itself to his as nature dictated in the conjunction of the sexes. It was not the sign of her surrender to an over-whelming desire, but rather a wild grasp at some excitement by someone who was desperately bored. Adulterous women, wrote both Stendhal and Byron, who were Charlie's masters in these matters, are not in love with their lovers but with love.

Had he known what thoughts were passing through Laura's head as she walked back from Bayswater to Lansdowne Square, he would have been complacently contented with his analysis of her state of mind. Just as she had made Charlie promise to pretend that the kiss had not happened, so she had decided to erase the experience from her memory; but even before she had reached Orme Square it had proved impossible to keep to her resolve. A number of different voices kept saying different things as if a dozen impudent genies had suddenly jumped into her brain. 'How wonderful! How shameful! Don't make a fuss about nothing. Did he really say he loved me or did I imagine it? He kissed me! So what? He probably kisses a lot of women. How monstrous! How dare he! But I don't really fancy him. He smells of cigarettes. And he doesn't shave properly. What on earth would people say if they knew! Think of Madge! If I had let him go on, what would have happened? He'll try again if I let him. I must avoid being alone with him. But what a curious flat. I'd like to have had a closer look. Was there a bedroom or does he sleep on that sofa? What a horrible smell! Francis would notice if I came back smelling of Gauloises. It makes life so complicated. And dangerous. But I mustn't think in this way. I'm married. Think of Lucy. And Johnny and Belinda. And Francis. He'd be so upset. But of course he would never know. It would never occur to him. He takes me for granted.'

Such were her thoughts as she walked back to Lansdowne Square.

The kiss took place on a Thursday. On the Friday the Mortons went down to Risley for the weekend. On the Saturday Eva Burroughs joined them for a professional visit: it was time to redecorate the drawing-room.

Until now we have seen Eva Burroughs play a walk-on part as a divorced interior decorator who had once had an affair with Charlie Eldon and had briefly tempted Francis Morton to betray his wife. This suggests she was pretty, and no one contests that despite slightly stocky legs she had been in the 1960s one of the loveliest debutantes of her generation. This beauty, as it so often does, had given her a distorted picture of her own intrinsic interest: men had listened to what she said in the vain hope that flattering the mind would deliver the body.

As a result, by the age of thirty-five she had become a consistently tedious woman who held forth at great length on any subject which came up in a flirty, girlish voice. She remained attractive in a buxom way with plump breasts that were often on display and a sexy manner which was essentially to conceal both from her lovers and from herself that she did not like sex at all. Charlie had sensed this when he had slept with her *faute de mieux* after a party. He had not been enthralled by her favours, and thereafter he had slept with her only five times more – half-a-dozen encounters being the minimum he considered civil. He explained after the sixth that he felt there was no marriage of true minds. She knew this was only a pretext: she had been dropped because she was boring before.

One quality she did possess, besides her talent at matching the colours of curtains and walls, was her loyalty to her old lovers. No man who had ever slept with her, or made a pass at her, or even given her a lascivious look, was ever forgotten: he remained her friend for life. This dogged loyalty extended not just to Charlie but also to Francis Morton. True he had not made a pass; true his desire for her had been of a most fleeting and lukewarm kind; but she had sensed that day in her bedroom in Fulham that he had fancied her, and she credited him in her mind with the noblest of reasons for resisting her – his love for Laura, his wife. Like many a lush she had a hallowed and romantic image of marriage and family life; and while time after time she succumbed to the advances of the husbands of her friends, she nevertheless believed that men and women could be and should be faithful.

Having been around for a while, and hearing all the gossip, she had learned what led to divorce. Without evolving an elaborate theory, she had become convinced that the three essential ingredients for a happy marriage were sex, money and something to do. The contrary qualities, in an obverse order – boredom, poverty and frustration – led to danger, and within the category of poverty she included stinginess: so many husbands were rich but mean.

One of the qualities that Eva liked in Francis was the triumph of his generosity over his instinctive thrift – not so much to her (she still lived on commission) but to Laura, who redecorated her houses at the rate that other wives spring-clean. He always insisted, of course, that she should get a bargain where she could – buying materials at sales, for example, and paint at a discount from wholesale stores; but if Eva suggested stippling or a *trompe-l'oeil* he would never veto her ideas on the grounds of expense.

One way and another – socially and professionally – Eva saw a lot of the Mortons and, though she was not privy to the secrets of the boudoir, she had placed a wager in her heart on the happiness of their marriage. But she also knew Charlie Eldon, and seeing him so often at their table made her suddenly afraid that her bet was at risk. She bore no grudge against Charlie, but it made her inexplicably unhappy to think that he was about to add Laura to the long list of his women. In a blundering way she began to pray that Laura would not fall; but then her earthier and more practical instincts began to measure her chances against her three principles of a happy marriage – sex, money and something to do.

Sex she could assume was as good or as bad as might be expected in a marriage that had lasted that length of time. Certainly Laura did not have the look of someone sexually sated, but nor did she have the nervy, ratty manner of the frustrated. Money, clearly, was abundant. But Eva knew enough about Laura to suspect that she had far too little to do. Thus that weekend at Risley, when Charlie sat smugly certain that his quarry was in the bag, she made up her mind to warn Francis that his pretty wife was at risk.

She knew, of course, that this was a hazardous thing to do. No one likes the bearer of bad tidings and Eva knew that she was risking a lucrative account. But she had what is called a good heart and so decided to risk Francis's indignation by warning him what was afoot.

Her chance came on the Saturday afternoon when Laura took Lucy to tea with some neighbours. Eva went to look for Francis and found him in the cellar, where he had gone to muse over his racks of rare wine. She suggested a walk and, with a wistful look at his bottles, he agreed. They went out in their boots into the garden where a small wicket gate led out into the fields, and from there followed a well established route which took them back to the house in half-an-hour.

'You know,' said Eva as they crossed the stream, 'there's been something I've been wanting to say but didn't know if I should.'

'About the house?' asked Francis mildly.

'About Laura.'

'Ah.' He nodded his head in a semi-ironic way.

'If you don't want me to go on, just say so.'

He gave a thin smile. 'Even if the husband is the last to know, he has to know some time.'

'Oh, it's not that. At least, not yet.'

'Not yet?'

'Have you noticed that Laura is seeing a lot of Charlie Eldon?'

'He's a very agreeable fellow.'

'You don't mind?'

Francis's face retained an expression of mild, defensive irony. 'I don't mind that she meets him. I would mind, I dare say, if she met him to go to bed with him.'

'I don't think she does. Not yet.'

'But she will?'

'Not because she loves him . . .'

'Then why?'

'She's bored.'

He nodded. 'I know.'

'If she is considering him it's only because she has time on her hands.'

'You think she does?'

'What?'

'Consider him?'

'Women do.'

'So I'm told. I can't see why.'

'As you said, he's very agreeable.'

'But not handsome.'

'That isn't always important.'

Again Francis nodded. 'So you think she should have something to do?'

'Yes.'

'A job of some kind?'

'Yes.'

'What do you suggest?'

'I don't know. I hadn't thought that far. What did she do before you were married?'

Francis was silent as he thought back to those early days. 'She took a degree in Slavonic studies.'

Eva was not sure what that meant but asked: 'Could she get some sort of job with that qualification?'

'Perhaps. I'm not sure.'

'She's awfully clever,' said Eva, to whom anyone cleverer than she was appeared brilliant. 'I'm sure she could do anything she wanted.'

'The only problem,' said Francis, 'would be to fit it in with the rest of her life. I don't think she'd want to change that.'

Eva went back to London before Laura returned from tea. Since Gail had the weekend off, Laura gave Lucy her bath and then dried her – patting her skin with the thick white towel with an abstracted expression on her face.

When Lucy was in bed she went to the kitchen to make the supper: for once they were neither dining out nor having anyone to dinner. The food had been mostly prepared in advance by dear Mrs Jackson, the gardener's wife, but she frowned all the same because she was cross that Francis had not offered to help either with Lucy or the supper. As she had come down from the nursery she had heard him on the telephone in the library, and while she realized that sometimes there was urgent business to be done for the bank, she resented him doing it while she slaved away as both nanny and cook.

Just as she was about to call him to come and eat Mrs Jackson's *quenelles*, Francis came into the kitchen with glass of vodka and tonic in one hand and a whisky and soda in the other. He handed her the vodka and then stood leaning against the chrome bar of the Aga.

'That was Andrew MacDonald,' he said.

'What did he want?' she asked irritably.

'You.'

'Me?'

'Not to speak to you – not now – but rather to sound me out about whether you might help him out at the Comenius Foundation.'

She frowned. 'How do you mean?'

'They need someone who knows Czech.'

'But my Czech is incredibly rusty.'

'He realizes that.'

She put place mats on the table. 'What would he want me to do?'

'Just general work in the office, and perhaps some translation for the magazine.'

'I couldn't do it full time.'

'He said you could choose your own hours.'

She came to the Aga and pushed him aside to take the food out of the lower oven. 'What did you tell him?'

'That you'd go and see him.'

'When?'

'On Monday. Is that all right?'

'Yes. I suppose so.' She frowned to hide her confusion and put the dish of *quenelles* on top of the oven.

This, then, was how Laura Morton came to work for the Comenius Foundation. She had only a vague notion at that time of what actually went on in their office in Pembridge Square. She knew that it was something to do with fighting Communism, and that Francis had persuaded Louards to contribute to its funds, but little more than that. She was rather pleased, all the same, at the idea of working there although it has to be said that her first thoughts were not of how she could help oppressed intellectuals in Czechoslovakia but of how wonderful it would be to escape from Gail, how convenient it was that Pembridge Square was so near to Lansdowne Square, and how impressed Madge would be that she was doing something which Madge could not do herself.

She went to see Andrew MacDonald that Monday morning and agreed terms. She was to be paid by the hour, and would work when she could, probably not on a Monday morning and certainly not on a Friday afternoon. The school holidays, it was understood, would be difficult but it was always possible that she could take work home. She left MacDonald's office at twelve and was about to drive back to Lansdowne Square when she suddenly remembered that she was to have lunch with Charlie.

The fact was that just as Eva had predicted, but more quickly than she could have hoped, the job had pushed Charlie out of her mind – not entirely out of her mind, of course, because the kiss was still a disturbing memory, but decidedly behind the job in order of preoccupation. She was a little thrown by this because already, at the weekend, before the job had been suggested, she had found herself involuntarily wondering what she should wear for lunch on Monday – something modest, of course, yet soft and appealing – perhaps a cashmere jersey which came up to her neck yet clung to the swelling of her pretty breasts.

That morning, however, she had thought first of her interview with MacDonald and how the image she should convey was of a serious, studious and industrious intellectual. Too much elegance, she knew, might create the wrong impression so she had dug out an old suit from the back of her cupboard made of grey gabardine which she had bought four years before to attend the funeral of her mother. She had worn it with a white blouse and a narrow scarf, almost like a businessman's necktie. Now, standing in Pembridge Square with a parking ticket in one hand and the key to the Volvo in the other, she dithered between running home to change and being late for Charlie, or turning up on time looking like a lesbian.

She dithered for only a minute but it was a minute which sealed her fate. She wanted to look nice for Charlie but she was also excited about the job, irritated by the ticket and above all very hungry. She therefore decided that he would have to take her as she was, got into the car and drove over the hill to South Kensington where they had arranged to meet.

Charlie was waiting, and she could tell at once that he was taken aback by her appearance.

'I'm sorry,' she said, sitting down briskly, 'but I had to go and see a man about a job so I thought I had better dress the part.'

'Is he an undertaker?' asked Charlie with an undertaker's expression on his face because he knew as well as Eva the value of Laura's boredom.

'No, no,' she said with a laugh. 'He's the director of the Comenius Foundation.'

'Ah,' said Charlie. 'That nest of spies.'

'They're not spies, are they?' she asked but with a gleam in her eye (what would Madge say to that!).

'They're fanatics.'

'No they're not. Francis supports them and you couldn't call him a fanatic.'

'He has a vested interest in the triumph of the capitalist system.'

'Don't we all?'

'Perhaps.'

'The work they do is impressive, really. I didn't realize until this morning. They smuggle the samizdat books out of Czechoslovakia and publish them here, but they're terribly short of translators.'

'Aren't there plenty of émigrés with nothing to do?'

'Of course,' she said, 'but Andrew – that's the director – said that it never works to translate into a language that isn't your own. And when it comes to English people who can speak Czech, well, there aren't very many.'

'I dare say.'

'You don't look very pleased.'

'I'm delighted. It's just that I had hoped to talk about other things.'

'If, by other things, you mean what you promised you wouldn't talk about, then I regard you as very dishonourable.'

'I haven't been able to think of much else.'

'Nonsense.'

'And you?'

'What about me?'

'Have you thought about what happened last Thursday?'

'A little.'

'And?'

She bit her lip and wondered what to say: she had thought so much about her first interview that morning that she had forgotten to prepare for the second.

Charlie took her hesitation for bashfulness. 'I know it took you by surprise,' he said. 'It took me by surprise too. And it lasted only a few seconds, but it's like pushing the button that sets off a nuclear bomb. That doesn't take long but it has tremendous consequences.'

'That's just the point,' said Laura, looking hungrily at the braised endives wrapped in ham and topped with cheese sauce which the waiter had just set before her. 'It's the consequences you have to think of – the horrible risk of a happy family exploding and dis-integrating . . .'

'That needn't happen,' said Charlie.

'It needn't but it might.'

'Husbands never ask if they don't want to know.'

'But they sense things, don't they?'

'Not if things go on as before.'

She blushed. 'I don't think I could do that, and anyway, that's not the point.'

'What is the point?'

'The point is . . .' She had her mouth full of endive. She swallowed it and began again. 'The point is, really, that I like you enormously but I don't really love you.'

'I had hoped you did . . . a little . . . enough.' Charlie put down his knife and fork. His grilled sardines were uneaten.

'To be quite honest I thought that perhaps I did, or might. I mean no one else since I married has ever kissed me, and hardly anyone did before I was married, and I'm prepared to admit that it stirred things up in my mind. But I think you're too good for me . . .'

'That's nonsense.'

'I don't mean too good, I mean too clever. I feel a little like a rabbit mesmerized by a snake that wants to gobble it up.'

He looked at her eyes, then at her throat. 'I do want to gobble you up,' he said.

'But, you see, I don't want to be gobbled up. I've been gobbled up by Francis and Johnny and Belinda and Lucy. I've been someone else's wife and someone else's mother now for eighteen years, and for the first time in my life I want to stand on my own two feet and be myself and perhaps in time . . .'

'Gobble someone up yourself.'

She blushed. 'That's not what I was going to say.'

'Think of me when you're hungry.'

'A rabbit can't eat a snake.'

'You won't be a rabbit. You'll be a snake.'

The rest of their lunch was awkward but Laura hardly noticed. For once in her life she felt in control. The self-respect that Charlie had encouraged by his attentions over the past months, together with the job she was to do which demanded skills she alone possessed, had given her the confidence to reach a decision which was both sensible and good. The terrifying prospect of going back to his flat, knowing quite well what it would imply, had now passed like a black cloud without any thunder and lightning. She tucked into her next course – a Dover sole – with the appetite of the righteous while Charlie, ever more lugubrious, merely picked at his rack of lamb.

FIVE

From past experience the officers of the Comenius Foundation knew that after the drama and excitement of a dissident's first arrival in the West there came an awkward period of adjustment. Coming from a nation where the state controlled every facet of life, it often came as a surprise to the Czech exile to discover that the British government, having granted him asylum, left him to sink or swim as he pleased. It was therefore up to the Foundation to help men like Birek both with money and advice; but its funds were inevitably limited, and so the allowance they offered for the first three months was no more than the government grant for a graduate student. It was left to Andrew MacDonald to explain these practicalities to Birek and advise him to move from the Alwyn Hotel to a hostel for overseas students on a street between University College and the Tottenham Court Road. By the standards of Eastern Europe, its amenities were good. The canteen was cheap and the rooms were clean. The only discomfort, if one call it that, was that he had to share a bathroom.

To understand the impression that London made upon Birek it is necessary to know a little more about him. Czechoslovakia, after all, as Neville Chamberlain discovered, is a small country about which the British know little and care less. It was only formed in 1918 from two provinces of the former Austrian Empire. Birek came from Bohemia and its capital, Prague. His grandfather had been a mediocre playwright who had made up for his lack of talent, as writers so often do, by espousing a cause that was fashionable at the time – the rights of the Czechs to a nation. He was even imprisoned for a month or so in 1905 in the sombre fortress of Brno. This minor discomfort proved a sound investment, for when Austria was defeated and the Habsburgs overthrown, old Birek and his friends became the heroes of the hour. In the new republic the garrulous old bore was hailed as one of the fathers of his nation. His plays in Czech were performed over and over again to audiences composed largely of German-speaking Jews.

The playwright's son Jaroslav studied law. Susceptible like his father to fashionable causes, he became a Communist at the time of the Spanish Civil War. To the horror of his bourgeois parents, he married a worker's daughter and went to live with her in the grim industrial town of Ostrava. When Chamberlain and Daladier abandoned the Czechs at Munich, it confirmed in the mind of young Jaroslav Birek that the Western democracies would never stand up to Hitler. He therefore decamped with his wife to Moscow and only returned to Prague in the wake of the victorious Red Army.

In 1946 he was given a teaching post at the Faculty of Law at Prague university, and at the same time was elected a Communist member of the Prague City Council. In 1948 he led his students on to Wenceslas Square to demonstrate in favour of the Popular Front. After the fall of Beneš, his loyalty to the Party paid off. His bourgeois superiors at the university lost their posts and Jaroslav Birek became a full professor. His lectures, according to his enemies, were like his father's plays – zealous but mediocre – but then the first decades of the Socialist Republic were not a time for original thinking among legal theorists.

In the 1950s the greatest achievement of Jaroslav Birek was to survive the Stalinist purges. Of course he performed all the expected intellectual contortions to conform to the changes in the Party line, but many who did as much disappeared all the same.

His middle-class origins, which might have counted against him, were mitigated by the background of his working-class wife: nevertheless the rumour went around that in Russia during the war Birek had been recruited by the KGB and was protected by his masters in Moscow.

Yet in the early 1960s, when liberal Communists gradually gained the upper hand, Birek suddenly burst out of his shell. He divorced the worker's daughter and married a young scientist, Katya Hudeckova, daughter of the celebrated physicist Pavel Hudeck. She bore him a son, Josef, in 1962, whose early years saw all the excitement which led up to the Prague Spring. He was too young to attend his father's lectures, but those he gave in the summer of 1967 calling for the subordination of Party to Parliament were among the clarion calls for the reforms of the Dubcek era.

Because of these lectures and the renown they brought him, and because he was not only a Communist member of the Prague Town Council but also the son of the bourgeois-nationalist playwright Pavel Birek, and possibly an officer in the KGB who would reassure Moscow, Jaroslav Birek was suddenly elected on to the Praesidium and soon afterwards made a member of the Central Committee of the Communist Party of Czechoslovakia. The liberals had high hopes of him; his students and former students came to his flat near Wenceslas Square where his wife Katya, returning from the laboratory with the fragrance of carbolic acid on her clothes found them drinking, talking and arguing while dandling her son Josef on their knees.

Katya was delighted. She outdid all the others in elation. Persecuted in her youth as the child of a bourgeois academic – only admitted to the university because of her unquestioned brilliance, and only given a job there which no one else could do – she was giddy with her dream of socialism with a human face. To reconcile the nation – to free the Czech spirit which had suffered for so long – to do away with the intellectual bullying and political intolerance which the dictatorship of the proletariat had imposed! A third way, between Communism and Capitalism! An oasis of neutrality between East and West! And she the pretty wife of one of the leaders of this renaissance of the Czech nation! Bliss was it in that dawn to be alive . . . but to be young was very heaven!

Then the Russians marched in. Jaroslav Birek was among those who were flown to Moscow to be harangued and abused by the Soviet leaders. He returned with the others at Svoboda's insistence and at the crucial meeting of the Central Committee in 1969 he sided with Husak and voted Dubcek down.

Was it realism? Opportunism? Or had his orders altered from the KGB in Moscow? Whatever the reason, the enlightened Professor now reimposed the bleak Marxist ideology in which neither he nor anyone else any longer believed.

Katya left him or, more accurately, refused to go with him when he was obliged for his own safety to move out of their flat off the Wenceslas Square to an apartment in the Hradcany Castle. She also kept Josef and Jaroslav Birek did not claim him. In contrast to some of his colleagues, he lived a life of some austerity in a small, sparsely furnished flat, as if he were one of those fanatic Jesuits who in the sixteenth century had directed the eradication of religious dissent.

Although Josef barely saw his father after the age of six, he was nonetheless protected by his hidden hand. Much as she now loathed her husband for his betrayal of the nation, Katya, his mother, did not forgo the advantages which she derived from his official position. She had a new Skoda, wore a fur coat and bought Scotch whisky from the shops reserved for the Communist elite. Josef was sent to a special school for the children of Party leaders and, when it came to his National Service, he was posted to the English language school run by Army Intelligence. He found no difficulty in gaining a place to continue his study of English at Prague university even though, by this time, he had expressed his scepticism about Marxism and had declined an invitation to join the Party.

It could be said that in choosing to oppose the regime, the young Josef Birek was only following in the footsteps of his father and grandfather who had both been dissidents in their time. One can also see, however – without delving too deep into his subconscious – that there were Oedipal forces at work. Not only had the young Josef Birek felt abandoned by a father whom he rarely saw, but who he knew was up in the castle which broods over the city of Prague – but he was also raised on his mother's contempt for her estranged husband. There was hardly a day when she did not castigate the absent Jaroslav Birek for his pusillanimousness before the Russians — investing her invective with all the scorn of a passionate woman for an impotent man.

Katya Birekova was a nervous handsome woman who had the contempt for bourgeois morals which you only find in members of the bourgeoisie. She had lovers, as we know from some of Birek's stories, and she paraded them publicly in Prague. No one knows what Jaroslav made of this provocation; there was little he could do; but such wanton ways in the mother cannot have been good for the fragile feelings of her adolescent son.

He remained living with his mother because she had a large flat in the centre of the city. If he had taken up with some pretty, friendly girl he might have escaped her overbearing influence but from the way he portrays them in his stories it would seem that those girls he knew were either as neurotic as he was himself, or cunning little opportunists who saw in the son of a member of the Central Committee their pass to hard currency and an easy life. He preferred the company of his male friends, some of whom were zealous Catholics. Birek himself was drawn towards the Church — he looked at times like a young monk — but his mother was as atheist and anticlerical as his father and killed his piety with ridicule.

A greater commitment to the Catholic religion might have given him a strong sense of who he was, for if Birek had reason to be confused about his own identity as aristocrat, bourgeois or worker in a worker's state, he also shared in the common confusion which the history of his country inevitably bestowed. Hus, the heretic, was their national hero yet the prevalent religion was of those who had burned him. The Austrians were their historic oppressors — the Habsburgs the tyrants — yet every elegant arch and joyful spire in the city of Prague, and every star in the halo of every statue of the Virgin in every little village square, proclaimed their culture to be that of the Austrian empire. The Germans were the hated enemies of their more recent history — yet some of their most celebrated writers such as Kafka had written in German, and German was the language of the literary culture to which they had once belonged. How often had Josef berated the ghost of his grandfather, the mediocre playwright and Czech patriot, for his Slavophile aspirations. Now that they knew rule from Moscow, how happy the Bohemians would be to be governed once again from Vienna!

And yet the West – that shimmering land, flowing with milk and honey, which Josef had glimpsed throught the windows of Austrian and Bavarian television – provoked equally contradictory feelings. Certainly, as a good-looking boy of sixteen, he had not been immune from a certain narcissism and had passed through the phase of coveting stone-washed Levis: but since they could be got for dollars on the black market, they soon lost their allure and became, rather, a source of embarrassment – the mark of materialistic vulgarity. By the time he was twenty Josef dressed like most of his fellow intellectuals. They wore shapeless jerseys or knitted woollen jackets, drab trousers and sandals. Some had their hair long, like hippies in the 1960s, and several sported a Günter Grass moustache.

Already, at this age, Josef had had a sublime conception of his own vocation as thinker and writer. He did not want to shirk his predicament as a Czech in the 1980s but rather wished to suffer as his contemporaries suffered, and express in his work all the anguish they felt living with the false myths and hypocritical values of the Communist regime. He could quite easily, as the son of his father, have obtained a post at a university if he had been ready to pay lip-service to the Marxist orthodoxy; but he publicly refused, preferring to take a job as a caretaker in a secondary school in the suburbs.

Here he also had time to write in the warm room which housed the central heating boiler. Time was now important, because Josef had started the novel which he was to bring with him to the West. He had great ambitions for this longer work – not simply to establish his reputation among his fellow Czechs, but to impress upon the world on the other side of the Iron Curtain that the spirit of his nation was still alive.

Like all young writers, Josef vacillated between insensate optimism and abysmal pessimism when he imagined the destiny of his novel. He hoped that it would get beyond the carbon copies of a samizdat edition put together in Prague. He knew that Czechs living in Munich had received some of his stories, and so he felt confident that his novel would eventually be published by an émigré press abroad. Whether it would make him rich and famous like Milan Kundera in Paris, or sell a few hundred copies to Czechs living abroad, he could not predict.

And if it was translated, how would it fare? The literature of the West, as much as the West itself, filled him with ambivalent feelings. Certainly the freedom to write and publish without any restraint had led to great power and vitality in much of the fiction which he read in the reading-rooms of the British Council and the American Embassy. Yet he was somewhat taken aback by the vivid depiction of the characters' sexual behaviour in novels like Updike's *Couples* or Styron's *Sophie's Choice*. The Iron Curtain had not only kept out capitalism; it had also protected the Czechs of Birek's generation from the obsessive eroticism of the Western world. Some of his friends lamented it but Birek was something of a prude. Pornography, however elegant, shocked him; and it was matched in his mind with the grossness of the Mercedes and BMWs which arrived from the frontier filled with loud-mouthed German tourists and were parked provocatively outside the expensive hotels.

Thus in thinking of the West – and considering going there, as they all did from time to time – he was moved at one moment by a feeling of ineffable superiority – of spiritual aloofness from Western grossness and indulgence – and at the next by a despairing sense of inferiority as if the capitalist world was a jungle in which he might not survive.

Yet when he thought of a lifetime's privation and compromise – of the boredom and isolation which he felt even among his friends; as he saw one and then another peel off to kowtow surreptitiously to the Party in exchange for a comfortable job in a literature faculty or a publishing house, or others be driven by the petty persecution which they suffered into a self-conscious cult of political martyrdom; and as he saw his own future going one way or the other, and no hope of ever being truly free; then the West became the lure – particularly, because he knew English, London or New York.

When word came to him that one of his stories had been published in Munich he was pleased; but the news that they had been translated into English and published in *Outrage* filled him with ecstatic delight. Two months later one of the couriers of the Comenius Foundation smuggled in the issue in which his second story, 'The Spider and the Fly', had appeared, together with one hundred pounds in ten-pound notes as payment for what had been published so far. Josef was quite dazed with astonishment and pride. He showed the magazine to his mother, who did not seem particularly pleased, and then passed it around some of his English-speaking friends. They too seemed more envious than admiring so he took the magazine back to his own room and propped it up, open at his story, so that he could revere it like a holy text and wonder, as he stared at it, about the translator whose name, Laura Morton, was printed beneath his own.

The ten-pound notes, which as hard currency had an inflated value in Prague, encouraged Birek to believe that he would not find it hard to earn his living in the West. If he was paid that for a couple of stories, what would he be paid for a long novel! As the pile of paper on his desk grew higher, so his determination grew stronger not just to have it published in the West but to take it there himself. A glorious future seemed to await him, and so when the novel was finished he left.

SIX

It was only on Birek's second night in London that he found himself alone and so ventured out of the hostel to explore the city that he had imagined so vividly when living in Prague. It was dusk and he walked west and then north and then west again, having seen Baker Street marked on the map and hoping that perhaps in that direction he would find the London of the Sherlock Holmes stories he had read as a boy in the flat of the colonel's widow. He had seen enough of London already to realize that the gas street lamps had been replaced by orange neon, and that horse-drawn cabs no longer plied for trade on the streets of the modern city; but he hoped all the same to discover something of the atmosphere which he had imagined from reading Dickens and Henry James.

He walked down Tottenham Court Road and was immediately drawn into the kasbah of electronic consumer goods where window after window displayed pyramids of sleek black and silver machines – radios, televisions, home computers, compact disc players, stereos, video recorders, satellite dishes, camcorders, intercoms, radio telephones and quadraphonic sound systems. He stopped, peered and marvelled at the power and elegance of these ingenious machines – then did quick calculations into Czech crowns to see how many months or years he would have had to work in Prague to equip himself with all these adjuncts to life in the Western world.

He turned from the shop windows to the street and crossed at a light in front of the stream of gleaming cars. Here again it astonished him to realize that in London luxury was so banal. His mind was still attuned to the streets of Prague where a trickle of identical Skodas had coughed and spluttered around Wenceslas Square. The sight of so many large limousines charging north out of London filled him both with amazement and awe. He knew only too well what it cost to buy a Mercedes or a BMW – not a question in Prague of working months or years but of labouring over several lifetimes. Yet here they were, one after another, driven not by the chauffeurs of a government department but by ordinary men and women.

He turned into Charlotte Street and at once was intoxicated by the cosmopolitan atmosphere of French, Italian and Greek restaurants. He remembered a Bulgarian restaurant in Prague with its surly waiters and hideous décor – the walls lined with blown-up photographs of resorts on the Black Sea – and contrasted it with the French bistros, Greek tavernas and Italian pizzerias which are found in that part of London. This, then, was liberty – not just for the English themselves but for those who came to England like Herzen, Kossuth, Hugo, Zola and now Birek – to work, to thrive, and to spice the life of the indigenous population.

Yet where was this indigenous population? He looked into the

74

faces of those he passed in the street and could see none of the blonde-haired, blue-eyed Anglo-Saxons he had expected. There were Chinese, Arabs, Africans, Indians, Malays and many a swarthy Mediterranean. Whenever he saw what he took to be an Englishman, he always heard a babble of some other Nordic language. He crossed Oxford Street into Soho where instead of windows filled with stereos, or a display of the bill of fare, his eyes met the splayed breasts and proffered groins of the naked women on the hoardings outside the nightclubs and strip-joints. An ordinary young woman offered him a 'nice time' which with a blush he declined. He decided, indeed, that it was time to make his way back to the hostel.

He went into what he thought was a chemist to buy some toothpaste and soap but discovered to his embarrassment that it was a 'sex shop' selling handbooks, artefacts and unctions whose use Birek had never imagined. The girl who served him looked at him as if he was an imbecile when he asked for toothpaste, and he retreated scarlet in the face to find himself, on the street outside, entangled in a group of French teenage schoolchildren who tittered at him as he walked away.

He found a genuine chemist on Charing Cross Road and bought not just toothpaste and soap but also razor blades, deodorant, shaving cream and paper tissues, and came out with little change from the first of the ten-pound notes that MacDonald had given him for the first week's expenses. He realized with a certain alarm how careful he would have to be with his money, and how if he wanted to taste even the most modest delights of this glittering city he would have to think of ways to earn more.

He got back to the hostel just as a busload of Nigerian students were checking in. He squeezed through the crowd in the foyer to fetch his key, and was handed a note by the distracted receptionist. He had had two calls, one from Miroslav Maier; another from a certain Mr Eldon who had telephoned to invite him to lunch the next day. With his brow creased as he tried to think who Mr Eldon might be, Birek went up to his room and after writing one or two letters – including one to Laura Morton to thank her for the party – he took a bath and went to bed.

*

Miroslav Maier called on him at ten the next morning, sent by MacDonald to make sure that all was well. Birek instinctively took against him, seeing in the seedy émigré his worst fears for his own future, but since Maier represented the Comenius Foundation he could hardly refuse his offer to show him around.

'Avoid taxis,' said Maier, his toad's head wobbling as they walked towards Gower Street. 'The buses are quite good. The tube is better.'

'So many people seem to have cars,' said Birek.

'Of course, of course,' said Maier. 'I have a car. But I don't bring it into the centre of London.'

'Where do you live?'

'In Hounslow, near to the airport.'

'Is it pleasant out there?'

'No, but it is cheap.'

'Is it more expensive to live in the centre of the city?'

'That depends.'

'Where we went to the party of Mr and Mrs Morton?'

Maier whistled. 'There, my dear fellow, the prices have gone through the roof.'

'To rent a house like theirs, what would it cost?'

'Four or five hundred pounds.'

'A month?'

'A week!'

Birek glanced furtively at Miroslav Maier to see if he was teasing him but saw from his expression that he was not.

They got on a bus which took them towards Trafalgar Square. 'But I do not understand,' said Birek, 'how a man can afford to pay so much each week simply for a roof over his head.'

'People like the Mortons do not rent their houses, they buy them.'

'But if it costs so much to rent such a house, how much would it cost to buy one?'

'Half a million, perhaps. Six hundred thousand.'

'And they have that much money?'

'My dear Birek, that is only their London house. In the country they have another much larger house with land as well and cottages for their servants.'

'It is really like something out of the history books,' said Birek.

'There are times,' said Maier, 'when you feel that you are living in a novel by Trollope or Jane Austen.'

'And Dickens?'

'Even Dickens.'

They got off the bus at Trafalgar Square and walked to the National Gallery.

'Take these Impressionists,' said Maier, waving to the wall of paintings, and exhaling malodorous air from his lungs. 'Each of those is now worth several million pounds, not because of their intrinsic value, but in obedience to the laws of supply and demand. It is the same with houses, with labour, with everything. You grow rich if you have something others value.'

'And if you have nothing, you stay poor?'

'Precisely. And since all I have is my knowledge of Czech, for which there is very little demand indeed, I remain poor and live in Hounslow.'

'What does Mr Morton possess that is in such demand?'

'No one really knows. He is a banker – *c'est tout*. The City, you see, is like a castle full of conjurors who spin gold from straw. Peasants like us are never admitted so we can never steal their spells.'

'Yet they did not seem like grasping people.'

'Of course not, because to them money is nothing new. His family, I imagine, always had some money and Laura's father was a very rich man.'

'So she is rich too?'

'Of course. You only find that delicacy and dignity in women with money.'

'She is very beautiful,' said Birek simply.

'Beautiful, yes,' said Maier with a sigh. 'And think, my dear fellow, that for two or three days a week I sit in the same room as that woman!'

'You are very lucky.'

'Lucky? As lucky as the starving man who works in a busy kitchen.'

'How can you be starving? You have a wife.'

'Did you meet my wife?'

Birek smiled. 'I can see that compared to Mrs Morton . . .'

77

'I tell you, Josef, it is a daily torment to have that angel constantly before my eyes and know that never, in a thousand thousand years, could I ever be her lover.'

'Nor anyone else,' said Birek chivalrously.

'Many have tried,' said Maier, 'but all have failed.'

'She does not look like a woman who would betray her husband.'

'In those circles, my dear Birek, little is made of the occasional affair. But in the case of our beloved Laura, there is no one qualified as her *cavaliere servente*. Even a champion Don Juan like Eldon was sent away with a flea in his ear.'

'Eldon?' said Birek. 'A man called Eldon has invited me to lunch.'

'You met him at the Mortons'.'

'Was he the man from the British Council?'

Maier laughed. 'No. He is a journalist but also a great friend of writers like Geoffrey Bartle and Ashton Lowe.'

'He told me on the telephone that I would meet them at lunch.'

Maier sniffed and gave a furtive look of envy at his compatriot. 'Then you're off to a flying start,' he said. 'Bartle, Lowe, Henriot – that's the inner circle of the literary smart set.'

'Bartle, I know, has a high reputation.'

'Of course. And Henriot is very successful too, thanks to the reviews he gets from Bartle and Lowe.'

'They are part of a literary school?' suggested Birek.

'You could call it that,' said Maier.

'Are they realists or experimentalists?'

'Back-scratchers,' said Maier.

Birek looked puzzled. 'Back-scratchers?'

'You must always remember, Josef,' said Maier, 'that the British are pragmatists. They don't form schools around styles but rather around cliques of old friends.'

'I see.' He paused, then added: 'But since I am not an old friend, I do not understand why I have been invited.'

'Because Eldon is an old friend.'

'But I am not a friend of Eldon.'

'No, my dear fellow, but you have a guardian angel called Laura Morton.'

*

78

Birek found his own way back from Trafalgar Square to the hostel where, shortly before one, Eldon came to fetch him.

'How are you getting on?' he asked as if he was not particularly interested in the answer.

'It is very exhilarating,' said Birek, 'but also confusing.'

'I dare say.'

They walked out into Tottenham Court Road and turned left towards Soho. 'Do you mind walking?' asked Eldon. 'It isn't very far.'

'Not at all. It is very kind of you to . . .'

'Laura thought you should meet a few English writers,' said Eldon, 'and since I had fixed this lunch some time ago, I thought I might as well take you along.'

'I am most grateful.'

'I should warn you,' said Charlie, turning to Birek with an ironic but well-meaning smile, 'that I myself have a particular loathing for literature of every kind.'

Birek blushed. 'Then why do you have lunch with writers?'

'One cannot desert old friends just because they turn into posturing frauds.'

'You would rather they were journalists like you?'

'Truth is to be found in hard facts, not pretentious fantasies.'

'You sound like Mr Gradgrind,' said Birek.

'Who is Mr Gradgrind?'

Birek hesitated, unable to believe that an educated Englishman was not familiar with the novels of Charles Dickens. 'Isn't he a character in *Hard Times*?' he asked.

'I dare say,' said Eldon. 'I've never read it.'

They crossed Oxford Street and walked through Soho Square – Eldon walking ahead with wide paces, Birek almost running to follow.

'Do you never take pleasure in art?' asked Birek.

'Less than in food and women.'

'They appeal to the senses but not the soul.'

'My soul expired when I was twenty-two.'

'Perhaps . . .' Birek began. He blushed, then said: 'Does Mrs Morton have a soul?'

Eldon did not slow his pace. 'I'm sure she would want you to call her Laura.'

'My first gaffe,' said Birek. 'I wrote to her this morning as Mrs Morton.'

'Hardly a gaffe. She'll be touched.'

'Touched?'

'Moved. Her feelings . . . favourably affected.'

'I see. I did not know that meaning of the word.'

Eldon stopped and pointed up to a blue plaque on a house in the street where they stood. 'Once the home of Karl Marx.'

'If only they knew what crimes would be committed in his name.'

'It was in that house that he seduced his wife's maid, disowned her bastard and led his legitimate children to believe that the father was Engels.'

'I didn't know.'

'The champion of the proletariat had a very bourgeois sense of propriety.'

They came to an Italian restaurant and went in. Eldon was greeted with a familiar smile by the hat-check girl. 'The two writers I expect to be here,' he said as he took off his coat, 'are Geoffrey Bartle and Ashton Lowe.'

'I have heard of them, of course.'

'They're both better self-publicists than they are writers – particularly Lowe, who's our resident performing Yank.'

'He's American?'

'Yes.'

'And Bartle?'

'He's Welsh though he always denies it.' Eldon took Birek's coat and gave it, with his own, to the hat-check girl.

'Eddie Henriot might also turn up,' he said as he led Birek into the restaurant. 'He's won a couple of literary prizes but I've never met anyone who's enjoyed one of his novels.'

'You haven't met the judges who awarded the prizes?'

Eldon smiled. 'I've met them all.'

A waiter led them to a table where three men sat drinking Negronis. Eldon introduced Birek. Geoffrey Bartle, who sat squatly at the head of the table, waved to an empty chair next to his and Birek sat down. Henriot, a leaner, furtive-looking man, gave a twitch which might have been a smile. Only the American, Ashton

Lowe, got to his feet, clasped Birek's hand and said: 'Welcome, Birek, welcome to the West.'

'I am really most glad to be here,' said Birek – flushing with emotion as he found himself admitted into this inner circle of English letters.

Bartle glanced at Henriot and raised his eyes as if to say: 'What kind of goose have we here?' but Lowe, who as an American could at least recognize sincerity, clapped him on the back with the same hand that had a moment before almost crushed his fingers. The two newcomers sat down and Eldon ordered a further round of Negronis.

'Have you heard,' Bartle asked Eldon, 'what Ash has just landed for a two-book deal?'

'It's confidential,' said Ashton with a sly grin.

Bartle leaned forward and said, in a pretended whisper: 'Seven three zero . . .'

'Go on.'

'Zero zero . . .'

'Zero,' said Henriot.

'Pounds or dollars?' asked Eldon.

'Dollars,' said Ashe. 'And I don't get it all at once.'

'You would think,' said Eldon, 'that they would either make it a million, or three quarters of a million. Why seven hundred and *thirty* thousand?'

'I guess that's what I'm worth.'

'Less than Jeffrey Archer or Shirley Conran,' said Bartle.

'Less than Schyler. Derrings paid him a million for a two-book deal.'

'Schyler!' cried Henriot in mock despair. 'He couldn't write the copy for a Tampax ad.'

'He was on the short list of the Axminster Prize for that last book of his.'

'That's only because Sally was one of the judges.'

'Has he fucked her?' asked Ashton.

'Who hasn't fucked her?'

'I haven't fucked her,' said Henriot.

'If you had, your book might have made it to the short list.'

'Have *you* fucked her?' Henriot asked Bartle.

81

'Take it from me,' said Bartle with a knowing nod. 'If you haven't fucked her, then you and Birek are the only ones here who haven't.'

Henriot turned to Ashton. 'Have you fucked her?'

'I'm afraid so.'

Henriot turned to Eldon. 'And you?'

'Charlie has fucked everyone,' said Bartle.

'Not *everyone*,' teased Ashton Lowe.

'No one fucks Laura Morton,' said Bartle. 'Her knickers are glued to her thighs. But Sally de Lacey – you *must* have fucked her?'

'The requisite half-dozen,' said Eldon.

'She certainly doesn't merit more,' said Lowe.

'I know someone who *hasn't* fucked her,' said Bartle.

'Besides me,' said Henriot.

'Besides you.'

'Who?' asked Eldon.

'Our Dave.'

'She wouldn't have him?'

'She was willing, and so was he . . .'

'A no show?' asked Henriot.

Bartle nodded sadly.

'He was probably too pissed,' said Henriot.

'He tried drunk and he tried sober.'

'No good?'

'A fiasco on both occasions.'

Since a waitress was waiting to take their order, Bartle now looked down at the menu. Birek glanced anxiously at Eldon, looking for guidance as to what he should choose. Eldon asked for six oysters followed by roast duck. Birek, seeing the price, chose a cheaper *scaloppine Milanese* preceded by carrot soup.

When the waitress had withdrawn, and while Eldon was pouring out the red wine which had been brought to their table, Birek turned to the three novelists. 'Tell me,' he asked, his youthful voice with its mild Czech accent cutting through the hubbub with precision, 'do you feel that the concept of God, and of the miraculous, can any longer be brought into the realistic novel as, for example, in the novels of Graham Greene?'

'Uh?' Bartle gawped at him with a look of bafflement on his face.

'Do we feel *what*?' asked Henriot, reaching for his glass of Valpolicella.

'I have noticed,' said Birek, getting into his stride, 'from the few contemporary English novels that I was able to read in Prague, that there is a certain measure of whimsical fantasy in the novels say of Rushdie or others of the magic realism school; and then there is the strict and invariable domestic realism of those novels written particularly by women, but I do not think that subsequent to Graham Greene – and indeed not in his later novels – there is any realistic depiction of the supernatural within the confines of realism as a stylistic form.'

Eldon tried to hide a yawn. 'Well?' he said to his friends. 'Can none of you enlighten our Czech friend?'

'Nope,' said Bartle. 'Greene was on his own.'

'I think,' said Ashton who fancied himself as a literary critic, 'that there isn't really . . . I mean to say, there isn't one of us who would claim a sufficiently comprehensive knowledge of the novels written by our contemporaries to be able to say definitively yea or nay.'

'What he means,' said Eldon with a sneer, 'is that none of them read books other than their own.'

'Unless we're paid to review them,' said Bartle.

'And how, may I ask,' asked Henriot, 'could Ash have got involved in that little fracas about plagiarism if he hadn't read Herder's novel?'

Lowe frowned. 'You had better explain to Mr Birek that it was I who was plagiarized, not I who did the plagiarizing.'

'I'm sure he took it in no other way,' said Henriot.

Birek looked confused.

'The fact is,' said Ashton Lowe in the emphatic tones that went down so well on television, 'there are thirty thousand books published every year in Britain alone, of which three thousand are novels. To read them all would mean reading eight or nine a day. So even with the best will in the world, one could not be expected to have a comprehensive knowledge of what is going on.'

'With so many books,' said Birek, 'how do new authors ever get noticed?'

'If you're Schyler,' said Bartle, 'by fucking literary editors like Sally de Lacey.'

'But surely,' said Birek, 'some of the literary editors are men.'

'Of course,' said Eldon. 'And you don't have to sleep with them as you might if you were an actor or in the fashion world. But you find after a while that you've all slept with the same woman, and it creates a kind of fraternity.'

'We call it the extended family,' said Henriot.

'Held together,' said Ashton, 'by the silken cords of shared affections and venereal diseases.'

'Until death us do part,' said Bartle.

'He is alluding,' said Eldon to Birek, 'to that unfortunate disease called AIDS. I dare say you were spared that behind the Iron Curtain.'

Birek blushed. 'I believe there have been one or two cases in Prague, but only among homosexuals who have travelled abroad.'

'Here,' said Bartle, 'it spread from the fist-fuckers to the teen-age slags. In some of those dungeon discos you can practically smell it in the air – wisps of the dreaded virus mingling with the fumes of cocaine and the clouds of grass.' He sniffed the air of the restaurant as if imitating a bloodhound. 'The acrid smell of pus and incontinence. Unclean! Unclean!' He laughed loudly and emptied his glass of wine.

Birek looked perplexed. 'Is it really widespread, this terrible disease?'

'Everywhere,' said Henriot.

'It's all those boogies,' said Bartle.

'Boogies?' asked Birek.

'Blacks,' said Eldon.

'Dem coons comin' floodn' in,' said Bartle, 'from dat dere dark continent of Aahfrika.'

'In Uganda,' said Henriot, 'they say half the population has got it.'

'They invented it,' said Eldon, 'by buggering the monkeys.'

'Dat is deir way of life,' said Bartle. 'Dey bugger dem dere monkeys, den dey knock up de wife, den dey knock up de girl friend, den dey knock up de girl friend's sister, den deir wife's cousin, den dey do come to ol' Inglad to sell deir crop of ko-kaine dat dey do smuggle in under deir kaftans, and den dey do spend de mon-eh on de bonking de whitie ladies in dat dere Shepherd's Mar-ket.'

Birek looked perplexed: he had not understood a word. 'Are you saying,' he asked, 'that in Africa it is not just the homosexuals who have AIDS, but also heterosexual men and women?'

'So we are told,' said Eldon.

'But surely those with the disease are not allowed to enter England?'

'How could you stop them?'

'By tests, surely.'

'For everyone who flies into Heathrow?'

'No, only those from Africa.'

'It would be thought prejudiced.'

'Why?'

'Because they're black.'

'It seems a very dangerous situation,' said Birek.

'Just think before you flirt before you fuck,' said Bartle.

'It suggests caution,' said Eldon.

'Never venture abroad without your Frenchies,' said Henriot.

'And put iodine pills into public lavatories,' said Ashton.

'You can't catch it from public lavatories,' said Eldon.

'That's what they *say*,' said Bartle. 'But would you borrow a toothbrush off someone with AIDS?'

'It's in the tear glands,' said Henriot, 'so why not in the sweat glands? Christ, there's AIDS in the steam of every Turkish bath in England.'

The thought of this plague did not diminish the appetite of Eldon and his literary friends for their food and drink. The oysters, soups and pâtés came and went; bottle after bottle of Valpolicella was brought and then emptied at the table. A new course came – the roast duck and *scaloppine* – and with it new topics of conversation. Not all were treated with the same reckless levity as they had shown towards AIDS. Bartle wept into his wineglass about the imminence of a nuclear Armageddon while Ashton explained to Birek that it was the tyranny of Ronald Reagan that forced him to live abroad. Henriot's loathing was for the iniquitous despotism of Margaret Thatcher, and as they moved on to rum baba, doppo espressos, grappa and brandy each became more fervent in his protestations of loyalty to the socialist cause.

Eldon remained detached: Birek was baffled. The bill arrived and each chipped in twenty-five pounds. Neither Eldon nor any of his friends offered to pay for Birek. The party broke up. Eldon went off to Fleet Street. Birek returned to the hostel feeling little wiser about English men of letters but forewarned and forearmed against AIDS – and the cost of lunch in the West End.

SEVEN

Andrew MacDonald, the director of the Comenius Foundation, was waiting in the foyer to take him to the Home Office. 'There should be no problem about political asylum,' he said as they sat back in a taxi, 'but we have to go through the formality of an interview.'

'Of course.'

'I wouldn't want to advise you as to what you should say,' said MacDonald. 'Just bear in mind that they have to satisfy themselves that you are a genuine political refugee.'

'Of course.'

'It's a good thing you're white, of course,' MacDonald went on, 'and that Czechoslovakia is a Communist country. They've all read their Le Carré. They're not so keen on these Tamils and Vietnamese.'

They arrived at the Home Office, which was not at all what Birek had expected. He had imagined some Victorian or Edwardian building with a wide entrance beneath the portico of a neo-classical façade. Instead he found a modern building of scarred concrete with high walls and overhanging parapets, designed as if to withstand an imminent insurrection. He was glad to have MacDonald with him to give his name to the sour receptionist and escort him past the grim security guards.

They went up four floors in the lift, turned left along an air-conditioned, neon-lit corridor and knocked on a door marked with the number 487. No one answered. MacDonald opened the door and led Birek in. The room was empty. 'This is where we wait,' said MacDonald, sitting on one of the blue chairs placed up against the wall.

There was no furniture in the room besides the chairs. Birek went to the window and looked down over Green Park. The wine he had drunk at lunch in Soho had left him feeling groggy. He longed to go back to sleep in his bed at the hostel. He repeated in his mind MacDonald's phrase – 'There should be no problem about political asylum.' What tense was that? Future conditional? Did that mean that there might be trouble? That his application might be turned down? That he might be deported to Czechoslovakia? In all the months and years he had spent thinking about flight to the West, it had never occurred to him that the West would send him back.

A woman entered. 'Mr Birek?' she asked.

'Yes.'

'Come this way, please.'

She did not smile. She seemed to Birek, as he followed her, like a nurse in a hospital taking a patient to see a specialist. He felt she might suddenly turn and ask for a sample of his urine.

MacDonald walked beside him with no particular expression on his face. The woman opened a door and then stood aside to let them enter. Birek went in first and found himself immediately face to face with two men and a woman. They were sitting in a row on the far side of a rectangular table.

The man in the middle of this group whom Birek took to be the presiding official pointed towards a chair in the centre of the room. 'Please sit down,' he said in an impersonal tone of voice.

The chair was about five feet from the table. Birek looked around to see if he might sit further away from his interrogators, but MacDonald had already seated himself on one of the two chairs at the back of the room, and the woman who had escorted them along the corridor was making for the other. She pointed to the chair in the middle of the room and Birek, seeing no alternative, stepped forward and sat down.

'The purpose of this hearing, Mr Birek,' said the presiding official who was a balding, bespectacled, middle-aged man, 'is to confirm that you qualify for political asylum according to the section of the requisite Act.'

Birek nodded. 'Yes.'

'You will understand, I am sure, that there are numerous foreign nationals who attempt each year to evade United Kingdom immigration regulations by claiming that they are persecuted in their native land.'

'Of course.'

'Now we know from Mr MacDonald who is here as your official sponsor that he and his colleagues at the Comenius Foundation have no doubt whatsoever that you are a genuine victim of official discrimination in Czechoslovakia.'

'Yes.'

'He cites your inability to get your work published in your own country.'

'Yes.'

The presiding official looked down at the papers on his desk, then up again at Birek over the rims of his spectacles. 'You will agree, I am sure, that a rejection slip – or even a bundle of rejection slips – is not in itself incontrovertible evidence that a writer is persecuted?'

'Yes.'

'If it were, then we would have to grant asylum to every third-rate writer who chose to make Britain his home.'

'Of course.'

'Do you have, by any chance, some documentary evidence to prove that your work has been banned or rejected for its political content?'

Birek shifted in his chair. 'I am sorry. I am not quite sure what you mean.'

'A letter from a publishing house, for example, saying that a book of yours is unpublishable because its political content is unacceptable?'

'No.'

'You did not bring such a letter with you, or such a letter does not exist?'

'There never was such a letter because there never was any question of publishing what I wrote in official publishing houses or magazines.'

'There never was any question?' He repeated Birek's assertion with mild irony.

'No.'

'So you never submitted anything?'

'No, well, one or two early works – a poem, once . . .'

'On what subject?'

'I beg your pardon?'

'What was the poem about?'

Birek blushed. 'Snowflakes.'

'I see. You submitted a poem about snowflakes and it was rejected for political reasons.'

'Yes.'

'The editor wrote to you, did he, to say that your treatment of snowflakes was ideologically unacceptable?'

'He did not say that exactly . . .'

'He simply rejected it?'

'Yes, but his reasons for rejecting it were ideological.'

The presiding official sighed and turned to the second man who said: 'Forgive me, Mr Birek, but how can a poem about snowflakes be ideologically unacceptable?'

'Because of its symbolic meaning. In the poem the fresh flakes of snow, like the youth of Czechoslovakia, are crushed by the boots of the militia.'

'Was this symbolism clear to the editor?'

'Of course.'

'And that was why he rejected it?'

'You must understand,' said Birek, 'that it is not so much the poem as the writer who is judged to be ideologically unacceptable or not. The publishers are either members of the Party or they are fellow travellers who accept the Party line. They would lose their jobs if they took the work of someone who was opposed to the Marxist ideology.'

Now the woman leaned forward. 'Is it not possible, Mr Birek, that your poem was rejected because it was a bad poem?'

Birek turned pale. 'No. That was not the reason.'

There was a brief moment of silence, as if time should be left for Birek's last statement to sink into the plastic walls of the air-conditioned room. Then the presiding official resumed his questions.

'Having failed to have your poem on snowflakes published, you then turned to what is commonly called samizdat publication?'

'Yes.'

'And all of your subsequent works were published in this form?'

'Yes.'

'Some of them, eventually, reaching the West?'

'Yes.'

'Where they were translated into German, English . . .'

'Yes. And Swedish.'

'And Swedish. I'm sorry.' He apologized with an irony that was imperceptible to the Czech. 'And this gained you a certain recognition abroad?'

'Yes.'

'Quite justified, I am sure.' The presiding official peered over the rims of his spectacles again – not at Birek this time but at Andrew MacDonald.

MacDonald nodded but said nothing. The presiding official looked back at Birek. 'These works of yours were published over what period of time?'

'Three or four years.'

'Three or four years.' He repeated the figure and made a note of it. 'And do you think that during this time the authorities were aware that you were publishing your works in this way?'

'I imagine so. They know everything.'

'The Secret Police?'

'Yes.'

'So they knew, presumably, that your work had been smuggled abroad and was published there?'

'Yes.'

'Is that against the law?'

'Yes.'

'Were you prosecuted?'

'No. They do not always prosecute.'

The woman now scrutinized Birek and said: 'Was this because of your father?'

Birek frowned. 'My father? No. It was because there was no evidence that I myself sent my work to be published abroad.'

'Are the Secret Police always so scrupulous about evidence?' asked the presiding official.

'In recent years there has been some semblance of legality,' said Birek.

'But your father is Jaroslav Birek, is he not?' the woman persisted.

'Yes.'

'A member of the Central Committee of the Czech Communist Party?'

'Yes.'

'To be quite honest, Mr Birek,' she said, 'it is difficult for me to believe that you could have been persecuted for your political beliefs with a father in that position.'

'It depends what you call persecution . . .' Birek began.

'It does indeed,' said the presiding official.

'There is no liberty,' said Birek, his voice rising a semi-tone. 'It is difficult to explain how such a pernicious system works, but just because writers are not tortured or imprisoned does not mean that they are not oppressed.'

'That may well be so,' said the presiding official.

The younger man now sat back in his chair and said to Birek: 'How did you earn your living?'

'I had a job – a manual job – as a school janitor.'

'Was that the only job you could get?'

'Without compromising, yes.'

'How do you mean? Without compromising?'

'I was qualified to teach English at a university, but to get an appointment I should have had to join the Party.'

'And stop writing subversive poems about snowflakes?'

'Yes.'

'And how do you intend to earn your living here?'

'I . . . I hadn't yet thought. In any way I can.'

'You have brought no money with you?'

'No. I . . . It was not possible.'

'I gather that the Comenius Foundation is prepared to help you up to a point.'

'It has very kindly offered to support me for a time.'

'Three months, I believe?' The presiding official looked towards MacDonald.

MacDonald nodded.

'And after that?'

'I have a novel which is almost completed.'

'You hope to have that published in London?'

'Yes.'

'And to earn your living here as a writer rather than as caretaker?'

'Yes.'

'You do not expect to be a charge on our social services.'

'No.'

'You speak English very well,' said the woman.

'Thank you,' said Birek.

'It must have taken some time to reach such proficiency.'

'Ten years.'

'You were taught as a child?'

'Yes.'

'And kept it up?'

'Yes.'

'With a view, perhaps, to visiting England or the United States?'

'With a view to reading what was published in the English-speaking world.'

'But you must have realized that English would be useful if ever you decided to emigrate?'

'I did not calculate in this way.'

'You did not plan to come West?'

'Not at first.'

'But subsequently?'

'Yes.'

'Just when and why did you make the decision?'

'Suddenly, in March.'

'Did any particular act of persecution drive you to leave?'

'No. It was just . . .' He hesitated.

'What?'

'The general situation.'

'But surely if anything has changed in Czechoslovakia, it is for the better?'

'Perhaps.'

'So what made you make up your mind?'

'I don't know. I had finished a novel and I felt that it would never be published in Prague.'

'You could sell it better in the West?'

'Not sell it. Publish it. I was so constrained by the knowledge that I was writing a book which would only reach a few hundred of my friends.'

'You thought it deserved better?'

'Yes. And I thought that if I escaped from the oppressive atmosphere of Prague, I would write a better book in the future.'

'So it was an artistic impulse, not a commercial calculation?'

'Yes. An artistic impulse.'

'But not flight from political persecution?'

'No . . . I mean, yes. The two go together.'

The presiding official sighed. 'I appreciate, Mr Birek, that you must have lived under certain constraints in Czechoslovakia but I am not convinced that they amounted to persecution for your beliefs.'

'Unless you live there,' said Birek, 'you cannot know.'

'I dare say.' The presiding official gathered up his papers, then glanced at his colleagues to see if either wished to put a further question.

'Tell me,' asked the younger man, 'why did you choose to come to England?'

'Because . . .' Birek hesitated.

'Because you spoke English?'

'No,' said Birek. 'They speak English in America and Australia too.'

'Then why?'

'Because I thought . . . I always thought of England as the land of liberty.'

'Of course,' said the presiding official, 'and so it is. But you will appreciate that the essence of liberty is the rule of law.' He stood, gave a supercilious smile and then, followed by the two other officials, left the room by a side door.

The woman who had brought them to the hearing now escorted

Birek and MacDonald to the lift. No one spoke as they walked along the corridor and MacDonald's face bore no expression. It was only when they had left the Home Office and were out in the street that he turned to Birek and said: 'You did very well.'

'I did very badly,' said Birek grimly. 'It is certain that my application will be rejected.'

'Don't worry about them,' said MacDonald. 'They're the bureaucrats and bureaucrats always side with the bureaucrats whichever regime they serve.'

'All the same, they decide.'

MacDonald hailed a taxi. 'They advise the minister,' he said, 'and then the minister decides.'

'According to the law . . .'

'Fiddlesticks. According to what will put him in the best light.' The taxi drew up beside them. 'And it wouldn't look good for a Tory minister to turn away a famous dissident – particularly if he's the son of a Communist leader.' MacDonald showed Birek into the taxi. 'And there's another thing,' he said before he closed the door. 'The minister happens to be an old school friend of Francis Morton, and will do anything that Laura asks him.'

Birek had no further engagements that night and so remained alone in the hostel. He ate nothing but lay on his bed, exhausted by the events of the day. He was an artist, after all, whose delicate nerves made even the most casual encounter an exacting business. In Prague he had led a semi-solitary life in the boiler-room at the school and at his mother's flat: now, in a single day, he had been flung into a crowd of unknown people – Maier, Eldon, Bartle, Lowe, Henriot, MacDonald and the three civil servants.

At nine he decided to go to bed. Feeling sticky after a day in a dirty city, and knowing that he must do something to calm his nerves before trying to sleep, Birek decided to take a bath. He undressed, put on his dressing-gown, took up his towel and a bar of soap, and set off for the bathroom at the end of the corridor.

The door was locked. He could hear someone singing inside. Birek went back to his room but left his door ajar. Five minutes later he heard the lock click open on the bathroom door. He rose quickly to claim it and was halfway there when a huge Nigerian came out of the bathroom and greeted him as he passed with a friendly 'Hello!'

Birek went into the steamy bathroom. He leaned over to put in the plug and as he did so remembered what Bartle and Henriot had said about AIDS and was seized by a horrifying panic. Everyone in Africa had it! The virus is in the sweat glands! It permeates the steam of Turkish baths! His heart beat faster. His breathing quickened. The imagination which served him so well in writing his stories now went to work to terrify him. He ran to the window, tugged it open and stuck his head out into the smutty air.

When his lungs were full he held his breath and looked back into the bathroom. A draught had blown the steam out of the window. He breathed normally and looked at the bath. It was clean but clearly many million microbes could have been secreted on to the smooth enamel. He must disinfect it, but how? His mind ran back to the medicines he had bought at the chemist in the Charing Cross Road. Mouthwash? No. Perhaps his hair lotion? That was absurd. Then he remembered the bottle of vodka which he had bought duty free on the plane from Vienna.

He ran back to his room, grabbed the bottle of vodka and a box of matches, and with both hidden under his towel he returned to the bathroom. He closed and locked the door, laid his towel on the cork seat of the chair, and then with a deft twist of his right hand emptied the bottle of vodka along the side of the bath, lit a match and dropped it into the bath. The whole tub burst into a blue flame which burned for a few seconds, then puckered out.

Birek picked up the dead match, put it into his dressing-gown pocket, closed the window and ran a deep bath. He lay in it for a long time, and when he finally went to bed, slept without dreams.

EIGHT

When Andrew MacDonald got back to the Comenius Foundation from the Home Office he found Laura Morton still at her desk. He drew up the chair from behind the desk of Miroslav Maier (Miroslav had gone home to Hounslow) and told Laura about Birek's interrogation. 'It always amazes me,' he said, his Scottish accent growing stronger because he was tired, 'that they're so damned rude – quite apart from anything else.'

Laura frowned. 'Why, I wonder?' she asked in her gentle voice.

'Oh, partly the conviction that the whole world wants to sponge off our Welfare State and partly instinctive sympathy for their opposite numbers in Prague.'

'But they aren't Communists, surely . . .'

'No. It's just a reflex bureaucratic distaste for oddballs like Birek.'

'Does that mean that they might not allow him to stay in this country?'

'I don't think that we should take it for granted.'

'Then we must go to work.'

'I seem to remember that you know the minister.'

'Yes.'

'Could you put a word in his ear?'

'Of course.'

'We must also think of some way for Josef to earn a living.'

'Can't the Foundation support him?'

'Not indefinitely.'

'Couldn't we give him a job?'

'And sack Miroslav?'

'No. You couldn't do that.'

'Have you read his novel?'

'Not yet.'

'Do you think he could get an advance?'

'Pritchard seemed interested.'

'Can you follow that up?'

'Of course.'

MacDonald went back to his office. Laura looked at her watch. It was twenty to six – probably too late to catch Pritchard at his office, but worth trying all the same. She stooped to take her address book out of her handbag to find Pritchard's office number. As she did so, her telephone rang. It was Charlie Eldon.

'Laura?'

'Yes.'

'I took your Czech to lunch.'

'You are sweet.'

'I thought you might like a report.'

'Yes. How did it go?'

'Predictably.'

'What does that mean?'

'I don't think it was quite what he expected.'

'He just wanted to meet some English writers.'

'He seemed a little taken aback.'

'By what?'

'By Bartle.'

'What did Bartle say?'

'The usual ribald stuff.'

'Didn't Josef find it amusing?'

'He's on the earnest side.'

'The Czechs have a particular sense of humour,' said Laura defensively.

'So does Bartle.'

'What about the others – Henriot and Lowe?'

'They're not very curious about what goes on outside London and possibly New York.'

'They found him a bore?'

'In a word.'

'How pathetic!'

'Pathetic, perhaps, but that's London literary life.'

'Poor Josef. He had such high hopes.'

'It may have been his first, but it won't be his last disappointment.'

Laura frowned. 'What should we do about getting his novel published?'

'Send it to Pritchard.'

'Shouldn't it go through an agent?'

97

Eldon hesitated. 'Yes, perhaps it should.'

'Which one?'

'There are several.'

'Who would you suggest?'

Again Eldon paused to consider the question. 'The best is probably Bartle's agent, Stephanie Parr, if she could be persuaded to take him on.'

'Do you know her?'

'I have met her.'

'How do I get hold of her?'

'I'll ring her, if you like, and prepare the ground.'

'That would be kind.'

'I'll talk to you tomorrow.'

'Good. And Charlie . . .'

'What?'

'Thanks again for taking Birek to lunch.'

She put down the telephone with a smile on her face – not a fond smile, however, but a smile of self-satisfaction. Women usually take credit for the passions they inspire in men and Laura was no exception.

It was at that quiet little chat at the end of her party that she had asked Charlie to take Birek to meet his literary friends and that Charlie without protest had agreed to do so. The wolf had been tamed to a lap-dog and now whenever she whistled he came to heel. It was an ignoble servitude for such a skilled seducer, and to save a little of his self-respect Charlie told himself that he was playing a waiting game; but an honest diagnosis of his true condition would reveal all the symptoms of *grand amour*.

When Laura had rejected him (over the Dover sole and the rack of lamb) he had done his best to shrug off the reverse and return to the life he had led before. 'There are more fish in the sea than ever came out of it,' he told himself and, in coarser terms than I care to use here, one woman is much like another. He therefore took out some of the women on his list of reserves but quickly discovered to his own dismay that all of them bored him both at dinner and in bed. The mere thought of Laura, prompted by something as insignificant as the sight of a Mercedes Estate, threw him into a sexual frenzy which no woman but Laura could calm. More degrading still, his heart beat faster whenever the telephone rang in the hope that it was her, and his spirits sank if, when he picked up the receiver, he heard the voice of anyone else. He saw her and spoke to her whenever he could, going time and again to the most tedious dinners and sitting next to the same old spinsters, all for that moment at the end of the evening when she would chat to him as her special friend.

He suffered the usual torments of jealousy – not so much of Laura's husband as of the men who worked at the Comenius Foundation – first Andrew MacDonald whose position of authority he must surely use to seduce her, then of Miroslav Maier whose lascivious looks she had described to him with an amused disgust. There he was, day after day, at the next desk: would he not, in time, wear her down? Charlie loathed him for daring to desire Laura and spent hours imagining the ways he would punish him if he ever had his way.

He was jealous of Birek even before Birek arrived in England, because Laura often talked about his wonderful stories. When he met him at Laura's party, and saw how young and delicate he was, his jealousy became less that of a lover than of a pettish, rival child. What right had this Czech to her affectionate smiles? What had he done to deserve her approbation? A few pretentious poems and mannered stories did not merit privileges of this kind.

But while a tamed dog like Charlie knew better than to bite the new puppy in the presence of his mistress, he retained an instinctive cunning and realized at once that Laura's patronage of Birek could be used to his advantage. She had contacts, certainly, among bankers and Tory politicians but it was Charlie who moved in the literary world. He therefore agreed to take Birek to meet Bartle, Henriot and Lowe, knowing that all three would find him heavy going. It would have been one thing to bring along an American celebrity like Updike or Bellow, or even a South American like Márquez or Vargas Llosa, but an obscure Czech who had only been published in *Outrage!* 'Christ, what a crasher,' would be Bartle's judgement and it was – delivered over the snooker table on the afternoon after the lunch in Soho and word went out to the London literati to watch out for Charlie's 'blank Czech' – otherwise known as 'Birek the bore'.

He showed the same double-edged benevolence in suggesting the services of Stephanie Parr. She was indisputably one of the best literary agents in London – pretty, brittle and audacious in her demands for her authors. She was particularly clever at suggesting to male publishers that the size of their advance was a measure of their prowess, and had often shown herself willing to consummate a contract in her bed at the Frankfurter Hof. She therefore established over the years a network of former lovers among publishers in London and New York who were happy to do business with an old flame, and her reputation for extracting large advances attracted the ablest authors like wasps to a tin of treacle.

She remained unmarried and, by the time Birek arrived in London, found lovers harder to come by: therefore her search for what Jung calls the *animus* – the reflection of all her own masculine qualities – had become internal, and had resulted, in obedience to the Jungian prognosis, in strong opinions on political questions which she did not really understand.

Since these opinions were shared by most of her friends or, more precisely, since she only befriended those who shared her opinions, she was spared the need to defend them. Thus racists, anti-feminists and Palestinian-liberationists – Reagan, Thatcher, Botha, Pinochet, Arafat, the Contras and the Pope – were all damned at dinners in Belsize Park without a squeak of contradiction or a murmur of dissent. It might have been better for Ms Parr and her friends if they had retained in their circle some of the reactionaries they despised, because punching the air is a frustrating pastime, and when fighting in the dark one's enemies sometimes seem more monstrous than they really are. Knowing that they exist, but never seeing them face to face, makes one suspect that they are hiding behind every shrub. How often, at those dinner parties in NW3, had Stephanie secretly longed for an unwary guest who would slip up about the Sandinistas or the PLO and suffer as a result a scathing diatribe to expose his fundamental anti-Semitism or racist-imperialist assumptions.

Charlie knew this; he also knew that in such progressive circles the Soviets as the champions of Cuba and Nicaragua tended to be given the benefit of the doubt; but he said nothing to warn Laura of Stephanie's shrill convictions. Even if he had, Laura would have felt that she had nothing to fear. She thought of herself as a liberal-minded person and so could not conceive of antagonizing anyone by inadvertently betraying an offensive prejudice. She thought that the white South Africans were beastly to their blacks while the English, on the whole, treated theirs well. Certainly, since so many of the young West Indians in London were muggers and thieves, negroes made her feel uneasy when she passed them in the street, and she could never understand people's objections to paying their fares back to Jamaica if they could not get a job in England; but she was satisfied in her own mind that this did not mean that she was prejudiced because she loved the Indians and Pakistanis who ran the grocer's shops on Holland Park Avenue and kept them open until ten at night.

Of course she did not care for the Irish but then no one did, and that was not racial prejudice because the Irish were white. She also had other minor aversions – for those, for example, who lived in North London. NW1 and NW3 conjured up an image of pretentious Jewish intellectuals; N1 the awful, arty Islington crowd and chippy bigots like Madge and Ben; while N5, N6 or N16 were like the outer circles of Hell. She was a little more tolerant of people who lived south of the river – she was sorry for them – but thought it a damned nuisance to have to drive all the way to Stockwell where there was a small colony of her less fortunate friends.

She therefore felt prepared to cope with someone like Stephanie Parr who she sensed would probably come from somewhere like Hampstead or Primrose Hill. She felt sure she could take her measure as soon as she heard her speak: like all the English of her class Laura had a sharp ear for the nuances of accent. No longer was it as simple as in the days of D. H. Lawrence, when a land-owner spoke one way and his gamekeeper another. Now the landowner's son came away from Eton or Westminster with the tones of an East End barrow boy while the gamekeeper's son, with his degree in computer studies, spoke more correctly than many a young duke. Only the experts could tell them apart but Laura was an expert. She sensed at once when she was telephoned by Stephanie Parr that this big-time literary agent came from nowhere at all.

First of all Ms Parr made the serious social error of asking her secretary to get hold of Laura before she herself came on the line. Secondly she spoke with a semi-American accent – not as neuter as a Canadian, but mid-Atlantic all the same – which in her professional life may have established her as a hard-hitting business woman but to Laura suggested that she had something to hide.

Her third solecism was to be too friendly over the telephone to someone she had never met before. 'Laura? Hi. This is Stephanie Parr. Yes, Charlie told me that you're looking for someone to represent Birek.'

'We are.'

'Well this is so exciting. I really love his work, and am just dying to read the novel.'

'It hasn't been translated yet.'

'We don't need to wait for that. We could probably get a contract on the basis of his stories and an outline.'

'That would be wonderful.'

'The best thing would be for you and me and Birek to meet together and see how we get along.'

'Yes. Good.'

'How are you fixed?'

'I beg your pardon?'

'Are you free for lunch?'

'Yes. Almost any time.'

'And Birek?'

'I don't think he's very busy.'

'I've got something I could cancel on Thursday. Would that be OK?'

'Yes.'

'Do you know Green's on Duke Street?'

'Yes.'

'He might like that English cooking.'

'I'm sure he would.'

'Shall we say one?'

'Fine.'

'I'll see you there.'

Laura fetched Birek from his hostel to take him to lunch with

Stephanie Parr. She had not seen him since her party three days before and found that he was not quite as she remembered him. That evening he had seemed heroic and triumphant – a champion of liberty acclaimed by his admirers. Now he seemed young and vulnerable. She had not realized that he was so pale and thin. He greeted her formally by shaking her hand and with a sheepish smile gave her a package containing the manuscript of his novel. As Laura thanked him, she noticed, with a certain satisfaction, that his eye took in the elegance of her grey coat, red scarf and shoes from Pied-à-terre. He himself wore the same sky blue suit that he had worn at the party: it looked even worse by day than it had by candlelight.

After greeting one another they set off down the Tottenham Court Road, dodging the crowds of tawdry shoppers as they looked for a taxi.

'It is astonishing,' said Birek to Laura as they walked past the windows of televisions, stereos and computers, 'that in Prague not even your life's savings could buy what you might want from one of these shops.'

'Here everyone has everything,' said Laura, 'and it's all Japanese.'

'Don't the British make televisions?'

'I don't think so. Not any more.'

'So if you buy all this . . .' – he waved his hand at the electrical goods in a shop window – 'what do the Japanese buy from you?'

She looked perplexed. 'I don't know. You'd have to ask Francis.' Then she suddenly added: 'Oil, I suppose. We've got masses of it underneath the North Sea.'

They passed the sex shop where Birek had tried to buy toothpaste. Laura felt a little embarrassed. 'I'm afraid this is rather a mixed bit of London,' she said. 'You have the British Museum, but also Soho with all those nightclubs and pornographic book shops.'

'And they are permitted?' asked Birek, glancing at the photograph of a naked woman in a lascivious pose.

'Yes,' said Laura. 'Nothing much like that is against the law these days.'

'Freedom is freedom, I suppose,' said Birek, sounding a little uncertain.

They found a taxi which took them to Duke Street. Stephanie Parr had not yet arrived at the restaurant but they were shown to the table she had reserved.

'I don't quite understand,' said Birek as they sat down. 'Is this woman we are to meet someone who might publish my novel?'

'No,' said Laura. 'She's just an agent.'

'There are no agents in Czechoslovakia.'

'Here they are very important.'

'She will send my novel to a publisher?'

'We hope she will get a contract straight away.'

'A contract?'

'And an advance.'

'You mean a publisher may pay some money to publish a book he has not read?'

'Yes. On the basis of the stories you have already written and an outline of the novel.'

'That would be encouraging.'

'But it is most important to have a good agent.'

'Why?'

'Well . . .' Laura hesitated. She wished Charlie was there to explain. 'You see publishers trust agents – the good ones, at any rate – and the agents are very good at creating an atmosphere of excitement about a book or an author so that publishers compete with one another and pay more than they might otherwise have paid . . .' Her explanation came to a lame end.

'For a book they may not have read?'

'Precisely.'

'I will try to make a good impression,' said Birek as Stephanie Parr entered the restaurant.

Laura recognized Stephanie Parr: the urbanity of her appearance gave her away. She was wearing an elegant blue suit with brass buttons – almost a sailor suit – which Laura had seen in *Vogue*. It confirmed Laura's suspicions that this woman was thoroughly vulgar, just as Stephanie Parr recognized in Laura the chintzy, mousy, blousy type that to her was the bane of British fashion.

The two women greeted one another with blasts of false warmth.

'I am so sorry to be late,' said Stephanie, smiling at Laura and then turning to Birek. 'And this is so *wonderful*.' She took hold of the hand he held out to greet her but kept hold of it for a moment or two. 'I am such an admirer of your work, and I am so excited to hear that you have a novel.'

Birek blushed. 'Yes. I brought it with me from Prague.'

'I have the manuscript in my briefcase,' said Laura. 'I mean to start reading it this afternoon.'

'Lucky you.' She sat down. A waiter come to ask if they would like an aperitif. 'Sure,' said Stephanie. She turned to Laura. 'What would you like?'

'Oh, just some tomato juice.'

'Spicy?'

'Yes.'

Stephanie looked at the waiter. 'One Virgin Mary. One Perrier water and . . .' She turned back to Birek.

'A glass of beer.'

'And one beer.'

'We don't serve beer,' said the waiter.

Stephanie frowned and looked back at Birek. 'They don't have beer.'

Birek blushed. 'I'm sorry.'

'Would you like a glass of wine?'

Birek remembered how he had felt after the lunch in Soho. 'No. Perhaps a glass of tomato juice . . .'

'Two Virgin Marys. One Perrier.' The waiter withdrew. Stephanie turned back to Birek. 'I saw the piece in the *Daily Telegraph* yesterday. It will certainly have aroused a lot of interest.'

'I am glad.'

'Calling you the new Kundera was really inspired because that is something publishers – particularly in New York – can relate to.'

Birek blushed. 'I do not like the association. There is a great difference, both stylistically and philosophically, between myself and Kundera.'

'Of course,' said Stephanie. 'Each writer is unique, but each publisher is not. They're all the same, and they're getting more and more like the movie moguls. They want to know what to expect from a book before they read it.'

'But it is a deception,' said Birek earnestly, 'to compare me to Kundera because Kundera was a Communist who then left our people in the predicament he had helped to create for them, and now charms the West with his whimsical cynicism.'

The waiter brought their drinks.

'From the public's point of view,' said Stephanie, sipping her Perrier water, 'Kundera is the best-known dissident Czech writer.'

'But he is not a dissident,' said Birek, as if it was important that Stephanie should understand the truth. 'He was a socialist opportunist who gambled, lost, and did not stay to pay his debt.'

'You can hardly blame him for being a socialist,' said Stephanie.

'Of course I blame him for being a socialist,' said Birek, 'and so do all those of my generation. All that talk of socialism with a human face was a contradiction in terms because socialism of any kind means the pre-eminence of collectivism and the human spirit rebels against collectivism! It is the eagle, not the ant! It longs to soar above the earth, solitary and proud!'

'Shall we order?' suggested Laura.

She and Stephanie now led Birek though the menu, explaining that this was one of the few restaurants in London which served English dishes like fish-cakes and sausages and mash. Birek therefore asked for shepherd's pie while both Laura and Stephanie chose fillet steak.

To Laura's relief the conversation now turned to lighter things. They discussed Charlie and Pritchard and a number of other common friends and acquaintances; then the state of British publishing; and then the large advances that Stephanie had secured for some of her authors. Birek ate and listened, and only asked questions if there was something he did not understand. For example when Stephanie told Laura that two of her authors had been forced to live abroad, he frowned and said: 'I do not understand. Were they exiled by the government?'

Stephanie gave one of her metallic laughs. 'Oh no, it wasn't as bad as that. It was just that they earned so much money that they had to move abroad to avoid the tax.'

'Do you pay no tax in other countries?' asked Birek.

'Not if you have a good accountant.'

'And the government can do nothing against you?'

'It can try,' said Stephanie.

Birek smiled and shook his head. 'You can have no idea how impossible it would be in Czechoslovakia to say of the government: "It can try." There, what it wants it takes and the individual can do nothing to prevent it.'

'Here, if you're clever,' said Laura, 'there are several ways of avoiding tax.'

'If I can get you the kind of advance I have in mind,' said Stephanie, '*you'll* need a good accountant.'

'But I would like to pay tax in England.'

'We'd all like to pay it if the money was spent on sensible things,' said Stephanie, whose agency was a subsidiary of Stephanie Parr Associates, incorporated in the Dutch Antilles.

'Is it not spent on sensible things?' asked Birek.

'Well . . .' Laura began.

'If it went on schools and hospitals and old age pensions, that would be one thing,' said Stephanie, 'but it's all squandered on defence.'

'If you had no defence,' said Birek, 'then you too might have the Russians imposing a government on your people.'

'It could hardly be worse than the government that the people have imposed upon themselves,' said Stephanie.

'To us in Prague,' said Birek, 'it seemed that Britain has now the finest leader since Winston Churchill.'

'That shows how little truth gets through the Iron Curtain.'

'Or how the most fortunate sometimes do not realize how lucky they are.'

He said this quietly – as if making a considered judgement about human nature – but Stephanie looked irritated. 'I think you should be careful, Josef, about jumping to conclusions about this country after only a couple of days.'

'Of course.'

'You can't judge Britain from the West End of London.'

'No.'

'If you went to somewhere like Sunderland, you might come to a different conclusion.'

'Do you come from there?' asked Birek.

'No,' said Stephanie, who had never been to the north of

England. 'But I have a good idea of what conditions are like in areas of high unemployment.'

'Of course,' said Birek. 'I am sure there are poor people, but . . .' He stopped and smiled. 'If you know my poem "The Next Delivery", you will know how I feel about these things.'

Stephanie looked at Laura for help.

'We published it last autumn,' said Laura. ' "And then I said/It is not bread/but the truth/that I await/in the misty queue/of the patient few/that coils around the city." '

'Of course,' said Stephanie. 'A very beautiful poem.'

Birek smiled at Laura, and then looked back at Stephanie. 'Do you not think that I am fortunate to have such a fine translator?'

'I certainly do.'

'Which of my works, do you feel, comes across best in English?'

A look of panic came on to Stephanie's face. 'You know I have such difficulty remembering the titles.'

'Of course.' Birek laughed. 'The author is like a mother. He always thinks others will remember the names of his children. But do you remember my story "The General"?'

Again Stephanie appealed to Laura.

'The one about the retired officer,' Laura prompted.

'Yes,' said Birek. He turned again to Stephanie. 'There is a passage there when I express the old general's thoughts – it is, I think, what you call a soliloquy . . .'

'Yes.'

'You remember it?'

'Er . . . yes.'

'Well there I tried to interpose a poem, as it were, in the middle of prose like a jewel in a setting of precious metal, but I am not at all sure that it works because the reader has come to expect the words to perform a function, and he cannot adjust his mind to the enjoyment of mere sounds and associations.'

Again Laura caught the trapped look in Stephanie's eye, and feeling that the lunch had not gone as well as she had hoped, she said to Birek: 'That's rather what Stephanie was saying about publishers. They like to know what to expect before they open a book.'

'Of course,' said Birek. 'It is natural, I suppose.'

The waiter brought the bill. All three attempted to pay it but

Stephanie Parr waved aside the offers of the other two and without looking to see how much the lunch had cost them gave the bill back to the waiter with her gold credit card.

'Where are you staying?' she asked Birek.

'At a hostel,' he said.

'What's it like?'

'It is very comfortable. Like a hotel. The only trouble is that the bathroom is used by Africans.'

Stephanie Parr's fingers froze on the buckle of her bag. 'How awful,' she said with a scathing irony that Birek did not appreciate.

'It was all right,' he said. 'I had some vodka which I poured all around the edge of the bath and then lit with a match and boom!' He used his hands to indicate a small conflagration. 'That is a good way to disinfect it, don't you think?'

Stephanie's face had hardened to a mask. 'Sure,' she said. 'Otherwise you might have caught some dreadful disease.'

'It was a surprise for me,' said Birek, 'that so many of them are allowed to come into England but liberty is liberty, I suppose.'

'It most certainly is,' said Stephanie: and without waiting for the waiter to return with her card she stood and walked towards the door.

Laura and Birek followed. 'But why,' Laura asked Birek, 'did you think you would catch a disease from sharing a bath with an African?'

'This new disease called AIDS,' said Birek. 'Apparently it is common in Africa.'

'But you can't catch it from a bath,' said Laura.

'Bartle and Henriot thought that you could,' said Birek.

'I think, my dear Josef,' said Laura, 'that you still have something to learn about the English sense of humour.'

They took leave of Stephanie Parr outside in Duke Street.

'I'll send you the outline as soon as I can,' said Laura.

'We'll be in touch,' said Stephanie Parr. Then she turned to Birek. 'Goodbye, Mr Birek,' she said with a finality which suggested that they were unlikely to meet again.

Laura and Birek walked up Duke Street towards Piccadilly. Birek looked cowed. For a moment neither spoke. Then he turned to

Laura and asked: 'Was she angry because I said that I had burned the bath?'

'Perhaps, yes,' said Laura awkwardly. 'I don't think she understood about your fear of AIDS. But don't worry. I'll tell Charlie. And he can tell her what Bartle and the others told you.'

'Did she think that it was because I was prejudiced that I would want to disinfect the bath?'

'I think so. Yes.'

'I am sorry.'

'Don't be sorry – at least you needn't be sorry so far as I am concerned. I mean I would have given a bath a good clean if it had just been used by . . . by someone I didn't know. But people here are very sensitive about race, and if you say something which seems to suggest that you find someone inferior . . .'

'I do not think that Africans are inferior.'

'No, of course you don't, but people in England are very quick to think that you do.'

'Why?'

'I don't know, really. I think it's because we treated them so badly in the past.'

'But we Czechs did not treat them badly. We had no empire.'

'I know. But there's also what happened to the Jews.'

'Where?'

'In Germany. You know. The concentration camps and all that.'

Birek frowned – a mixture of perplexity and irritation. 'But it was not the Jews in England who were exterminated,' he said. 'There were no concentration camps on your soil.'

'I know,' said Laura, 'but all the same you have to be careful what you say to people like Stephanie about blacks or Jews or Mrs Thatcher.'

'It is ironic,' said Birek. 'In Czechoslovakia it is dangerous to criticize the government. Here it is dangerous not to criticize the government.'

'I know,' said Laura. 'It does seem slightly absurd.'

NINE

Laura put Birek on to a 19 bus to take him back to the hostel. She herself then took a taxi to Lansdowne Square and looked out of its window at the trees in Hyde Park feeling inexplicably sad. She probed her mind for the source of this melancholy and quickly found it in the expression she had seen on Birek's face as he had got on to his bus – a mixture of confusion, disappointment and a sense that he had let her down. She imagined him returning to the solitude of his dingy room at the hostel, and although she knew that he was to have supper that night with Miroslav Maier in Hounslow, and that through Maier he would meet a circle of Czech émigrés, she nonetheless sensed that their company would only exacerbate his sense of loneliness. His particular sensibility made him more vulnerable than most to the banality and vulgarity of men like Maier: he should be protected by those of a like kind.

The house was empty. Gail had taken Lucy straight from school to tea with some friends. Laura went into the library, intending to start work at once on Birek's novel – not just because the task was urgent, but because it would allow her to feel that he was still in her company; but the very silence of the house reminded her of its size, and of the two empty bedrooms on the top floor which were only used by Johnny and Belinda on the odd nights during the school holidays which they did not spend at Risley. Why on earth, she wondered, should not Birek stay in one of them instead of in a squalid hostel?

Francis might object to a lodger – he complained as it was about Gail – but it would not be for long and Birek was so gentle and unassuming that his presence would hardly be noticed. With this thought in mind she went up the two flights of stairs to the children's floor and went into Johnny's bedroom. It was still filled with the clutter of his childhood. There was a wooden castle in one corner and an old Sinclair ZX computer gathering dust on the top shelf of his book-case. On the wall was pinned a banner of Arsenal Football Club, two souvenir street signs of Carnaby Street and a portrait of David Bowie. She opened his wardrobe and saw the small blazer he had worn at his London day school, then looked in the drawers where there were four shirts, three pairs of socks and pushed behind the socks two cigarettes in a crumpled carton.

All this could be moved to make room for the few clothes that Birek would have brought with him from Prague – indeed his visit would be an excellent opportunity to clear out the mess. She looked at the bed. It was narrow but big enough for a slender young man. She did not imagine that he would be so tactless as to invite girls back to his room. She went to the desk. Again it was small – bought for a ten-year-old boy – and there were some Batman stickers which would have to be scraped off; but it looked out over the trees of the communal garden and would be a much more pleasant place to work than a room in the hostel.

She went down to the kitchen, made herself some tea, and took it on a tray to the library where she had left the manuscript of Birek's novel. She found, however, that her mind wandered – perhaps because the description of spring in the Bohemian forest with which the novel opened was written in such dense prose, or perhaps because she was still preoccupied with the idea of having Birek to stay.

She tried to envisage what it would be like. He would have to share the nursery bathroom with Gail and the children: he could hardly object to that – they were white, after all. She would have to warn him to keep out of Francis's way when he got back from the bank in the evening; and suggest, perhaps, that he did not come down to breakfast until after Francis had left in the morning. That would leave time for him to see her before she left for the Foundation. But could she still come down in her dressing-gown, she wondered? And would he drink coffee or tea?

The thought of Birek at breakfast made Laura smile, but her reverie was interrupted by the return of Gail with Lucy. The party had apparently not been a success. The little girl came in clutching the bag of sweets which had been her going-away present with a grim look on her face. When Lucy was angry, everyone in the household quailed, but Laura was now so inexplicably cheerful that she determined to get to the bottom of Lucy's ill humour and to do so volunteered to give her a bath. Gail went to her room to prepare for another night out and Laura, while she poured in the bubbles and helped Lucy out of her school uniform, gently asked questions to elicit that Lucy's friend Alice who had given the party had snubbed her in favour of an older girl.

The daughter's sulk did not last for long: it could not withstand Laura's good humour, nor the unexpected bounty of her being there to bath her when it was not even Gail's day off. Laura read her two chapters of a 'My Little Pony' story, and kissed her goodnight with a special affection before going downstairs to take a bath in her own bathroom. That evening, however, she did not lie on her bed reading the *Evening Standard*, or even wallow in the oily water of the bath, but quickly changed into a black skirt and grey cashmere jersey and went down to the kitchen to prepare supper.

She had originally intended to heat up a seafood pie from Marks and Spencer's which she often did when she had been busy, and perhaps boil up some frozen peas; but knowing how to raise the spirits of her husband as well as her daughter, she prepared aubergines for a first course and at the same time defrosted some Cumberland sausages. She loathed these tubes of gristle but Francis loved them: he also liked root vegetables, so she peeled both carrots and parsnips, and made a dressing for the salad they would have with their cheese.

She did not consider that she was being devious in taking trouble in this way. It is part of the art of marriage of wives and husbands to manipulate their spouses' moods – wives with food, husbands with flowers, and both at times with an affected languor. Moreover it usually works, even if the one is conscious of the other's calculation, and that evening Francis became quite benign. He came home grumpy, as he always did, but after a fresh bath, free from oily unguents, a glass of whisky, Channel Four news, a good supper and a shared bottle of wine, he listened with a smile, as he helped Laura load the Miele, to her account of the lunch with Stephanie Parr. When she told him about Birek and the bath Francis actually laughed, which was a rare thing for him to do.

'He sounds a little naïf,' he said to Laura.

'He's awfully young,' she said, 'and horribly sincere.'

'He'll have to learn to keep some of his thoughts to himself.'

'I know. But it's difficult to tell him that.'

'He'll learn from experience.'

'My worry is that he'll lose all the likely friends before he makes them.'

'That's very pessimistic.'

'Charlie took him to lunch with some writers and I'm afraid it wasn't a success.'

'They took against him?'

'Bartle found him a bore.'

'He probably didn't laugh at Bartle's jokes.'

'Perhaps he didn't understand them.'

'That's the trouble. You can understand a language without catching the sense of humour.'

'Give him time,' said Laura as she filled the electric kettle.

'Once he's made a few friends of his own . . .' Francis began.

'I know,' she said, 'but that takes time. And meanwhile he's so wretched in the hostel.'

'Because of the blacks in the bathroom?'

'Not just that.'

'Can't he go somewhere else?'

'I suppose he could rent a bed-sit in Balham, or something like that. And if he was here as a student, I dare say that that is what he would do. But being an exile – having cut himself off from his country, his family, everything – and being rather proud and oversensitive, as writers often are, I think Balham would kill him.'

'He should take a room in a family of some émigré Czechs.'

'He's sick of Czechs.'

'Then an English family.'

'You don't think . . .' The kettle came to boil. Laura poured the hot water into the two mugs in which she had already put granules of decaffeinated coffee.

'What?'

'Do you think we should have him here for a bit?' Her tone was casual and reluctant, as if she was weighing up whether or not to ask a maiden aunt for Christmas.

'Where would he sleep?'

'In Johnny's room.'

'And Johnny?'

'He would probably have gone by the holidays, and anyway Johnny usually goes straight from Eton to Risley.'

Francis picked up his mug of coffee. 'It would certainly be a pity,' he said, 'if Birek's only experience of the Western world is a hostel off the Tottenham Court Road.'

'He might wish he was back in Prague.'

'We wouldn't want that.' He moved towards the door of the kitchen.

'Shall I suggest it, then?'

'What?'

'That Birek come to stay.'

'If you like.' He looked at his watch. 'But you'll have to clear some of the rubbish out of Johnny's room.' With that he took his mug of coffee up to the library to drink it while watching television.

In the beginning of May when Birek moved from the hostel to the Mortons' house the weather suddenly changed from the squally tail-end of winter to a warm English spring. Blossoms flowered on the trees which lined the streets and tulips and primroses bloomed in the communal gardens.

This capricious change in the climate enhanced the contrast for Birek between the hell of Tottenham Court Road and the heaven of Holland Park. Even Laura, who went off as usual three days a week to the office of the Comenius Foundation, regretted having to remain in the stuffy room she shared with Miroslav Maier. Since she was now working on the translation of Birek's novel, and had to consult him almost every day on the exact meaning of a word or a phrase, it seemed absurd not to use the library or even the garden at Lansdowne Square; but she was wise enough to realize what people might say if just as Birek became her lodger she stopped coming to the Foundation.

She also knew that she could always consult him in the evening, although Birek was extraordinarily tactful and somehow arranged to go out whenever Laura and Francis spent an evening in. Nor did she see him on those mornings when she went to the Foundation because he followed her advice in keeping to his room until after the household had dispersed in the morning. Indeed, after a couple of weeks Laura became quite annoyed that she saw so little of him. So ingenious was he at keeping out of the way that one morning Laura went up to Johnny's room to reassure herself that he was still staying under her roof.

It was a Friday, when Laura did not go to the Foundation but packed and prepared for the weekend at Risley. Francis was at the bank; Lucy was at school; Gail was out; Fatima, the daily, had not yet come. Birek, she knew, had left the house without eating any breakfast: she had heard him creep down the stairs while she was dressing. She knocked on the door in case he had come back unobserved, but since there was no answer she went in. The room was empty. The bed was made and the window had been opened an inch or two to let in the fresh air. She stood for a moment struck by how little Birek had made the room his own. The few relics of Johnny's childhood which had been there when he arrived, like the Arsenal banner pinned to the wall, remained where Laura had left them. The only sign that someone else now used the room were the books and magazines on the desk and chest-of-drawers – some in English but others in Czech, published by émigré houses in London.

On the bedside table there was a paperback copy of Waugh's *Decline and Fall* and beneath that a Czech Bible. She picked up the Bible. It seemed well used. She put it back again under the novel, afraid to leave evidence that she had been rummaging around among his things. Nor did she rummage, exactly, but her curiosity drove her to open one of the drawers that had been emptied for his clothes. There lay two drab shirts, three well-worn pairs of underpants and four pairs of nylon socks – all much scruffier than the old clothes of Johnny's which she had given to Fatima to either keep for her children or throw away.

The poignancy of Birek's dingy garments, and the possessions limited to a few books, brought tears to Laura's eyes. She thought of the drawers in Francis's dressing-room filled with tailored cotton shirts, well ironed boxer shorts and fluffy woollen socks. She wondered if any of them would fit Birek, comparing in her mind's eye the sagging stomach of her husband and the slender form of the young Czech. She picked up a pair of Birek's underpants, as if to judge the size. She felt like going off at once to Harrods to order a dozen new ones as she would for Johnny and Belinda, but then realized that this might be tactless and so put back the underpants and closed the drawer.

She had planned to drive down to Risley that morning, leaving Gail to fetch Lucy from school and then deliver her to Francis at Paddington Station. She changed her mind, however, for no particular reason, and was sitting in the study when at twelve Birek returned to the house.

She saw him come up to the front door and left the library as he entered as if to fetch something she had left on the hall table.

'Oh, hello,' she said with affected surprise.

'Hello.' He smiled.

'We hardly seem to see you,' she said.

'I do not want to get in your way.'

She laughed. 'I sometimes wonder if you are really staying in the house.'

'But I am,' he said, blushing, 'and I am so grateful to you, but I know that having a strange person in your house is often awkward . . .'

'You're very tactful,' said Laura, 'but you mustn't take tact to extremes.'

'I am sorry.'

She looked at her watch. 'Let's have some lunch in about half-an-hour – just a sandwich in the kitchen – and then we can go through some of your book.'

'Of course.' He nodded and then went up the stairs while Laura returned to the library.

She had by now read through the novel three times, and had completed a rough translation of the first two chapters. She should already have sent the outline and a sample chapter to Stephanie Parr and hesitated only because neither of the first two chapters seemed likely to arouse the enthusiasm of a busy publisher. Some of the later ones were undoubtedly more dramatic – although dramatic was perhaps too strong a word for a plot which in itself was surely meant to signify the unchanging pace of rural life.

She wondered if she dared suggest to Birek . . . But what? He undoubtedly knew what he was doing; there was an admirable consistency in the style and integrity in the construction; and it would make Laura sound dreadfully superficial if she were to suggest that the long descriptions of natural phenomena – particularly of the geological strata in the outcrops of rock – would strain the patience of the reader. Nor would she want Birek to think that she did not appreciate the point he was making about time and civilization. It was just that it was extraordinarily difficult to translate such passages into lively English prose.

It was a pity that in the novel there were so few of the psychological vignettes which were found in his stories. Why did writers think that a major work had to be long and boring? Not that Birek's novel was long and boring, but there was a tendency, which one might ascribe to his youth, to labour the philosophic theme, and so both smother the plot and crush the characters under the weight of their symbolic meaning.

It was not warm enough to eat in the garden so Laura spread an impromptu picnic out on the kitchen table. Gail returned at one, but since she was always on a diet she never ate in the presence of others but only gorged herself secretly when no one was looking. Therefore Laura and Josef were left alone with the pâté, Camembert and French bread. There was even an open bottle of Riesling in the door of the fridge from the night before which both of them drank mixed with Perrier water.

They talked about the book – about nuances in the meaning of certain words – and Laura saw the relief in the expression on his face when she told him once again how much she admired what he had written.

'And will Stephanie like it, I wonder?' he asked.

'I'm sure she will,' said Laura with as much conviction as she could muster.

'Do you think that she will comprehend the significance of certain scenes?'

'Such as what?'

'For example Karel's attempt to burn down the House of Culture?'

'I'm sure she will,' said Laura.

'You do not think that it is too obviously a misunderstandable symbol?'

'How do you mean?'

'It could be taken to signify that he is against the culture of the socialist state.'

'Is that not what you meant?'

'Of course. But he is also against all culture – socialist, capitalist or whatever – because it appropriates the dreams and the poetry of the individual for the community.'

'Of course.'

'Karel wishes his art to be the dream of one person, communicable perhaps to only one other person. A real passion between two souls, like love, not a subject you study or teach or use to decorate a social system.'

'I think that comes across.'

'And the scene with the Party Secretary is also important because the man is kind. He has the choice of deciding whether what Karel has done is sabotage or madness, and he wishes it to be madness because for sabotage he would be imprisoned – perhaps shot. And Karel too is happy to be thought mad, because to him art must be a kind of madness – something which seems crazy to everyone else, again like love.'

'Does love always seem mad to everyone else?'

'Yes, of course.' He leaned forward, a little pink in the face: the hock and seltzer was taking effect. 'Not love as such, but love in the particular. For example you love Francis and your friend . . . Madge?'

'Yes, Madge.'

'She loves Ben.'

'Well . . .'

'And to you, she is mad to love Ben, and to her you are mad to love Francis, because she cannot understand your love and you cannot understand hers.'

'Unless I was to fall in love with Ben, and she with Francis.'

He blushed. 'Yes, that could happen. And the work of art – that too can be appreciated by more than one person, but the appreciation is still a personal experience, it is not a communal experience.'

'Perhaps that's just as well,' said Laura. 'We don't all want to fall in love with the same person.'

'No.'

She filled Birek's glass with wine, then poured a little into her own. 'You don't feel,' said said, returning to the novel, 'that Karel is a little unkind to Yvonna?'

'But she too wants to claim him for the collectivity. She thinks she loves him, but in reality she only wants a husband and a father for her children. Karel rebels against this. He thinks that love must be pure, without a social function . . .'

'That is a dangerous philosophy.'

'Of course. The lover, like the artist, is the wicked elephant.'

'Rogue elephant.'

'I am sorry. Rogue elephant.'

'What you say,' said Laura modestly, 'could be used by a Don Juan to justify his bad behaviour.'

Birek brushed back a lock of black hair that had fallen over his face. 'That is the risk, but it is better to take that risk for the purity and integrity of love.'

'Is it common . . . I mean to say, have you come across love of that kind?'

'In myself?'

'Yes.'

'No.' He laughed as if relieved to be able to say this. 'Did you think that the character of Karel was a self-portrait?'

She blushed. 'No. Not necessarily.'

'One reason I came to the West,' said Birek, 'is that unlike Karel I could not fall in love in Czechoslovakia.'

'Why not?'

'You know, there were nice girls, there were pretty girls, but they were all, to me, very uninteresting because their experience was so limited that they could not be interesting. For love there has to be something mysterious, something unknown. The beloved has to embody areas of life or experience that the lover desires to comprehend, and among the girls of my own age in Czecho-slovakia, there was no one who could do this.'

'Perhaps you set impossible standards?'

'No. Because I knew that such a woman could exist. That old lady, for example – the one who taught me English – she was interesting because even though she had been just the wife of an officer, she had grown up in the old Austrian Empire which for all its faults was a very lively society. And even my mother, who is Czech, came from the intelligentsia, and though she was a Communist when she was young, she had *chosen* to be a Communist and so she could choose, later, to be free, not just of my father but of the whole ideology.'

'And the younger generation in Prague? Can't they choose?'

'How? What can they know when they can only learn and can only read what the state allows?'

'They can't all accept what they are taught.'

'And they don't. They reject it. But what can take its place? Western values, to them, come from Austrian television. *Sachertorte* and blue-jeans and Mercedes Benz. That is what the West means to them. But that kind of materialism is quite as banal as Marxist-Leninism.'

'Of course,' said Laura, reaching for the bar of Lindt chocolate which she had hidden from Lucy on the top of the fridge. She then turned back to Birek and said with a smile: 'We must try and think of some mysterious young women for you to meet here in London.'

Birek laughed. 'Please, no. Let it take place whatever takes place. Just now, I am quite happy.'

'So am I.' She said it without thinking, immediately blushed and glanced at Birek to see how he had taken it. He too had blushed. Their two eyes met: then Birek looked towards the window and Laura started talking in an almost hysterical way about her children and Risley and how generous life had been to her, as if the happiness she had referred to was of a general sort, not linked in particular to sitting in her kitchen with Birek.

Yet it was, and when she stood to go to the stove and make some coffee, she darted a glance at his long legs and his handsome face with its high Slav cheekbones and small straight nose, and with a wantonness that surprised her because it was novel she wished that it was summer and that he was lying by the swimming-pool at Risley so that she could see rather than imagine his pale body.

TEN

Risley Hall, which had been Laura's childhood home, was an elegant limestone rectory built at a time when the clergy were close to the aristocracy in the social order. Indeed the incumbent who had rebuilt the house soon after the Napoleonic wars was the younger son of a local grandee, Lord Diston, and Risley was a small village on the edge of the Diston estate. There was no larger house in the village and so the rectory not only played the role of the manor but looked the part with its symmetrical classical façade.

Despite its proximity to the church it was set back from the village street and its privacy was protected by a tall red-brick wall. To the left of the house there was a large courtyard with a tithe-barn, stable, saddle-room, coalhouse and fold-yard which served as a garage. Although there was a small lawn at the front of the house, and a walled kitchen garden on the opposite side to the courtyard, the larger lawns ran from the south side and faced on to open country. This garden was totally private – protected from prying eyes not just by the red-brick walls but by the rectory itself. To the left, beyond the courtyard, there was a tennis-court and to the right, concealed by trees and bushes, the swimming-pool.

The inside of the house was equally elegant and ordered. There was a door at the front which was rarely used but, when it was, opened into a spacious hall. A drawing-room ran down the full length of the east side of the house; on the west side there was a library at the front and a dining-room at the back while the kitchen was in a Victorian wing which linked the main house to the court-yard. The library was panelled: the drawing-room had glazed doors at one end which opened on to the lawns on the south side. All these rooms on the ground floor had tall sash windows with shutters and panes of glass which, if seen in a certain light, showed a roughness and irregularity which betrayed their antiquity.

The view from the terrace on the south side of the house was of perfect English countryside – arranged as if by an artist with no other house in sight. To Laura this outlook was completely familiar but she never took it for granted, and every Friday evening, when she arrived from London, she would breathe in the fresh air and gaze at the view to refresh her body and rest her mind.

Her father, the explorer, had bought the house soon after Laura was born. His wife, Laura's mother, was a cousin of the Distons and so felt that she had roots in the county. When Sir John had died, Laura's mother had continued to live at Risley with Laura's brother Crispin. It was always understood that Crispin would inherit the estate and it was some consolation to Laura, when her mother died, that the house would remain in the family and that the weekends with granny might be replaced by weekends with Uncle Cris.

But a month after the funeral Crispin told Laura that he was going to sell Risley and live in Morocco. Laura was dumbfounded. To sell Risley was to sell the past. And to live in Morocco! Why? Suddenly, and for the first time, she looked at her brother not as a member of her family whom she had always taken for granted but as a bachelor of forty-three who had done nothing with his life but look after his mother. Why had he no job? Because he had plenty of money without one. Why had he no wife or girl friend? Because he managed very well with his friends of the same sex.

All this threw Laura into a depressed state of mind. A house in London was all very well but it could hardly be considered a home. As she lay in her bedroom in Lansdowne Square, listening to the faint roar of the traffic on Ladbroke Grove, she felt disgust for life in the city with all the concrete and carbon monoxide, the dog shit on the pavements and the constant crowd of weird people. It had been tolerable when there was Risley as both lung and bolthole; now it was unendurable.

Francis talked of buying a cottage somewhere else in the country but for Laura such a hovel would not be the same. It was not just the house at Risley but all the loyal servants like dear Mrs Jackson and the friends from her childhood who lived nearby. She was therefore inconsolable – hard hit, it was said, by the death of her mother. Every evening Francis would come back from the bank to find her lying gloomily on her bed. One evening, however, when the pillow was still wet from one of her bouts of weeping, he sat down beside her and said: 'I talked to Crispin today.'

'I never want to talk to him again,' she said.

'I made an offer for Risley.'

She looked up astonished. 'An offer?'

'Yes. And he accepted.'

It had taken a moment for Laura to realize quite what this meant, and when she did she had wept all the more – the tears of helpless joy. Never before had she felt so fond of her husband, and when her tears had subsided she tried to reward him with an unstinting embrace; but it was Francis's misfortune that though offered the role of a romantic hero who had spent recklessly to buy happiness for his wife, he was too dogged a banker, and too honest a husband, not to betray what was passing through his mind. When she looked up he did not see the affectionate expression in her wet and grateful eyes, but continued to concentrate on the balance sheet in his mind. 'With property appreciating at the present rate,' he said – to himself as much as to her – 'it would be absurd to dispose of an asset like Risley unless it was absolutely necessary. There is, after all, your reversionary interest in your father's estate which amounts to a quarter of the value of the house. We will have to raise money to buy the balance, but that won't be difficult, and some of the interest can be found in the children's trusts.'

He had mumbled on and Laura, though a little taken aback at this way of looking at her childhood home, was nevertheless content. She had never before dared dream that Risley might actually become hers. Now she was to have it as her second home – a house with nine bedrooms! How nice it would be to have their friends to stay, but what on earth would she say to Madge? Perhaps that her mother had left it in trust for the children.

One of the duties which went with living at Risley Hall was going to church on a Sunday. The church, after all, was only at the end of the garden and while neither Laura nor Francis was pious, both thought it incumbent upon them, as the owners of the largest house in the village, to attend the morning service. Both had been brought up as Anglicans and so took that form of worship for granted. Laura liked the hymns and took her children to the same pew as her parents had taken her. Francis went more from a sense of form. He saw the Church of England as a kind of club which a man must join if he lived in the way he had chosen. It had certain rituals and traditions which formed part of the English way of life.

His image of himself as an Englishman was more important to Francis than many of his friends supposed. He loved his country and tried where he could to preserve its traditional identity. He had asked Laura to marry him partly because she had conformed to his vision of what an English wife should be. He had bought Risley not just as a good investment or as a gift for his wife but because it rooted his family in their native land. Life in London was all very well but the house in Lansdowne Square was too close to the Pakistani grocers, Greek restaurants and Caribbean steel bands to be considered a part of England. In Risley there was a church, a pub and a village green; the sound of the hymns and the psalms, like that of the cricket ball against the willow bat in the summer, was the musical accompaniment to the English way of life.

The old vicar, the Reverend Alfred Popplethwaite, had fitted this concept of religion. He had been a close friend of Laura's parents – almost the only man admitted by the crotchety old explorer in his later years – but even on Sir John's deathbed he had talked to him about fishing, not God. He himself had died soon after Laura's mother and had been replaced by a clergyman of quite a different kind.

The Reverend Giles Jermain fitted the new order as exactly as the Reverend Alfred Popplethwaite had fitted the old. He was in his early thirties and already a little bald. He rarely wore a dog-collar but identified himself as a minister of religion by the wooden crucifix hanging on a leather thong around his neck. He came from a middle-class home in Bristol and had gone straight from school into a seminary. There he had adopted radical views of both society and religion. Once ordained he had served as a curate in a derelict parish in Stoke. Here his provocative sermons denouncing capitalism had caused quite a stir, but rather than upset the bishop, as they might have done in the old days, they rather gained his esteem; and in due course he was appointed to the living at Risley with the specific mission to shake the complacency of this rural parish.

The Mortons' first brush with Giles Jermain had been over the christening of Lucy. Johnny and Belinda had both been baptized at the font of Risley parish church, and they assumed that Lucy would be too. But when Laura telephoned the new vicar from London to ask which Saturday would suit him, he told her almost curtly that she would have to call on him to discuss the question further.

The vicarage at Risley had been built in the early years of the twentieth century when the Church Commissioners had decided that the cost of running the rectory was too much for the incumbent. It was as small and mean as the old rectory was large and gracious. Laura was shown into the cramped parlour by the stocky, unfriendly wife of the Reverend Giles Jermain. She sat on a plastic sofa looking at a poster showing conifer forests overprinted with the word 'Peace'.

Eventually the vicar came in. He greeted Laura without smiling, then looked around as if surprised that no one else was in the room. 'Is your husband not with you?'

'No,' said Laura. 'I'm afraid that he has a hundred and one things to do.'

'I see,' said the vicar, sitting down on an armchair facing Laura. 'And the baptism of his daughter is the one hundred and second . . .'

'He didn't think that you would need to see us both.'

'As a rule,' said Giles Jermain, 'we like to talk to both parents because raising a child in Christ is both their responsibility.'

'Of course.' She looked down to conceal her irritation and saw that he was wearing sandals over grey socks.

'In the past, you see, baptism was seen as a mere formality, particularly, if I may say so, by people like you.'

Laura frowned but said nothing.

'Now, before we baptize a child, we have to be sure that the parents really intend their child to be a member of Christ's Church – to bring it up in the faith and the love of Christ, as one of his children in his family here on earth.'

'Of course.' Laura wondered how long this was going to take: she had to take Lucy to Pewsey.

The balding cleric fixed her with a strange glance – malevolence coated with compassion. 'You can reassure me, can you, that this will be the case?'

'Yes, I think so, I mean, yes.'

He opened a notebook which he had brought with him to the parlour and laid it out on the teak coffee table with splayed legs upon which there was no coffee because none had been offered.

'Can you tell me where you were confirmed?'

She thought back to her school days and the giggling sessions with the chaplain. 'At St Mary's, Calne.'

'In the school?'

'No. In the parish church.'

'By which bishop?'

'The Bishop of Salisbury.'

He noted this down. 'And your husband?'

'I don't know, I'm afraid. I'm not sure that he actually was confirmed.'

The vicar hesitated and tapped the tip of his felt-tipped pen against his teeth. 'It seems a little incongruous, doesn't it, that he should want to raise his child in a religion in which he is not confirmed?'

Laura frowned. 'But I was. Isn't that enough?'

'Perhaps.' He scribbled something down. 'And tell me,' he went on. 'What church do you go to in London?'

'In London?'

'Yes.' He looked up into her eyes with the same gaze of implacable compassion.

'Well, we don't often go in London because we're usually down here at weekends.'

'And here, I know, you go to church on a Sunday, but clearly, because you aren't here during the week, you don't play much part in the Christian community.'

'We have the fête at the Old Rectory every year,' said Laura lamely.

'Yes, of course, and I'm sure the Parish Council is most grateful. But that is not quite what I meant by playing a part in the Christian community. I thought that perhaps, in London, you belonged to a Bible study group or a prayer circle or something of that kind.'

Laura blushed, with anger rather than shame. 'No, you know, with three children, and the kind of life we lead . . .'

'Yes,' he said. 'I can imagine that you are kept very busy.' The sarcasm was unconcealed.

Laura bit her lip to control her temper. 'Clearly,' she said with a humble lowering of the head and clasping of hands at her knees, 'clearly our Christian life is not all that it should be, because one is so easily distracted by superficial things, but we are both aware of our shortcomings and certainly, when it comes to our children, determined to bring them up to be better than we are.'

This grovelling was enough. Triumph replaced malevolence behind the vicar's regulation expression of compassion. 'Very well,' he said. 'Let's go ahead.'

'Is the date I suggested all right?' asked Laura sweetly.

'It's perfect. We already have the Bottomly twins booked in for that afternoon, and there's a West Indian family who have been friends of mine since my days in Stoke who have been kind enough to ask me to baptize their baby as well.'

'And would they . . . are they, these days, baptized together?'

'Very much so, yes.'

'We had rather hoped for a separate ceremony . . .'

'Out of the question, I am afraid.' He stood up to see her to the door. 'Gone are the days when the parish church could be used as the private chapel of the lords and ladies of the manor.'

Never before had Laura been put in such a rage as she was that morning by the Reverend Giles Jermain. She returned to the Old Rectory pale and quivering – not just with outrage at his impertinent and antagonistic questions, but also with shock at the way in which she had given in to his demands. 'Now I know,' she said to Francis, 'what life is like under a totalitarian regime.'

Francis was more amused than annoyed by what she reported. 'You should be a little more understanding,' he said. 'It's the only chance, after all, for the poor fellow to throw his weight around. How do you think he feels, seeing us in the rectory, while he is confined to that dreadful vicarage at the bottom of the village with silage over the wall? The radicalism of the clergy is always in inverse proportion to their social standing. When Risley was a good living, they were the buttresses of the established order. Now a man like Jermain gets paid little more than a farm labourer. No wonder he bullies us a bit when he gets the chance.'

With this line of reasoning Francis insisted that Lucy's christening went ahead; and while Laura never forgave Giles Jermain for humiliating her over the christening, Francis continued to be entertained by his aggressive radicalism. He was almost the only member of the congregation at Risley parish church who paid close attention to the vicar's sermons. The vicar may have thought that he was taking his homilies to heart – they were directed, after all, at comfortable Christians like the Mortons: in fact Francis always made a bet at breakfast as to what the subject of the sermon would be. He had noticed, after a time, that the Reverend Jermain's themes were usually taken from some story in the Sunday newspapers. If there was a scandal in the City, then the vicar would denounce capitalism. If there was a rise in unemployment, it would be the turn of the Conservative government. While the expression on the faces of the other parishioners would become alarmed, contrite or more often bored, Francis's would suddenly break out into a smile when he heard the words that won his wager.

ELEVEN

After her lunch with Birek in the kitchen of her house in Lansdowne Square, Laura left for Risley. She fetched Lucy from school on her way out of London and her mood remained cheerful until the effects of the wine began to wear off, making her irritable and sleepy. She had to stop at a service area to drink some coffee to keep herself awake. They left the motorway at Hungerford and reached Risley at half-past five. Mrs Jackson was waiting in the kitchen with a simmering kettle ready to make tea. Lucy kissed this cosy lady and then ran up to her room to change out of her uniform while Laura, who now had a slight hangover, took her tea into the library where Mrs Jackson had lit a fire.

At seven she joined the other wives of bankers and stockbrokers waiting for their husbands in their Volvos, Mercedes and Range Rovers at Westbury Station. At ten past seven Francis arrived from Paddington and climbed into the car carrying his briefcase and a copy of the *Spectator*.

'How was the drive down?' he asked as Laura drove off.

'Abominable.'

'Jams?'

'Bumper to bumper all the way.'

'I was ready to take Lucy on the train.'

'It was easier to take her straight from school.'

'Why didn't you come down this morning?'

'I had things to do.' She said this in such a way as to exclude any enquiries as to what these things might be.

'Is there anything on this weekend?'

'The Grays to lunch tomorrow, then dinner with the Hamptons.'

He nodded but said nothing. Sometimes Francis wished that their life in the country was less social – that the frenzy of a week in London could be followed by some repose; but he remained committed to the role that living at Risley had thrust upon him, and so was obedient to the invitations from those neighbours who relied upon the Londoners to liven things up at weekends.

That night, at least, they were to dine alone. Francis went first to kiss Lucy good-night, then changed from his suit into the old jersey and corduroy trousers that he always wore at Risley. Mrs Jackson had left a fish pie on the Aga and had set two places on the kitchen table. Since it was time to eat Francis skipped his usual glass of whisky but opened a bottle of Moselle. He drank most of it himself. Laura would only drink water.

Among the many advantages of living at Risley was the established circle of friends and neighbours. Some of these were the bankers and brokers whom Francis knew from the City or the Friday evening train; but others were friends from Laura's childhood – her cousins the Distons, for example, but also girls from school or the pony club who were now wives and mothers like Laura. Of these she saw most of a pretty, cheerful woman called Emma Jenkins. Emma had a daughter the same age as Lucy. Every Saturday morning the two little girls went riding together from a stable in Pewsey while their mothers had a cup of coffee in the Red Lion Hotel.

There is little that can be said about Emma Jenkins to save her from caricature as the archetypal county lady in headscarf and green wellington boots. She always drove a Range Rover and was never out of a quilted waistcoat until the 1980s when like everyone else she defected to the greased raincoat which then came into fashion. Her husband Jimmy farmed five hundred acres in the vale of Pewsey and while damning the scroungers who cheated on social security managed to extract huge subsidies from both the Ministry of Agriculture and the European Commission.

They had a large rather ugly house about five miles from Risley and a flat in South Kensington which they used about six times a year. Emma preferred to drive up and down to London in a day, and Jimmy had a mistress near Hungerford and so never had a reason to go to town. They were both in the centre of the hectic life of the county and when Laura met Emma for coffee she would prattle on like the gossip column in the *Daily Mail*. Laura was a little ashamed of the pleasure she took in catching up on local scandal, but since Emma was hardly the person with whom she could discuss the problems of translating Czech prose, she simply prompted her and listened and allowed herself to be amused.

That Saturday, as they sat in the Red Lion, the two women talked less about what had happened than about what would happen at a dance to be given by the Distons at Diston Park in June. June was still some way away but a ball of this kind was sufficiently rare to stand out on the social horizon. Both Laura and Emma had promised to give dinners and they now chatted about who might come and what they would wear.

'I'm damned well going to buy a new dress,' said Emma. 'I haven't had one for ages.'

'Then I will too,' said Laura.

'But you've got that pretty blue dress that Francis bought for you in January at the Caroline Charles sale.'

Laura laughed. 'That was two years ago, and it wasn't blue, it was pink.'

'No,' said Emma. 'I saw him *this* January. He bought one of those blue dresses with a flouncy skirt. You know . . .'

Laura frowned. 'Are you sure?'

'Positive.'

'Well he didn't give it to me.'

'Oh God, then I've put my foot in it. He's probably got a girl friend like Jimmy.'

'It sounds most unlike Francis,' said Laura.

'They're frightfully crafty when it comes to a bit on the side,' said Emma cheerfully. 'But don't let it get you down. Just find yourself a lover at the ball.'

Laura was taken aback – not by the idea that Francis might be having an affair but by how little the thought upset her. She did not become dizzy or distraught. The lounge in the Red Lion, with its horrible sixteenth-century beams, did not swirl around her as it was supposed to do when women receive an emotional shock. She simply poured herself another cup of coffee out of the heavy metal pot and then went on chatting as if she had heard some gossip about someone she hardly knew.

Even when she got back to Risley and saw Francis she felt no twinge of anger or jealousy. She was in the kitchen, helping Mrs Jackson prepare lunch, when Francis came in from his tour of inspection of the farm. Since their farm manager was behind him, and since Laura had to greet him in front of her husband, it was hardly the moment to confront Francis with what she had learned. Nor could she mention it in front of the Grays at lunch. When they left Francis disappeared to buy some piece of machinery before the shops closed. At tea there was Lucy, and when she was put to bed and Laura went to change for dinner with the Hamptons, Francis had had his bath and was down in the library.

It was only in the car on the way to the Hamptons that Laura and Francis were finally alone. She looked at him, and opened her mouth to speak, but then suddenly decided that if he had a mistress it was his own affair. She knew he would never leave her: he was too fond of the children and Risley was in her name. If, after nearly twenty years of marriage, he had embarked on a little adventure, it would be unkind of her to end it so soon. She also thought – but this thought was right at the back of her mind – that it might be useful to have a secret like this in reserve.

*

The next morning, at breakfast, Laura said to her husband: 'You know we must get Josef down for the weekend. He really ought to see something of the country.'

Hidden behind the *Sunday Times*, searching for the theme of the sermon, Francis was alerted by the tone of calculated inconsequence with which his wife had made that remark. Though as insensitive as most men to the nuances of feeling, and as short of what is properly called feminine intuition, he had been alerted by Eva Burroughs to the possibility that his wife's affections might stray from home. He had also been listening to Laura's offhand remarks at breakfast for almost twenty years, and so could sense at once, from a small variance of her vocal inflection – a deeper breath before the statement and a little too much air behind the words – that what was meant to sound by-the-way was really the fruit of substantial premeditation.

'You don't think we see enough of him in London?' he asked.

'We hardly see him at all.'

There was a long pause. Then Francis said: 'It's handy having someone there at weekends to frighten off the burglars.'

'I know.' Laura was as respectful of property as her husband. 'But there are weekends when Gail's there. He could come down then.'

There was another pause. Francis stole a glance over his newspaper to see what expression was on Laura's face. It was one of gracious detachment, as if she was posing for a cosmetics advertisement in her colour magazine. His eye fell to the emaciated African of the cover. 'It'll be something to do with the famine,' he said.

'What?'

'The sermon.'

'Why?'

'Because of the article in your magazine.'

Laura closed it and looked at the cover. 'I hadn't noticed. But I'm sure you're right.'

'A fiver?'

'No. You're sure to win.'

The sermon was indeed about famine, not just in Africa but endemic throughout the Third World, and in a manner that was both inspired and direct Giles Jermain ascribed all the evils which beset these unfortunate nations to the debts they incurred with Western banks. His theme was familiar enough – the congregation had heard it before – but on this occasion, perhaps to shake the complacency of his flock, the balding young vicar took his argument to extremes. 'What is wicked?' he asked rhetorically. 'What is evil? Is it something remote from our daily life – back in history, perhaps, in the concentration camps, or far away on the other side of the world, in foreign dictators wearing fancy uniforms who do nasty things to their people? Or is it in things which *we* do, or are done in our name, here and now, every day of our life, which we do not even realize are evil, like exacting our pound of flesh from nations that have only skin and bone?

'Do not think,' he thundered in his stylized West Country accent, 'that the God who judges the living and the dead is as selective in what he sees as you are. You may deceive yourselves but you cannot deceive him. You can shrug your shoulders and say that all this is none of your business, but God can see into your heart. He can see the cowardice and the laziness and the greed. You can say, perhaps, that you do not really understand complicated issues of international finance, and that you leave it all to the government to know what's best; but isn't that what the Germans said during the last war? Isn't that what people always say to get themselves off the hook for crimes committed in their name? And make no mistake about it – these *are* crimes, committed by you and me, crimes against the weak and the helpless, crimes which cry to Heaven for vengeance – a vengeance which will come, sooner or later, if not in this world, then in the next . . .'

Francis, of course, had heard sermons of this sort before, not just from this pulpit but from armchairs in London drawing-rooms. The preachers in the armchairs were not vicars, because no one knew vicars in London, but were rather rancorous socialists like Madge's husband Ben; and Francis was always protected from their moral assaults by his expert knowledge of the matter in hand. No one knew more than Francis Morton about Third World debt because it was Francis who, in his early years at Louards, had pioneered the recycling of the sudden surpluses belonging to Arab emirs which followed the great rise in the price of oil. At that time the wretched nations of Africa, Eastern Europe and South America had been clamouring for investment, so Louards had lent them the Arabs' money. Clearly Louards had to pay interest to the emirs and so was obliged in its turn to charge interest to the governments which borrowed; and it would, at the time, have seemed intolerably condescending to suggest to such newly independent nations that they were perhaps borrowing beyond their means.

Until that particular Sunday Francis's conscience had been clear; but that morning, as he listened to the Reverend Giles Jermain and sensed the indignation of the congregation against the heartless sinners in the City of London; and as he thought of the hungry and the diseased in those unfortunate nations who had indeed suffered not just from the profligacy and corruption of their rulers, but also from the implacable realities of the economic order, he began for the first time to wonder whether he did not, after all, bear some moral responsibility for their condition. Had he not known, in his heart, that most of the grandiose projects for which Louards had lent money would never work because there were not the diligent technicians to make them work? Had he not known, too, that a large part of the loans would in any event never go towards the projects to which they were allocated, but would find their way into Swiss bank accounts to be spent on Mercedes-Benz and villas on the Côte d'Azur?

He pondered these questions in an unusually gloomy frame of mind as with wife and daughter he walked back from the church to the delightful house which he had only been able to buy for his wife with the money he had made from Third World debt. He went into the drawing-room and his eye fell upon the vivid picture on the front of the Sunday colour magazine of a plaintive African holding her baby – a little bundle of skin and bone – to the shrivelled nipple of her dried-out breast. The supplement lay on the sofa. He remembered discussing the material for the loose cover with Eva Burroughs: it had cost £25 a yard.

He sat on the costly sofa and turned over the magazine to hide the despairing African and reveal an advertisement for fitted kitchens instead. He picked up the newspaper and let his eye run up and down the columns searching for some scandal or disaster to distract him from his grumbling conscience. There was nothing.

He picked up another section – the business news – which usually entertained him, but here again all the stories about takeovers and share fluctuations only depressed him. Was this all there was to life – buying, selling, lending, borrowing – just to make money for ruched curtains, loose covers, fitted kitchens and holidays abroad?

The third section was culture. Here at last was his salvation – because was not that the justification for the covering on the sofa, the ruched curtains, the Regency desk? Risley might not be Versailles but it was a little pool of civilization which together with all the others formed the sea of cultural abundance in the English nation.

His eye scanned the columns of criticism – plays, exhibitions, operas, concerts – and came to rest on a review by Geoffrey Bartle of a new novel. It was clear from the first sentence that Bartle did not like it. The hero was a master of fox hounds who, wrote Bartle, was 'so unrepresentative as to be unreal'. 'The so-called upper classes,' he went on, 'the blimps in their red coats or the bankers in the bowlers, are all right in soap operas on television, but they can hardly provide the substance of a work of art. The icing only decorates a cake: real art, like real life, must be a slice of the cake itself.'

It was an absurd, tendentious review – written in Bartle's celebrated sneering style to demolish a middle-brow author who was too old and unfashionable ever to be asked to review a novel by Bartle – but its effect that Sunday, following the vicar's sermon, was to throw Francis Morton into an even deeper gloom. Outside the sun shone on the bright green lawns, throwing dark liquid shadows of the trees onto the well-tended herbaceous borders; but what good was this exquisite scenery if the drama itself was a tragedy and the leading man unreal?

He lay back on the sofa with a deep sigh of self-pity. On the one hand, he thought, I am a sinner – an architect of the genocide in the sub-Sahara; yet I am also a brittle crumb of icing sugar – irrelevant, insignificant, insubstantial . . . So this is what I have worked for! This is my reward! Tears came into his eyes as Laura came into the room.

'I just rang up Josef,' she said as she picked up the colour magazine lying next to Francis on the sofa. And then, as if he had asked why, she added: 'I just thought I had better check up that everything was all right.'

He did not reply. She did not notice but flicked over the pages of the magazine. 'Don't you think,' she said, hesitating at an advertisement issued by the Tunisian Ministry of Tourism showing a beach almost as barren as the arid desert on the facing page which was to illustrate the article on famine, 'that we might see if we can't change the villa we've booked on Paxos for something a little larger so that we can have a few people to stay?'

Again Francis said nothing. Again Laura did not notice. 'I'm not sure that there are any bigger ones on Paxos, but I think you find them on Corfu.' She flicked over a few more pages. 'It's just that Johnny and Belinda will get frightfully bored if it's just us on our own . . .' Flick flick. 'It'll be more fun for them if we mix the generations.' She flicked to the end and threw down the magazines. 'God, they're boring, these magazines these days. There's nothing in that one that could be the slightest interest to anyone.'

TWELVE

Birek spent that weekend alone in London. He had now been in England for more than a month, and the hospitality arranged by the Comenius Foundation had run its course. The MacDonalds and the Maiers had had him to their homes at least once, while the British Council had given him complimentary tickets to the National Theatre, Covent Garden and the Festival Hall. With a sense of duty done they all now left Birek to sink or swim on his own.

It was known that he was staying with the Mortons and this knowledge in itself checked the flow of invitations. Andrew MacDonald was relieved that a protégé of the Foundation who was as young and sensitive as Birek should have been taken under such an ample wing. So too were the officials at the British Council. Miroslav Maier was envious and he expressed his envy by telling those émigré Czechs who had been eager to befriend Birek that Birek had better fish to fry – that he had been taken up by the English aristocracy and considered himself too important to mix with a set of seedy Slavs. 'He led a privileged life in Prague,' Miroslav confided to one of his friends, 'and now he expects the same kind of treatment in London. He turned up his nose at the room I found for him in Hounslow. He said it was too far from the centre of town!'

As with all successful calumnies, Miroslav's had a grain of truth. When Birek had gone to Sunday lunch with the Maiers, he had taken a bus, then an Underground, then a bus again. The journey had taken him an hour and a half. Birek had told Miroslav that he felt as if he had travelled halfway back to Prague, and had then added that he did not feel that Hounslow was part of London. He had found something dismal about the Maiers' pseudo-Tudor semi-detached house, and about the lodgings they had suggested in a modern semi-detached house on one of those indistinguishable streets which form part of the suburban sprawl around London airport. If Birek had had no choice, he might have taken it, but already by the time he saw it he was established in Johnny Morton's room on the top floor of the house in Lansdowne Square and had come to appreciate the advantages of living close to the centre of town.

Sincerity is the enemy of tact, and Birek's preference for a room in Holland Park only exacerbated the rancour of Miroslav Maier. The rumours he started about Birek's disdain for his fellow exiles successfully isolated Birek from the émigré community. Birek, however, hardly noticed that he had been cold-shouldered in this way. He had known enough Czechs in Czechoslovakia: his passion was now for England and the English. He would like to have seen more of Charlie Eldon, and Charlie's literary friends, but Charlie was abroad and Birek was content to wait until he returned. The whole of London, after all, was spread out around him – and it was the city that weekend which he set out to explore.

He had seen the obvious sights already – the Houses of Parliament, St Paul's Cathedral – and since it was part of his duty as a lodger to deter burglars by being seen coming and going from the house in Lansdowne Square, he confined himself to long walks around the borough of Kensington. On the Saturday morning he wandered through the crowded market on the Portobello Road, astonished at the number of antiques and *objets d'art* laid out on the little stalls. He went as far as the seamier streets beyond the viaducts which carried a railway and a motorway from London to the west. Here in North Kensington some shops were boarded up and the stucco of the houses was crumbling. There was rubbish in the gutters and a look of defeat on the faces of the impoverished passers-by.

He turned left on Golborne Road and left again on Ladbroke Grove, following this thoroughfare back to the arches of the concrete viaduct where four or five bums sat clutching half-drunk bottles of cider. Their eyes were bloodshot, their faces bloated, and as Birek passed he could smell the stale urine on their sodden clothes. He hurried on past the shoddy shops and the greasy cafés to Blenheim Crescent — the outer rampart of the choice area in which the Mortons had their home.

For lunch he ate a pizza at Notting Hill Gate. He then walked along the Bayswater Road past the ugly concrete building which was the embassy of his native land to the Round Pond in Kensington Gardens. It was a warm afternoon. The park was filled with people of every kind — young couples arm-in-arm, shuffling old men, Arabs in kaftans with their veiled wives, Americans, Frenchmen, Germans, Italians, Spaniards, Poles and people whose language he could not recognize from the phrases he overheard as he walked past. Every now and then he saw a uniformed English nanny pushing her charge in a shining pram. This sight delighted him because it proved that the England he had imagined, after reading so many nineteenth-century novels, still existed unchanged at the heart of this cosmopolitan metropolis.

Beyond the pond, through the haze of the warm afternoon, he could see the elegant brick façade of Kensington Palace; to the left the spire of St Mary Abbot's church, and then the modern block of the Royal Garden Hotel. This horizon appealed to Birek as a symbolic display of everything he had hoped for in England — tradition in harmony with the spirit of the age. What had been wretched in Prague was not just the restrictions on liberty imposed by the regime but the provincialism which came with its cultural isolation from the West – the rise among writers and painters of vainglorious second-raters whose only talent was in sensing the limits to which their fashionable dissidence could go.

In London Birek felt that he was free of that horrifying mediocrity and provincialism. Here anything could happen – certainly one could sink to the level of the down-and-outs he had seen beneath the arches of the motorway; but one could also rise on one's wits alone to a fame and a fortune that were unimaginable in Prague. And because it was warm, and he was young, Birek felt extraordinarily optimistic about his own prospects – or rather the prospects for his novel – and in his fantasy, as he walked from the Round Pond towards the Serpentine, he imagined buying a house on Stanley Crescent – smaller than the Mortons', of course, but equally elegant – and giving a party for Laura Morton of the kind that Laura had given for him.

Laura was rarely out of his mind as he walked through the Park that afternoon. It was only to be expected that this woman who was so beautiful and so kind should preoccupy him, and if his feelings for her went beyond the gratitude one would expect from a guest, they still stopped short of anything improper – not because Birek was incapable of coarser longings, nor because his Christian beliefs inhibited him from illicit desires, but rather because his youth and temperament preferred fantasies of a noble and romantic kind. He imagined a reversal of fortunes whereby he, Birek, like the Count of Monte Cristo, could save Laura and her children from bankruptcy and shame. He even made up stories that were sillier still – a kidnapping of Lucy in which he risked his life to save the child and return her to the arms of her mother; or a rapist who broke into the Mortons' house and was only prevented from subjecting Laura to unmentionable humiliation by the timely return and courageous pugilism of Josef Birek.

There was a rapist at large in Kensington at that time whose favourite haunts were the shrubs of the communal gardens. There were also terrorists in the streets of Kensington – Sikhs, Iranians and Irishmen. All this had been told to Birek during his briefing about the burglar alarm and had excited his imagination, but his fantasies were innocent: never did Laura reward him for his heroic acts with anything more than a look of gratitude in her huge blue tear-filled eyes.

It was also true, however, that Francis Morton played a very modest supporting role – indeed most of his scenes were lost on the cutting-room floor. But those very qualities which made Laura so admirable in his eyes – her composed beauty, her measured manner, her stylish clothes – also made her admissible only as the object of chaste veneration. It was the citizens of Sodom who wished to seduce an angel, and Birek was very far from such depravity. All he wished was in some way to render her a service like a knight in the days of courtly love.

He left Kensington Gardens by the Albert Memorial, walked back towards Kensington, and was caught in a herd of Saturday shoppers which carried him down to the Earls Court Road. He stopped outside the Odeon cinema, wondering whether to go to a film, but then seeing the price of a ticket, remembering his limited resources, and recalling too the video tapes in the library at the house in Lansdowne Square, he walked back through Holland Park and spent the evening at home.

The next morning Birek went walking again right across Kensington towards Knightsbridge. In a pretty square he came upon a Gothic church which because it referred to the times of 'mass' on the board outside seemed to belong to the Roman Catholic communion. He sat through the service, some of which seemed unfamiliar; but the priest wore colourful vestments, incense billowed from the thurible, and so Birek took Communion confident that it had been consecrated by a priest of his own religion.

After the mass he accepted the priest's invitation to come into the parish hall for a cup of coffee and some biscuits. There was no evidence of a wife, which seemed to confirm that this was indeed a Roman Catholic church; but when Birek asked the young curate he said: 'Oh dear me no, we're C. of E.' He spoke with a slight lisp and was clearly popular with the younger parishioners – particularly the young men. Several of them had affected mannerisms – Birek thought that they might be students of drama – but they were extraordinarily welcoming, as Christians often are just after the Sunday service. Two young men even asked Birek if he would like

141

to come back to their flat for Sunday lunch but Birek, conscious of his duties as caretaker, declined their invitation.

Once back at Lansdowne Square, he switched off the burglar alarm, locked the door and went down to the kitchen to make himself a sandwich which he ate while listening to Bach on a compact disc. There was something particularly agreeable about having the run of such a large and lovely house, not just because when he was there he felt enveloped by Laura, but because everything in it was so fine. The Mortons' taste was conventional: indeed, given the furniture and the paintings they had inherited and Eva Burroughs's décor, there was little scope for a display of their taste at all; but both Francis and Laura had a feel for quality and the money to pay for it. The furniture, the china, the cutlery and the kitchen machines were all solid and well made. Coming from a country where everything was shoddy, Birek was inordinately impressed.

After lunch he watched a recording of *La Règle du Jeu* on the Mortons' 22" television. He had the tact to realize, however, that he should not be found lounging in an armchair when they returned from the country. Therefore as soon as the film had finished he tidied the sofa upon which he had been sitting, glanced around the library for any other evidence of his use of the room, and then went out once again to stalk round the city – being careful to set the burglar alarm before he left.

He went to see the film at the Odeon cinema which he had considered the day before, and came back at nine after eating a supper of Kentucky Fried Chicken at Notting Hill Gate. He knew that the Mortons were back because the Mercedes was parked outside the house. He went in, hoping to creep up to his room without disturbing any of the family, but just as he reached the second flight of stairs which led up to the children's floor, he heard an angry woman's voice shout out: 'Then bloody well cook her something yourself.'

Birek stood immobile on the stairs. After two days quite alone he was in a vulnerable condition for any social encounter, but to hear this harsh command from a voice he was obliged to recognize as Laura's at once alarmed him. He realized that he had stumbled upon a conjugal quarrel, and wanted to creep away before Laura realized that he had been a witness to it, but just as he was about to turn and go back down the stairs, Francis appeared above him. He hesitated for a moment, then came down, raising his eyes and shrugging his shoulders as he passed Birek on the stairs.

Birek had no choice but to go on. When he reached the landing he heard Lucy sobbing, then Laura's irritable voice saying: 'Oh do stop blubbing, darling. Daddy's *making* you some supper.' Again Birek hesitated – loathe to see Laura in a bad mood – but he could not reach his room without going past the bathroom, and since Francis was behind him there was no retreat. If he remained where he was, he was sure to be discovered as soon as Laura came out onto the landing. He therefore walked on and as he came to the bathroom door, said a brief and quiet 'Hello'.

Laura was sitting on the closed lavatory with Lucy wrapped in a towel upon her knee. Her face was red from the heat of the bath; her hair had half-fallen over her face; and the sleeves of her jersey had been pulled up to the elbow to reveal the delicate gold hairs on her forearm. She was frowning down at her daughter whose eyes were red from crying, but the moment Laura saw Birek the furrows left her brow. 'You,' she said simply in her old soft tone of voice.

'I am sorry . . .' Birek began as if he was to blame for her bad mood.

'Don't be silly,' she said quickly. 'Come in and tell us about your weekend.'

'It was fine.'

He came into the bathroom and sat uncomfortably on the edge of the bath.

'Good. So was ours, until the drive back.'

'Was it bad?'

'Worse than ever. And then we always have the same struggle every Sunday night . . .' She looked down at Lucy. 'I give her a huge tea before we leave so that she can go straight to bed when we get to London.'

'But Mummy . . .'

'And what happens? She says she's hungry.'

'But I *am*.'

Laura smiled and jogged the little girl on her knee. 'If you were really hungry, you'd eat an apple or a banana or a bowl of cereal.'

'I'm hungry for something *hot*.'

'And you're getting something hot. Kind Daddy is at this moment bent over the stove.' She looked at Birek and smiled. 'He's putty in her hands.'

'That's understandable.'

'But it makes her think she can always get her way.'

'I won't, Mummy, I promise.'

Laura finished rubbing her daughter with the towel and pushed her, naked, off her knee. 'I just hope you find a husband as nice as your father.'

'I'm going to marry Johnny,' said Lucy with a flirtatious look at Birek who, unfamiliar with the naked female form, even in a child, blushed and looked away.

'Anyway,' said Laura, taking a nightdress from the towel rail and putting it over her daughter's head, 'find your slippers and go down to Daddy in the kitchen.'

Lucy scampered out of the bathroom. Laura stood up and folded the towel. 'Have *you* had some supper?' she asked Birek.

'Yes. I had something . . .'

'Was everything all right over the weekend?' She put the towel on the towel-rail.

'Yes.'

'If you're free next weekend, you must come with us to the country.'

'I would like that very much.' He followed her out on to the landing.

'We should hear from Stephanie Parr some time this week,' said Laura, pulling down the sleeves of her jersey and brushing back the wisps of her hair.

'That will be good,' said Birek. 'The sooner I have a contract the better.'

'Are you so impatient to leave us?' She turned down her mouth in an ironic smile.

'No, of course not,' said Birek, blushing. 'But I know it is an imposition to have a stranger in your house.'

'It most certainly is,' said Laura.

Birek looked abashed.

'But you're hardly a stranger,' she added with a mocking smile.

'Thank you, but all the same . . .'

'You mustn't be foolish,' she interrupted with an affected severity in her tone of voice. 'We all think of you as one of the family. We would be very sorry to see you go.' Then, as if he was indeed her son, she kissed him lightly on the cheek, smiled, turned and went down stairs.

Birek now went to his room and sat at his desk in a state of great confusion. On the one hand he felt elated as if he had just been given a sniff of cocaine; on the other he felt ashamed because he was hit for the first time by a strong physical longing for Laura Morton.

It was not the kiss – the peck on the cheek – which had ignited his passions but rather the sight of Laura in the bathroom, hot, cross and dishevelled. The angel had been revealed as human – he had seen the little blonde hairs on her forearm beneath her rolled-up sleeve – and the small beads of steam and sweat on her cheeks; and all at once he had longed to stroke her arm and kiss her cheek and lick the moisture from her skin.

What else he longed to do can easily be imagined – we are all pawns in nature's pursuit of the procreation of the species – and it was his sudden possession by images of Laura Morton without her clothes that shamed and delighted him in equal measure. She was wonderful but she was married. She had befriended him and how did he repay her? By horrible and delightful daydreams of illicit contortions on his narrow bed.

He turned his eyes towards that bed and saw, as he did so, the Czech Bible on his bedside table. Thou shalt not commit adultery! Thou shalt not covet thy neighbour's wife! Yet he did covet her – he could hardly suffer another minute of life without her here, compliant, in his arms. Yet she had a child. Three children. And a husband. What ingratitude to Francis who had given him a roof over his head to take advantage of his hospitality to lust after his wife. Yet what right had such a boring man to a wife like Laura Morton? Thus the young stag countered the Christian's conscience until finally Birek went to bed – exhausted by the struggle between ecstasy and remorse.

He crept out of the house the next morning without daring to go down for breakfast in the kitchen. He went instead to a café at

Notting Hill Gate where he had a greasy English breakfast of bacon, eggs, sausages and tomatoes. He then walked over Campden Hill to the Kensington Public Library where he could read undisturbed.

Undisturbed! Refreshed after sleep, the temptations of the night before returned to torment him with a new vigour. Birek capitulated at once. His eye was on the page of his book but his lips were fixed in a gentle smile as he imagined a dozen different ways in which an encounter with Laura could lead to the consummation that his body desired. He gave in so easily because it was so inconceivable that the fantasy should ever become fact. Though the angel in his mind had come down to earth, shedding her wings as she shed her clothes, he did not once envisage that the real Laura Morton would love him in return.

Certainly she was fond of him – he could be sure of that – but with the same fondness she might feel for one of the friends of her son. She also admired his writing – he could concede that without conceit – but admiration and affection did not add up to love. The very qualities which Birek admired in Laura – her dignity, her pride – made it seem quite absurd to hope that his love for her could be returned.

This separation in his mind, which took place that day in the public library, between Laura Morton in the flesh and Laura Morton in his fantasy, made it easier for him to treat her normally when he returned that afternoon and when he saw her on and off during the week to discuss her translation of his novel. Indeed he felt so at ease by the Thursday morning that he decided not to go to the public library but to work in his room. It was raining: water trickled down the gutter outside his window; and though he spent some of his money on a new pair of shoes with rubber soles, he had no umbrella and felt ashamed of his Czech raincoat.

He went down to the kitchen at half-past nine to make himself a cup of instant coffee and eat two slices of white toast and marmalade. The house was silent. No one else seemed to be at home. While he was eating, Fatima, the cleaning lady, arrived and began to chat in an incomprehensible Spanish accent. Birek finished his breakfast, washed the cup and plate, put the marmalade back in the cupboard and went up to his room. He worked in a desultory manner – the only sounds the dripping of the rain and the vacuum cleaner as Fatima cleaned the stairs. Birek found it difficult to concentrate. He was working on a story set in Prague, but the character he wished to portray, based loosely upon a teacher in the school where he had worked as a caretaker, refused to come to life in his imagination. Nor could he conjure up the touch and smell of the classroom in Prague. They had been driven from his mind by the aroma of Floris bath essence which lingered on the landing outside the Mortons' bedroom.

At one he was hungry and thought of walking out to find some lunch, but it was still raining so he went down to the kitchen to eat some bread and cheese. The house was silent. Fatima had gone. He ate an apple, then boiled the kettle for a cup of instant coffee. He took this up to his room to continue work on his story, but after an hour's more work – despite the coffee – he felt drowsy and went to read on his bed. The rain dripped from the leak in the gutter. His lids grew heavy. He dozed off.

He awoke with a jump. For a moment he did not know why. It was still raining. There was no other sound until he heard a gentle knock on his door. 'Yes, come in,' he said, lifting his legs onto the floor. The door opened. Laura came in.

'Am I disturbing you?' she asked.

'No.'

She left the door ajar and went to the window as if she had climbed the stairs to see the rain falling over the communal garden. 'I thought you might be here, on such an awful day.'

'But you went out,' said Birek.

'Yes. I had lunch with Gerald Pritchard. Do you remember? The publisher you met at the party.'

'Of course.'

Birek already knew enough about Laura's wardrobe to see that she was wearing the kind of elegant suit that she kept for sallies into the West End.

'Do you mind if I sit down?' She asked this with a smile, moving towards the chair at the little desk by the window.

'Of course not.'

'I'm afraid the news is discouraging,' she said softly.

'About the novel?'

147

'Yes.'

'Did Stephanie send the outline to Pritchard?'

'No. She sent it back to me earlier this week, saying that she did not think she was the right person to represent you.'

'I see.'

'I didn't tell you at the time because I thought it might depress you. I wanted Gerald to read it and give us a second opinion.'

'What did he say?'

'Well he read it in twenty-four hours, which is a compliment in itself.'

'There were only two chapters.'

'I know, but publishers are often very slow.'

'He did not like them?'

'He liked them very much, but said that to judge from the outline and the two chapters this was not the work to launch you on the English market.'

Birek sagged on his bed. 'I see.'

Laura moved her chair an inch or two so that she could take hold of his hand. 'You mustn't be got down,' she said. 'First of all, those are just two opinions. Secondly, it may well be that my translation is unsatisfactory.'

'No, no,' said Birek, his voice choking as he struggled to suppress the tears, 'it is the book, I know, which is too long and too serious for English readers.'

'*I* think it's wonderful,' said Laura, now moving to sit next to Birek on the bed so that she would not have to stretch to keep hold of his hand.

'But you are *kind*,' Birek moaned. 'You would not say anything to hurt me.' He looked up. The tears trembled on his lower lids.

'Dear Josef,' she said, pulling him towards her.

He fell into her arms and felt for the first time the soft bulge of that bosom which he had imagined a thousand times.

'It does not matter,' he murmured.

'No,' she whispered, lifting his head and nuzzling her face against his cheek.

They kissed, then Birek, as if shocked at what he had done, started back and looked into Laura's eyes. 'I am sorry.'

She smiled. 'You're almost an Englishman.'

'Why?'

'Always apologizing for nothing at all.' She leaned forward and gave him a long, sweet kiss on the lips.

He clasped her violently to his chest. 'I love you so much.'

'Yes,' she whispered, moving her hands around his ribs to the sinews of his back, then pulling his shirt tails from his trousers so that she could feel not the cloth but his skin. Both breathed heavily into one another's ear.

'But this is wrong,' muttered Birek.

'Don't be silly,' murmured Laura.

'You are married. Your husband . . .'

'Everyone does it,' she said, a little breathless, as she guided his hand where it would never have dared go on its own. They writhed on the bed for some minutes – at times raising their bodies to remove some garment, at others hampering this practical action by impatient embraces and caresses, and on occasions almost toppling together on to the floor. There came a moment when, half-undressed, Laura rose from the bed and tiptoed across the room to close the door. Then, with a smile he had never seen on a woman's face before, she returned in the gloomy light of the wet afternoon and they made love on Birek's narrow bed.

THIRTEEN

Our reasons for doing things are often so complicated that it tests both the skill of the novelist and the patience of his reader to go into them as thoroughly as would a psychoanalyst or a social worker. It is therefore best not to do so but leave most of the skins on the onion. Above all it destroys a story to go into subconscious motivation: the author has to declare himself a Freudian, a Jungian, a Kleinian or an Adlerian, or any combination of the four, and then write what is, in effect, a paper for the Institute of Psycho-Analysis in New Cavendish Street.

Yet even if he discounts the subconscious, he cannot simply race on with his story after an incident of the kind described in the previous chapter. Unless a male author is an out-and-out misogynist, he is always half in love with his heroine and feels he must defend her honour. Yet in Laura's case it is not easy. For a wife to betray a husband who despite his paunch is a reasonably decent fellow; for her to break the vow she took – admittedly some time ago – to remain faithful to him until death, must lead to a measure of condemnation even in this tolerant age.

Why did Laura Morton sleep with Josef Birek? Was it because she had drunk half a bottle of Burgundy at lunch with Gerald Pritchard? Was it because she saw the sad look on Birek's face and wanted to cheer him up? Or was it simply because she loved him and because she loved him wanted to make love to him? To resist such an impulse is to defy nature and grapple with those instincts which are fundamental to the survival of the species. Add pity to the impulse – give it, in other words, a tint of altruism – and fire the blood with a few glasses of good wine, and one is well on the way to a victory over any inhibitions which modesty and morality have imposed.

Yet the reason she gave Birek – that everyone did that sort of thing – was perhaps the most honest and accurate, not because she thought that Francis had a mistress and wanted to emulate him but because Laura had felt for several years that she had missed out on the sexual revolution. She was born in 1947 and had married twenty-one years later in 1968, that *annus mirabilis* when youth rose up against authority all over the world – in Paris, in Prague, in London and in New York. The clamour against Stalinism, Gaullism or the war in Vietnam was also a revolt against restraints of any kind – particularly the code of sexual morality which confined sexual pleasure to marriage. 'Make love, not war', or 'Fuck, don't fight', were the slogans chanted at President Lyndon B. Johnson as he pondered his nation's intractable involvement in the political conflicts of South-East Asia.

If Laura and Francis Morton had not been blown off course by this change in direction of the wind, it was because they were carried along by the strong current of tradition. Not principle but disdain made their circle slow to emulate the long-haired pot-smoking free-loving hippies. The conventions of the 1950s were also the code of their class. They got tipsy on gin and orange, heavy-petted beneath the hoods of their Triumph Spitfires and MGBs, and only jumped the gun by a month or two once their engagements had been announced in *The Times*.

The danger of getting pregnant was then the real reason why decent girls either did not sleep with their boy friends, or if they did, did so in such terror, and with such control, that it was never the sublime experience they had expected. Certainly pessaries existed, and the pill was on the way, but neither was commonly prescribed or asked for by well-brought-up girls from respectable families. Abortion remained a criminal offence, but could be arranged as a last resort in great secrecy and at great expense.

The effect of these *moeurs* was to bring husband and wife together with little or no experience of physical love. Sometimes things went well, sometimes badly: mostly they had a jolly time until morning sickness set in, or the first baby brought broken nights and drained their once limitless libido. All this might have been fair enough – every generation goes through the same sort of thing – had not the conventional young couples like the Mortons been living through this phase of sexual disillusion on the fevered atmosphere of the sexual revolution. The publication of *Lady Chatterley's Lover* was like the first act of an erotic extravaganza. All at once they were surrounded by books, films and advertisements depicting couples writhing in orgasmic ecstasy. When they switched on their television they saw programmes extolling the virtue of sexual fulfilment. When they opened a newspaper they read articles on the vice of sexual restraint.

They did their best, but sexual habits once formed are hard to change. Most of the things that Francis once saw in someone else's copy of *The Joy of Sex* he thought improper and unhygienic. He was not and did not want to be a sexual athlete and there had been times when he had been embarrassed in Laura's presence by erotic scenes on the screen. Throughout the long decade of the 1970s, when the sexual revolution had raged unchecked, the Mortons had settled down to a conjugal life of a conventional kind. They were generally more excited by doing up houses, raising children and going on holidays with their friends than by what had become known by the blunt and simple term 'sex'.

It was impossible, however, to live through those years amid the acclamations of orgasm as the highest good, and not feel at times that one had missed out. Francis had loved his wife as dearly as any husband, and he had recognized and admired that beauty which she had so methodically preserved; but there had been times when he had considered that had she been a little more energetic or a little less reserved, then he might have felt encouraged to embellish instinct with art; and Laura, in her turn, as she complied with their conjugal routine, forgot the ecstasies of the earlier years and began delicate little daydreams of imaginary lovers.

They remained decidedly imaginary until Charlie Eldon presented himself as a candidate for her inspection, but he failed, as we have seen, to oust the phantom lover and impose himself as a real one. It was partly thanks to the advance intelligence given to Francis by Eva Burroughs, and partly thanks to Francis's own idea of sending Laura to the Comenius Foundation, that Charlie's intentions had been frustrated; but there was another factor to which Laura herself alluded in the last snatch of conversation during that lunch at which he was rejected. She had said that she was afraid that he would devour her, or words to that effect, and that she had already been devoured by Francis.

Francis, to an impartial observer, was very far from the ravenous wolf of Laura's terminology; but it should be remembered that when he married her he was energetic and ambitious whereas she had been indecisive and shy. He had been dominant, she submissive, and their love had thereby confirmed that natural pattern which is found throughout nature and some would say follows the Creator's design.

What it established, however, was a desire that was only aroused in response to the desire of another; whereas the kind of love Laura began to imagine was one in which she would take the initiative and have control. Why, she asked herself, should women always wait on men – particularly when the only men likely to approach them are their dreary husbands or professional seducers like Charlie Eldon? Why should they not choose for themselves the kind of shy and delicate young man who would never dare declare himself or make a pass? A man, in other words, like Josef Birek?

During the first days of that week, when she had been back in London, she had also been possessed by two other pertinent ideas – the first that she would be justified in betraying Francis because Francis was betraying her; the second, that she would soon be forty, an age after which a young man like Birek might not want her. If she was to have an adventure, it must be now or never. Otherwise a wrinkled face and sagging bosom would oblige her to be chaste until she died.

Both these thoughts were brought forward to justify what she had in mind. She saw Francis every evening, and her intuition told her over and over again that the idea that he had a mistress was absurd. The Caroline Charles dress was a mystery, but there was certainly some innocent explanation, and she had only to ask him about it, either for that explanation to be given, or for his faithlessness to be established as a fact. She would be able to tell, she was sure, if Francis tried to tell a lie; but Laura, at that moment, because of Birek, did not want to know for certain either way. If Francis had no mistress, then she would have no excuse, and if he did have a mistress then she might have to do something about it which would disrupt the convenient arrangements which she had so skilfully made.

So too the 'now or never' was only another way of deciding to strike while the iron was hot. She had preserved her body so well until now that another year or two would not make that much difference to its chances of attracting a member of the opposite sex. But when one means to take such a large step in such a particular direction, it is only to be expected that one looks for every reason for doing so; and so Laura, by that Thursday, had made her case to herself and had accepted it, and had awaited only the courage and the occasion to make Birek her lover.

Did she have scruples? Certainly not of a theological kind. It is the charm of the Church of England that its God of love obscures the God of judgement. Adultery, to Laura, was rather an ugly word from the Old Testament which had nothing to do with her feelings for Birek. Although on the one hand she told herself that she had the right to deceive Francis because he was deceiving her, on the other – in the kind of consistent contradiction with which a woman's intuition invariably overrules the rationalizations of her conscious mind – she did not really consider that she *was* deceiving Francis because Francis and Birek were so entirely different.

Of course it would be awful if Francis found out, because he would feel horribly hurt, but she knew that in reality she was not harming him, or risking her marriage in any way, because Josef was not a rival to her husband or a threat to their family life. He was not someone who could conceivably carry her off to be his wife in another home: indeed he prevented her from falling for someone who might, and so in a sense could be said to have saved her marriage.

When Lucy returned from school at ten to four that Thursday afternoon, she found her mother resting in her own room. After prattling about her day at school, the little girl went down to watch television while Gail prepared her tea in the kitchen.

Laura remained on her bed in a state of befuddled rapture. She had crept down from Birek's room in her underclothes and now lay under the duvet as if it was the lid of a casserole containing the scents and sensations which remained on her hot body. At around five she heard Birek come down the stairs on his way out of the house. She smiled as if the sound of his footsteps on the creaking floorboards was a precious possession she had recently gained. She longed for some tea but did not want to get dressed and go down to the kitchen.

Finally, at half-past five, she got up and ran a bath. She was loath to wash off Birek but felt it would be poor form to greet Francis while still sticky from another man. She therefore immersed herself in the usual oils and unguents, delighted for the first time that the trouble she took to smell nice was no longer to please herself alone. The more a woman admires herself, the more benevolent she can feel towards her lover, and while Laura was quite aware of her good fortune in having such a handsome young man in a room above her own, she was also conscious of her own munificence from his point of view. The very costliness of the bath essence, and the softness and beauty of her honey-coloured skin, made the thought of what she had bestowed upon the destitute Czech many times more appealing.

Francis returned at seven to find Laura already changed. If he noticed that she was ahead in the evening's routine, he seemed to make nothing of it. He changed, as usual, into a jersey and slippers, then ran his own bath. Laura was acutely ordinary in the way in which she talked to him, concealing with the skill of Mata Hari any evidence of the sins of the afternoon. Both her manner and her mood were just what they might have been at the end of any other day, except that just before Francis went into the bathroom, and she left the bedroom to put Lucy to bed, Laura remarked that Birek's novel had been rejected.

'By Pritchard?'

'Yes.'

'No good?'

'Too difficult.'

'That means, I suppose,' said Francis, 'that he'll be with us a little longer.'

'We can't really turn him out,' said Laura and then she sighed as if having him in the house was a bore.

Laura was astonished, in the weeks which followed, at her own ingenuity and audacity. At ten the next morning she set off with Birek for the country leaving Gail to fetch Lucy from school and deliver her to her father at Paddington Station. They arrived at Risley in time for lunch – a sandwich in the kitchen while chatting to Mrs Jackson. Then, when Mrs Jackson had gone back to her cottage, Laura showed Birek around her house. Since it was hers – her childhood home – she felt even more at ease than she had done in London, and when they reached the prettiest guest-room with its large four-poster bed, nothing seemed more natural than to use it for the purpose for which such beds were made.

How wonderful it was to make love with a man whose only purpose, he whispered, was to make her happy and bring her joy. Not for a moment did he try to dominate her, own her or make some point about his male prowess. His gestures were always gentle, and he moved in obedience to her guiding hand. His eyes expressed only love, delight and incredulity that this rapture was not a dream – that she was indeed lying naked beside him beneath the blue chintz hangings chosen by Eva Burroughs.

Lying naked in the bright light of that summer afternoon was for Laura a double delight – not just to feel that her own body was free from all constraint, and the object of such reverence in another, but to look once again at the long slim body of her lover – touch the warm ivory of his hairless chest, to follow the ridges made by his ribs and stroke the skin of his stomach. She gazed at him in wonder, thinking how understated were the representations in painting and sculpture of what in life could be so monstrous on such an innocent young man. Yet what was monstrous did not intimidate her, as it might once have done on another man, because Birek was so obedient and gentle. All he had was hers, for her to use as she liked, and crouching over him like a panther she devoured him inch by inch, sniffing and kissing his wonderful skin from his eyelids to his toes, and then without any embarrassment trying those variations which they both had read about in American novels.

She straightened the bed before she left the room – she had to think about Mrs Jackson – but continued the tour arm in arm with her lover. In the garden they walked apart, and at tea in the kitchen, when Mrs Jackson had returned, they spoke the lines of two people who were barely friends.

At six she went to meet Francis and Lucy at the station, leaving Birek alone in the house. When Lucy was in bed the three ate supper together. Once again Laura behaved in such a normal way that she inwardly applauded her own performance. Birek was just Birek: perhaps the only change in his behaviour was that he avoided Francis's eye. Francis, too, behaved much as he always behaved on a Friday evening – tired after a week in London.

The weekend passed like any other weekend except that Laura had Birek in tow. She took him to Pewsey while Lucy went riding and showed him off to Emma – not as her lover, of course, but as the celebrated young dissident who had recently escaped from behind the Iron Curtain and was now sitting tamely drinking coffee in the Red Lion Hotel. Emma gave her a look as if to ask the only question that a woman's best friend wants answered, but Laura gave nothing away – which is to say that she met Emma's look with a look of her own, a look intended to be one of astonishment that such a question should even be asked, but which may have had a trace of triumph: Birek, after all, was very good-looking.

After lunch at Risley, Francis took Lucy to Marlborough in pursuit of the elusive spare part for the broken mower. Laura thought that Birek should see something of the country, so they drove in the Land-Rover onto the Downs. There they walked over fields and through woods – hand in hand when hidden by the trees. They came to a barn half-filled with bales of straw, and hidden from view behind the half-closed door, they kissed ferociously as if they had not met for a month. The kissing stimulated desires which could only be satisfied in the usual way, so Laura, with a courage which itself excited her, slipped off her knickers (so much for Bartle's theory that they were glued to her thighs), hitched up her skirts and herself undid the buttons of Birek's trousers.

There were guests that night at dinner – the Saunders and the Wades – and Birek was mostly silent, not just intimidated by the raucous county talk, but exhausted by so much exercise in the country air. Luckily the next day was Sunday and a day of rest. Birek went to church with the Mortons and decided from the absence of vestments and incense that this was certainly a Protestant church. They lingered at Risley until after tea, and then all drove back to London. Lucy was as fractious in the Mercedes as she always was, but this time nothing she did could make her mother cross.

By the Monday Laura felt starved of time alone with her lover, but such time was not as easily arranged as might at first have been imagined. Though she was mistress of the house in Lansdowne Square, and Birek was living under her roof, there were not many moments when the two of them could be sure of being there alone. Francis left at a quarter past eight; Gail and Lucy at a quarter to nine; but Fatima came at nine and Gail was back soon after.

The only certain moment when Laura could be sure that Gail was not secretly scoffing in the kitchen, or lurking in her bedroom, was the half-hour or so in the early afternoon between Gail leaving to fetch Lucy and returning with her charge. Something could be done in half-an-hour, as Laura and Birek discovered on the Monday, but it was disagreeable to have to hurry what could be prolonged with such delight. On the Tuesday Laura remained all day at the Comenius Foundation, and only managed a quick kiss on the landing upon her return; but on the Wednesday she asked Andrew MacDonald if she could work at home that afternoon on the translation of Birek's novel. MacDonald of course agreed, whereupon Laura telephoned the mother of a friend of Lucy's to ask if Gail could take Lucy to tea. The mother also agreed – it was common enough to shunt nannies and children around in this way. Laura then telephoned Gail and told her to take Lucy on from school to her friend. At half-past three, when she knew Gail would have left, Laura drove home. Birek was waiting. So the pattern was established and continued throughout that summer term.

Who knew what was going on? So far as Laura was concerned, no one could know – or at any rate no one could be sure – because she took so much trouble not to give herself away. Of course some might suspect, but '*Honi soit qui mal y pense.*' It was natural enough to send Lucy to tea with her friends, and reasonable to tell the people at the Foundation that it was easier to discuss her translation with the author himself in the library of her own home.

What was harder to account for were the changes in her own behaviour and appearance. She suddenly looked so well – flushed, animated, energetic and five years younger. Gail was the first to notice – not just Laura's good health but also her constant good humour and the gentle tone with which she talked to her lodger. She also remarked upon the sudden increase in Lucy's tea-time invitations, and grumbled to the other nannies about the way she was made to drive hither and thither across London in the Mortons' Golf. She sensed that it was just to get them out of the way and was able, with the other nannies, to 'put two and two together'. Most of the nannies kept gossip of this kind from their employers, but there was one where the household was of a progressive, fraternal, Christian-name, *Guardian*-reading kind. She told the mother and the mother told the world.

Eva Burroughs heard the rumour; so too did Madge, who had already had her suspicions because Laura looked so well. She had put it to Ben, who at first had dismissed it as a ridiculous idea because, as he put it, 'sex isn't Laura's thing'; but when he saw her one evening with a bright, laughing look in her eye, he too came to give credence to the rumours on the grounds that 'only a fantastic amount of fucking could bring about a change of that kind'.

Laura was quite oblivious to their suspicions and took ever greater risks with her reputation. When Francis left for his annual visit to the Gulf to tell the emirs what he was doing with their money, she had candlelit dinners with Birek in restaurants like La Résidence, Monsieur Thompsons or La Pomme d'Amour. None of these was the kind of place where one went to be seen, but they were all of the sort where one *might* be seen, and seen they were by people who knew Laura well enough to say with a snigger to other friends that she was taking advantage of Francis's absence abroad to work on her Czech translation after hours. They also went to the cinema together – once on their own, once with Madge and Ben; and on this occasion Laura had been particularly cheerful, as if boasting to the dreary Islingtonians that life was more racy in Holland Park.

After these evenings out they could not make love in Birek's bedroom because Gail was next door watching her portable Sony. Nor would Birek consent to trespass upon Francis's *letto maritale*, which he somehow thought worse than making love with his wife. In any case, they had already made love in the afternoon, and enough should have been enough, and it was, yet it was not, and twice they ended up, furtive and breathless, behind the sofa on the drawing-room floor.

Francis returned – weary from his sweltering journey and two weeks of incessant courtesy to inscrutable Arab emirs and their ministers of finance. He kissed his wife in a formal way, and embraced his daughter with greater affection, and when he saw Birek he frowned but greeted him, all the same, with the same kind of politeness that he had shown to the Arabs on the Gulf.

Did he suspect? It was a question that Birek often put to Laura and Laura sometimes put to herself. She thought not – in fact she was sure – although he drank more whisky, that night of his return, than he had ever done before, and fell asleep on his back when they went to bed before Laura had put down her book. That meant that he snored, which kept her awake and made her long to climb the stairs to her delicate lover above; but she stayed where she was and eventually kicked her husband who snorted, grunted, then turned on his side and breathed more quietly through his nose.

FOURTEEN

At the end of May, Charlie Eldon returned from the Middle East and at once heard the gossip about Laura and Josef Birek. Since Charlie had predicted that Laura was ripe for an affair, the news did not come as a surprise. The cynic in him felt pleased that his assessment of her frailty had been proved correct: and the opportunist calculated that once a breach had been made in the ramparts of Laura's chastity, it would be easier for others to follow behind. Yet beneath the cynicism and the calculation was the suffering of a man who was still in love with Laura Morton. His trip abroad had been undertaken partly to try to forget her, and the jealousy he felt towards Birek proved that it had not worked.

Constancy of this kind is often admired by women who see in the power it appears to accord to one of their sex flattery of the entire gender: but Charlie's passion said less about Laura than about the tenacity of his own aspirations. Some men's ambitions are satisfied by a promotion or an accumulation of wealth: but others' perception of their own worth comes only from the women who love them. Constancy, in such cases, reflects vanity not love. So it was with Charlie. He still loved Laura, and suffered when he thought of Birek; but he took care not to show his feelings. It was bad enough to be scoffed at because the Czech had succeeded where he had failed: it would be worse if he showed that he cared. His instinct was to wait, and to see less of Laura in the meantime, but Laura telephoned him as soon as she heard he was back and asked if they could meet to discuss Birek's novel.

Charlie, despite his aversion to Birek, agreed to meet her for lunch. When he saw her walk towards his table – smiling at him with an almost wanton confidence in her own appearance – he lost any doubts that he might still have entertained that the rumours about her liaison were true. Yet the very glow which gave her away also compounded his jealousy: how dare the little Czech make her flourish in this way?

With the tactlessness of the besotted, Laura – after a few cursory questions about Charlie's travels – started to talk about Birek and the prospects for his novel. She explained how Pritchard had turned it down, and how Stephanie had declined to represent him. 'I know it's because of what he said about blacks,' she said to Charlie, 'and that was *your* fault.'

'Why my fault?'

'You should have told him that Bartle was joking.'

'I cannot be held responsible for Birek's lack of a sense of humour.'

Laura frowned. 'He doesn't lack a sense of humour.'

'Has he made you laugh?'

'Of course.'

'Not just by tickling you?'

'No.'

She said this, then blushed, because the way in which she had said it implied that Birek *had* tickled her. Anyone other than Charlie might not have noticed what she had given away, but Charlie missed nothing and so asked at once: 'Is he a good tickler?'

She blushed again. 'What do you mean?'

'Does he make you laugh more when he jokes or when he tickles?'

'He's never tickled me,' she lied.

'Really?' asked Charlie. 'Living at such close quarters, I would have thought that there must be a certain amount of slap and tickle . . .'

'Don't be absurd.'

She said this as an actress speaks her lines, and again anyone less experienced in the nuances of feminine behaviour might have taken her denial at its face value, but Charlie knew that people only keep secret the things of which they are ashamed. If Laura was in love with Birek, she might feel she should deny it for the sake of convention, but at the heart of her feminine nature she would feel triumphant at the conquest of such a young and handsome man, and so prudence would be battling with a longing to proclaim her passion to the world.

'I know when I am beaten,' he said with affected humility. 'I defer to the better man.'

'You just can't conceive of a man and a woman not sleeping together,' said Laura.

'Not when they see one another as much as you and the Czech.'

'He's called Josef.'

'I'm sorry. Josef.'

'I am very fond of him, and I want to help him, and so do we all at the Foundation.'

'Does he tickle everyone at the Foundation?'

'So far as I know he tickles no one at all except, perhaps, Lucy . . .'

'He's as close as that, is he? One of the family.'

'Yes. Like a . . .' She searched for the word.

'A son?' Charlie suggested.

'A cousin.'

'A cousin!' Charlie repeated what she had said in an ironic tone of voice.

'Listen,' said Laura, 'you can believe what you like . . .'

'Thank you. Then I will.'

'If people want to gossip, they can . . .'

'They do.'

'Who?'

'Everyone.'

'What do they say?'

'That you and the Czech are having an affair.'

Again she blushed – a mixed blush of embarrassment and delight. 'I can't help gossip.'

'You needn't encourage it.'

'It would be absurd to kick him out of my house just because of gossip.'

'It would be inconvenient, certainly . . .'

'Oh do shut up.'

He smiled and relented. 'What can I do to help him?'

'Get his novel published.'

'What is it like?'

She hesitated: it was easier to defend Birek than his book. 'It is difficult, I'll admit, but compared to the kind of trivia which gets published every day . . .'

'It's a masterpiece!'

'Not a masterpiece, no, but it has some wonderful passages and as an expression of a contemporary sensibility from behind the Iron Curtain . . .'

Charlie yawned.

'There must be publishers other than Pritchard,' she said.

'Yes. Pritchard was a mistake. He's much too cautious.'

'Then who?'

'Orloff.'

'Why Orloff?'

'Because he's the only publisher in London who will publish a book without reading it. He's a White Russian and a passionate Zionist so he hates the Soviets and will buy anything which shows them in a bad light.'

'If he's a White Russian, why is he a Zionist?'

Charlie shrugged his shoulders. 'Perhaps to make up for what his ancestors did to the Jews.'

'But Josef isn't Jewish.'

'That doesn't matter. So long as what he writes is anti-Communist . . .'

Laura frowned. 'We don't want him to become a pawn in the cold war.'

'We all have to be a piece in some sort of game.'

'Are books never published because people might want to read them?'

'Only thrillers and spy stories. Birck's only asset is his cachet as a dissident and Orloff is the man to cash it in.'

'If you think that's the best way,' said Laura.

'Most first novels,' said Charlie, 'sell less than a thousand copies. Orloff, however, sold twenty thousand of Shamrayev's *Permafrost* and I have yet to meet anyone who got beyond the first page.'

'Lots of people will read Josef's novel from start to finish,' said Laura defiantly.

'I'm sure. What's it called?'

'We haven't settled on a title.'

'He must have given it one in Czech.'

'It doesn't translate very well.'

'What is it?'

She blushed. '*The House of Culture.*'

'You'll have to come up with something better than that.'

'We will.'

'But Orloff's your man. It sounds right up his street.'

'What about an agent?'

'Don't bother with one. He won't pay much for it anyway.'

'Shall I just send it in?'

'No. It might never reach him.' Charlie hesitated. 'Do you know him?'

'I've met him.'

'Then ask him to dinner with a duchess, or if you can't drum up a duchess, some other title will do.'

'Would he come?'

'Of course.'

'And would you?'

'If you like. And perhaps I should bring Zorn. I know that Orloff is longing to poach him from Pritchard.'

Laura, who already made the distinction in her entertaining between 'grand' and 'simple' dinner parties, as well as 'supper in the kitchen' for her intimate friends, went into the usual pre-production routine for the grandest of grand dinners in honour of the Orloffs. She first asked Roly Roper, an old friend of Francis from Eton who if not a duke was at least the heir to a dukedom and had a wife who already behaved in a ducal way. She then asked Heinzi von Strugel, a banker of Austrian origins with an émigré title and a pretty wife. To kill two birds with one stone she also invited Henry Abbot, the junior minister from the Home Office, to both reward him for and remind him of the help he promised over Birek's naturalization.

The novelist Zorn had a wife, but with Charlie and Birek she had two extra men so there were slots for two single women. She took out a list of deserving spinsters, and had just rung Eva Burroughs when the other place was snatched by her friend from the country, Emma Jenkins, who was coming up to London for Wimbledon, got wind of the dinner and asked herself.

Laura's dining-room in the house in Lansdowne Square could seat sixteen in comfort – eighteen at a pinch. She toyed with the idea of asking Madge and Ben, not to add to the glamour but to be dazzled by it, but then she remembered how Ben had got drunk and obnoxious at her party for Birek so she decided it would be safer to leave them out. With her list thus complete it only remained for her to book the butler and the two ladies from Louards and telephone the jolly girl who did the cooking on occasions like this and brought all the food in her Honda van.

With the logistics of her dinner safely in their hands, Laura could concentrate on the social side of things. In deciding where each should sit at her large table, she rose above any feelings that Roly Roper might have about the prerogatives of his rank, and placed Orloff on her right as guest of honour. Since Zorn would be new to her, and Orloff might like him within range, she put him on her left: but she also wanted Orloff to talk to Birek so she put Annabel Roper next to Orloff and Birek next to her. Now the danger arose that Francis would hold court with his old Etonian cronies at the other end of the table and with their private jokes and jargon make everyone else feel ill-at-ease. She therefore mixed them all up as best she could with Francis flanked by Mrs Orloff and Emma next to Theodore Zorn.

Everything was ready well before the night. Her only anxiety as she contemplated her soirée was Birek's sky blue suit. *She* found its ghastliness endearing, and there was something to be said for fostering his image as an impoverished émigré; but she had also to acknowledge that when she had sat with him in the Louards box at Covent Garden the week before, the blue suit was something of an embarrassment. She had noticed several of her friends look askance at his eccentric appearance. Those who knew he was a dissident might have seen it as the battle-dress of a hero, but even a hero, at some point, must surely change from his battle-dress into a smart uniform. After reading so many nineteenth-century novels in which women displayed their lovers at the opera, she had looked forward to that performance of *Don Carlos* more than any other, and the truth she had had to acknowledge as she analysed her disappointment upon her return, was that the evening had been ruined by Birek's sky blue suit.

Yet dressing him in another suit was a delicate operation. Since he had no money of his own to buy one, the most natural thing would be for Francis to send him along to his tailor, and had Birek not been her lover, then Laura might have asked him to do so; but she felt it would be indelicate – a breach of some unwritten code of conduct – to have her husband pay for her lover's clothes, and remembering the Caroline Charles dress that Francis had bought for *his* mistress, she decided in a flurry of feminist defiance that *she* would buy Birek a new suit in time for the Orloff dinner.

Of course Birek had feelings too, and she realized that it might not be easy to persuade him to accept a gift of that kind. He was already so dependent upon her for his board and lodging; he might well feel humiliated if she clothed him as well. She considered this problem for some days. Should she simply guess his size, buy the suit, wrap it up and give it to him as an advance birthday present? Or explain to him that his Czech suit had been all very well for the first few weeks, but now seemed like an affectation?

It would have helped if she had sensed that Birek himself was conscious of the tawdriness of his wardrobe, but in his innocence he seemed quite unaware of his shabby appearance. As the day of the dinner grew closer, Laura grew increasingly desperate, noticing how it embarrassed him when she paid the bill after lunch in a restaurant which the waiter had handed to him. Birek had been working in Kensington Library and Laura had suggested lunch to get away from Gail.

'If Orloff likes my novel,' Birek asked as they walked out into Kensington High Street, 'how soon do you think it will be before there is a contract?'

He was still smarting about the bill: she could tell from the way he clenched his teeth. 'A month or so, I should imagine,' she said in a soothing tone of voice.

'And with a contract would come an advance?'

'Yes.'

She had not thought it necessary to repeat what Charlie had said about Orloff's frugality; but just as they passed a shop window displaying men's clothes, she seized upon what he had said to further her plans about a suit.

'You know,' she said, stopping on the pavement as if a thought had just come to her, 'since we are not going through an agent, we should perhaps think about how best to get a decent sum of money for your novel.'

The shop by which they were standing happened to be a branch of a chain which sold ill-made but elegant Italian suits.

Laura's son Johnny bought his clothes there: shirts and shoes as well as suits.

Birek looked confused. 'You do not think that I should try and find another agent?'

'Charlie thought not,' said Laura. 'But he also said that Orloff was canny. The last thing we want is for him to feel that you are desperate for money.'

'But I am,' he gave a feeble laugh.

She smiled. 'It's certainly high time that you received what you deserve, but I am afraid that here in the West one sometimes has to be devious in getting it.'

'What do you think I should do?'

'Well for one thing,' she said in a businesslike tone of voice, 'you should probably buy a new suit.'

Birek blushed. 'Yes.'

'They're not expensive.' She took his arm. 'Come on. We'll buy one now.'

'I don't think . . .'

'I'll lend you the money.'

'I couldn't accept . . .'

'You can pay me back when you get your advance.'

'I really wouldn't . . .'

'You can pay interest, if you like,' she said with a laugh, leading him to a rack of double-breasted suits.

'Very well,' he said sadly. 'If you really think it is important.'

'I do,' she said, and with great gusto she set about finding him not just a suit but also three shirts, a couple of ties, a pair of black shoes and some cotton socks.

As a result, in her eyes, he looked doubly handsome when introduced to Orloff – not affluent, perhaps, because he wore his new clothes with a certain gaucheness, but not the penniless refugee who would accept anything Orloff had to offer.

It was possible, of course, that the celebrated publisher did not notice what Birek was wearing, or even appreciate, at first, who he was. He was more interested, as had been anticipated, in the Mortons' more aristocratic guests – not so much Roly Roper as Heinzi and Sophie von Strugel. Apparently a von Strugel had fought a duel with an Orloff during the Congress of Vienna and having this in common made the two men instant friends. Too late did Laura realize that she should have put Sophie von Strugel on Orloff's other side, for though she was as English as Annabel Roper, she had responded quite well when Orloff, calling her *Gräfin*, had kissed her hand.

Mrs Orloff was a quiet, inoffensive woman of indeterminate nationality who had been married to her husband for thirty-five years. Her lips were fixed in a placid smile, and her eyes showed no expression. She appeared almost surprised when Francis engaged her in conversation, as if she was a chauffeur whom someone had mistaken for a guest.

Soon after the Orloffs, Charlie arrived with Theodore and Augusta Zorn. Never before had Laura taken such a quick dislike to two people as she did to the Zorns. It cut no ice with her that Zorn's novels sold millions of copies on both sides of the Atlantic; that a whole generation had guffawed over Zorn's scatological wit; that Zorn's words and phrases were now part of the common language of anyone half-literate in the Western world. Instead she saw on his face a concentrated distillation of vanity and paranoia. He strode into her drawing-room with a look which asked: 'What the Hell am I doing here?'; but if Zorn was bad, his wife was worse, because Theodore was at least handsome in a Levantine way. He could also crack a joke and, if those around him were sufficiently sycophantic, could twinkle his eyes and smile.

Augusta, on the other hand, was as heavy and ugly as an orangutan, with fuzzy, unkempt hair, a thick neck, and heavy breasts on a stocky figure hanging loose beneath a knitted dress. She was, Laura, had been told, almost as famous as her husband – not as a novelist but as a champion of women's rights. Coming from a country where money is to be made from immoderate opinions, she had outflanked all the earlier feminists with her vociferous denunciations of the male sex. Her public liaisons with militant blacks and lesbians did not bother Zorn, who was busy 'balling' his female admirers. There were no young Zorns – feminists rarely have children – but the Zorns' marriage survived as a good double act for the television breakfast shows.

When Laura realized quite what Charlie had brought into her

house she glanced at him with an astonished look, but Charlie did not catch it: he was talking affably to the junior minister. She then looked towards Francis, her expression now potentially apologetic, but he was going around with a bottle of champagne filling the empty glasses.

It was now that Laura realized that her party might be a disaster. It was not just that the Zorns would not be impressed by Roly Roper, the heir to an English dukedom: it was that they might actually dismiss the dear old buffer as a reactionary and a snob. Nor could she be sure, as she would be with European guests, that the Zorns would be tamed by Francis's Burgundy or the jolly girl's *boeuf en croûte*. Americans, after all, drank milk with their supper which was often just a peanut butter sandwich. When Emma bounced in, red in the face from Wimbledon, Laura's unease turned to despair. Rather than mix her guests, she now wished she had herded the two different species into their own corrals. She made for the door to change the cards but as she did so the butler entered and announced that dinner was served.

The die was cast: there was nothing she could do but hope to hold things together at her end of the table. At first all went well. Zorn had met his match in Emma, who had never heard of him and said so. This so staggered the illustrious American that he listened in silence to her account of the day's play on the centre court of Wimbledon. Meanwhile Orloff turned politely to Laura and asked her about her work at the Comenius Foundation.

This enabled her to mention Birek's novel – a little sooner, perhaps, than she had intended.

'And who is to publish it?' asked Orloff.

'That hasn't been decided.'

With an involuntary reflex of professional excitement, Orloff leaned closer to his hostess. 'You know, I would be most interested if you thought Orloffs the right house for a work of this kind.'

'I would have to ask Josef,' said Laura, glancing down the table towards her protégé. 'It is his book, after all. I am only the translator.'

'Of course, of course,' said Orloff. 'And is the translation completed?'

'More or less. But if a publisher wanted another translator . . .'

'No, no,' said Orloff, already calculating his costs. 'Quite the contrary. If the novel is already translated, it makes it much easier for those of us who do not read Czech to form an opinion.'

'I am prejudiced, of course,' said Laura in a low and conspiratorial tone of voice, 'but it seems to me to be a quite exceptional novel.'

'Should I talk to him this evening?' asked Orloff.

'Why not?'

'Is there an agent involved?'

'No. Coming straight from Prague, Josef is quite ignorant about how things are done in this country. So am I, for that matter.' She gave Orloff her best disingenuous smile. 'I am sure he would trust you to pay what his novel was worth.'

'Of course, of course,' said Orloff, his eyes alight with excitement at the chance to secure a successful novel without paying an exorbitant advance.

Once Zorn had got over the shock of sitting next to a woman who had never read any of his novels, he settled down into a very disagreeable mood, and as soon as he could he talked over Emma to Charlie, who was sitting on her other side. 'You haven't told me about Israel,' he said to Charlie. 'How did you survive among all those Jews?'

'It wasn't easy,' Charlie replied.

'I bet it wasn't,' said Emma.

This brief exchange happened at a moment when the butler at one side of the table, and one of the waitresses on the other, cut into the company with dishes of sliced *boeuf en croûte*, thereby isolating the six guests around Laura, and making them all witness what was said. All but Emma, of course, knew that Zorn was not only a very celebrated American novelist, but also a very celebrated Jewish American novelist who was thereby licensed to crack doubtful jokes about his fellow Jews. Emma, however, like so many English county girls, had on the one hand imbibed mild anti–Semitism with her mother's milk while on the other she found it difficult to know who was a Jew and who was not. Thus when Zorn made a remark of a kind she had heard a dozen times from her husband's City friends, she had taken it – and Charlie's answer – at face value.

Zorn realized at once that she had meant what she said. 'Have you been there?' he asked.

'To Israel? No.'

'Too many Jews.'

'Yes. And too hot. And too dangerous. Tommy Joliffe went there on a scuba-diving holiday in the Red Sea, and he said they make you wait for hours at the airport.'

'How tedious,' said Zorn in a phoney British upper-class accent.

'A bloody bore,' said Emma.

'Better, perhaps, than being blown up in the plane,' said Charlie.

'Sure,' said Emma. 'But who wants to get involved in other people's quarrels?'

'Other people's quarrels!' Zorn exploded, bringing his fist down on the table. 'Is that a way to describe the oppression of a people over two millennia?'

'I am sure,' said Laura in as calm a tone of voice as she could manage, 'that Emma did not mean to disparage the suffering of the Jews.'

'Of course I didn't,' said Emma who belatedly had realized that she had put her foot in something somewhere along the line.

Zorn, however, was not so easily placated. 'Don't sell yourself short!' he said to Emma. 'Be honest. You think the Jews are a bloody nuisance . . .' (this too was spoken in his British accent). 'Like the Egyptians, you tolerate them as long as they make your bricks, preferably without using too much straw, then drive them out into the desert.'

'I didn't drive anyone anywhere,' said Emma, tucking into her food.

'Some chose to go to Palestine,' said Orloff quietly. 'It was a return to the promised land.'

'Come on,' said Zorn. 'Who would have even thought of going to live in swamps and deserts in Palestine if they hadn't felt threatened in Christian Europe?'

'With good reason,' said Charlie.

'But they went to Palestine,' Orloff insisted, 'because it was the Promised Land.'

'Promised by whom to whom?' asked Zorn.

'By God to Abraham.'

171

'Come on,' said Zorn disparagingly. 'Would you seriously put that forward in a court of law?'

Birek, who had been listening to the conversation with some interest, now leaned across the table and asked Zorn: 'So what is the justification for the state of Israel if it is not the promise of God to Abraham?'

'The same as it is for anyone else. The Jews are a people. They deserve a state.'

'But not all peoples have a state,' said Birek, 'and not all states are based upon a single people.'

'You Czechs have a state.'

'But not the Kurds or Ruthenians.'

'You can't compare the Jews to the Kurds or the Ruthenians.'

'Perhaps not. But who decides if a people should have a state?'

'If you're a Czech,' sneered Zorn, 'the President of the United States.'

'And if you're an Israeli, the Congress?' asked Birek.

'If you're an Israeli,' growled Zorn, 'you decide for yourself with a gun. But I wouldn't expect a Czech to understand about fighting for one's country.'

Birek blushed and his jaw wobbled as he clenched his teeth. 'Isn't that the philosophy of fascism – that might makes right?'

'Go on! Abuse me! We Jews are used to abuse! You Christians have been at it for hundreds of years!'

Now Birek's blush turned into a scowl. 'No one can deny,' he said, 'that the Christians have misused the Jews, but it was the Jews, I think, who first misused the Christians.'

'Like who?'

'Like Christ himself, and then St Stephen . . .'

'So we started it all! So we are to blame for Auschwitz and Buchenwald!'

'You are not to blame, but nor are the Christians.'

'So who built the camps?'

'The Nazis.'

'Who were Christians.'

'Who were pagans.'

'And were the Popes pagans who pushed the Jews into ghettos in Rome and made them wear the Star of David as a badge of shame? And were the Spaniards pagans who burned the Jews who would not apostasize?'

'No, they were Christians – in name, at any rate.'

'Not just in name. In fact!'

'Not in fact,' snapped Birek, 'since Jesus commanded us to love our enemies and turn the other cheek.'

'So who told them to burn Jews?'

'The Jews told them to burn Jews,' said Birek. 'The whole concept of anathema, of intolerance, of slaughtering one's enemies, comes not from Jesus but from the prophets of Israel!'

'I can't believe it. Am I here? Am I hearing this?' Zorn turned around to appeal to his audience. 'I am being told that the Jews themselves are responsible for Auschwitz! That they built the gas ovens! Pinch me, someone, quick, because if this is a dream, I want to wake up.'

There was a horrible silence – the kind of silence that every hostess dreads, and which proved to Laura, as if she had ever doubted it, that there was much wisdom in the old adage that one should never talk at table about money, politics or religion.

'It would be better,' said Orloff, as if he was reading her thoughts, 'if we talked about something else.'

Laura turned to him gratefully but noticed, to her dismay, that he had gone quite pale in the face.

What did they talk about next? She could not later remember. She only noticed a cool formality in Orloff's tone of voice. Zorn, after his outburst, sat in injured silence while Charlie, it seemed, dared not talk to Emma for fear of being compromised by her anti-Semitic views. Nor was Augusta Zorn to be outdone by her husband. When dinner came to an end, and Laura led the ladies up to the drawing-room, Francis encouraged the men to remain behind for a while to finish their brandy and cigars. Ms Zorn stayed too to harangue them on the iniquitous oppression of women by the sexist traditions of the British upper classes.

This quickly drove the men out of the dining-room. Some of the old Etonians lingered on the stairs; the others joined the women in the drawing-room. Laura still hoped that something could be salvaged from the catastrophic evening. She took Henry Abbot, the junior minister, to the sofa by the window and quickly brought their conversation to the question of Birek's right of abode in the United Kingdom.

'I'm doing what I can,' said Abbot, in the confidential tone of voice that politicians like to adopt to show that they are very much in the centre of things.

'Your officials, apparently, have something against him.'

'I can deal with the officials all right, but we've run into some trouble from the Foreign Office, which thinks that Birek's defection is a damned nuisance.'

'Why should they think that?'

'Apparently his father is one of the more liberal figures among the old guard, and until his son scarpered was thought to be Gorbachev's choice to succeed Husak.'

'But surely,' said Laura in the kind of solemn voice she thought appropriate for discussing affairs of state of this kind, 'surely that should have nothing to do with Josef's right to remain in England.'

'In theory, nothing at all, but in practice it creates a complication.'

'Isn't the damage done so far as the father is concerned?'

'The damage is done, but there are some at the F.O. who think that we should not be seen to have done it.'

'But we had nothing to do with his defection.'

'I know.'

'And they must know.'

'Of course. But the enemies of Birek's father can still use it against him.'

'And could use it against him if Josef had remained in Vienna.'

'Precisely. And that is our case. And we shall win it.'

Having done what she could with the junior minister, Laura now reapplied her mind to the question of Orloff. She looked around the room, hoping to see the publisher and her protégé together, but she saw that Orloff was talking to Zorn and Birek to Annabel Roper. She therefore rose from the sofa on which she had been sitting with Henry Abbot and went to prise the second couple apart. 'Do you mind?' she said to Annabel while taking hold of Birek by the arm, 'I think that Josef ought to have another word with Mr Orloff.'

They crossed the room to Orloff whose wife was now at his side.

'I know you wanted to talk to Josef,' said Laura.

'Oh yes,' said Orloff as if he had forgotten him.

Laura let go of Birek's arm and turned to lead Mrs Orloff away, but before she could do so Orloff took hold of her hand and said: 'We had such a lovely time. It was most kind of you to have asked us.'

'Must you go so soon?'

'I am afraid we must.'

'It really has been a most lively evening,' said Mrs Orloff. 'Isn't Zorn amazing?'

'Yes,' said Laura. 'He is amazing.'

'Did you sign him up?' Mrs Orloff asked her husband as they turned towards the door.

'I think he's interested,' said Orloff as he turned his back on Laura.

Laura stepped forward to follow him but Birek held her back. 'Please don't,' he said.

'We can send him the book anyway.'

Birek shook his head. 'He won't publish it.'

Laura did not contradict him.

'Once again,' said Birek sadly, 'I said the wrong thing.'

'If Charlie hadn't brought those loathsome Americans . . .'

'No,' said Birek. 'It was my fault. I should have learned by now to watch what I say.'

FIFTEEN

Charlie left with the Zorns soon after the Orloffs. With Birek now the only stranger among a group of old friends, the atmosphere immediately lightened. Roly, Heinzi and Harry Abbot, their glasses filled, chatted away as if they were back at school; while Emma, who had felt muzzled after her gaffe at dinner, gossiped with Annabel, Eva and Sophie von Strugel. Laura sat on the sofa with Birek and Harriet Abbot while Francis moved from group to group, filling his guests' empty glasses.

Since this was now the role he played at his own dinner parties – particularly later in the evening when the staff from Louards had been paid off and sent home – no one noticed that he took no part in their conversation. Certainly those who remained were all his friends, but the evening had so clearly been arranged by Laura for her own purposes that even those old school friends of Francis seemed to have moved into orbit around her.

They were also constrained by the rumours they had heard about Laura's affair with Birek. Such things were common enough in their circle – both Roly and Heinzi had had notorious affairs – but somehow a deceived wife cuts a more dignified role than a husband with horns, particularly where the lover eats at his table and sleeps under his roof. There were more conventions to be respected, so none of these old friends of Francis would ever ask him if he knew that his wife had gone astray: instead they behaved as if they had heard that he had incurable cancer. They all smiled and joked as he filled their glasses but other emotions were hidden behind the *bonhomie*. Heinzi was actually angry to see Francis shuffling around serving drinks at a party given by his wife to further her lover's career. The others were less angry than curious. Did he know? How could he not know? And did he know they knew? None of them looked him in the eye in case they gave the game away. Emma, who was known to be Laura's confidante, was questioned in whispers by Sophie von Strugel but was not able to say. 'But he *must* know,' said Sophie, 'since everyone else does.'

'But surely, if he did,' said Annabel Roper, 'he wouldn't have him living in the house.'

'The husband is always the last to know,' said Emma – and that old adage closed their conversation which in any case was risky since the subjects of their conjecture were all in the room.

Did he know? The omniscient author should certainly be in a better position than Emma Jenkins to tell his readers yes or no; but he himself can be faced with an ambivalent state of mind. Adultery, like death, is often something we would rather not face. If we recall the dejection Francis had felt after the sermon, that Sunday morning, on Third World debt – when Laura had telephoned Birek to see that all was well, and had then talked about taking a larger villa in Greece for their summer holiday – we might say that Francis had in a sense been the first to know – that he had known, indeed, before Laura and Birek themselves: but in another sense, not having found them *in flagrante delicto*, he did not know even now. He may have had his suspicions, and had he acted upon them he might have arrived at the facts; but Francis, after a lifetime in banking, had learned to distinguish between knowledge which was useful and knowledge which was superfluous.

If he was to establish that Laura was sleeping with Birek, he would be obliged to choose between doing something and doing nothing about it. If something, what would it be? They could separate, perhaps divorce, but from that, he knew, he would gain little and lose almost everything that he liked in life – not just his wife but also his home and everything that the word implied – the house in London, which would have to be sold to divide their assets; the house in the country which was Laura's; and above all his children.

He had seen the effect of divorce on the families of his friends. Whatever rights a father was given to see his children at weekends or during the school holidays, the love which comes from daily contact was inevitably replaced by a polite and artificial affection. He had seen divorced husbands in Kensington Gardens taking their daughters like Lucy for their weekly walk – love battling with boredom as they filled in the hours the court allowed. He had also remarked upon the adolescent children of his friends who from the moment of their parents' separation had changed from confident young men and women, eager for life and determined to flourish, into baffled and cringing adolescents – distracted from their studies by their anxiety about their home, condemned by their parents' example to expect nothing from life but rancour and sorrow.

What home would they have if divorce led to the sale of the house on Lansdowne Square? Francis had done the calculations a number of times. He would move to a mansion flat and Laura to a smaller house south of the river. That in itself was no catastrophe – people could be happy in the humblest homes – but who would his children see at the head of the table instead of their father? A sallow Czech – for a time, at any rate. And who would his loneliness draw to his mansion flat? Some desperate spinster like Eva Burroughs.

For the sake of his children alone, Francis was inclined to look the other way – to pretend to himself for as long as he could that however things seemed, Laura had stopped short of sleeping with Birek. Francis had little imagination, and on the many occasions when he knew that his wife and the young Czech were alone together, he was not tormented by images of their bodies entwined. He did sometimes notice the flushed and breathless condition in which Laura sometimes returned from a walk on the Downs, but he put that down to the effects of the fresh air: and the absent-minded half-formed smile which was now so often on her lips when he found her in the bath on his return – that too could be ascribed to the relaxing effect of the hot water.

Not all the evidence, however, was open to such an innocent interpretation. He noticed, for example, that when Laura looked up when he entered the room, she would look down again with her expression unchanged, while when it was Birek who entered her features would move into a delightful smile. This observation did provoke a tremor of jealousy, but the very weakness of the tremor made him still more inclined to ignore what that smile implied. Jealousy, after all, though abused these days as a primitive emotion, is only the obverse of love. Where jealousy is feeble, so too is the affection which inspires it. Thus Francis was obliged to acknowledge, by the detached way in which he considered the possibility of his Laura's infidelity, and by the greater anxiety he felt about losing his children than about losing his wife, that perhaps he did not love her as much as he had always assumed.

This made him ashamed. He remembered how much they had loved one another in the early years of their marriage; and how they had looked upon their life together – the buying of houses, the birth of their children – as a joint enterprise with the promise of some magnificent but unspecified fulfilment. But where had it led beyond the accumulation of money and a clutter of possessions? He thought back to when Johnny had been a baby – when for a year or more neither had had a good night's sleep; when the weekends had not been spent at Risley but in painting and papering their little house in Chelsea – and realized that their happiness had been in the domestic trivialities of those early years.

Had Birek been a professional seducer like Charlie Eldon, or perhaps one of those friends in the City with whom Francis had always felt a certain rivalry, then outrage might have been one of his emotions; but Birek was so timid and passive – so gauche, so young and so confused by his compromising position – that Francis could hardly feel outrage – indeed he felt more inclined to pity him as a Joseph who had succumbed to a Potiphar's wife.

Thus when the guests finally left that evening, Francis did not mind that Laura and Birek lingered for a moment in the drawing-room after he had gone up to bed. What could they do there, after all? Hold hands? Kiss? They could hardly make love on the drawing-room floor!

That evening, as it happened, Laura came up some five minutes after Francis – a frown on her face and the mascara running from her eyes. He glanced at her over his book as she wiped the tinctures from her face: she looked sober, anxious and tired. At one time they might have chattered about their party – judging whether or not it had been a success – but Francis at that moment cared more about the social life of Barchester than about that of Holland Park, and Laura too seemed preoccupied with questions that had nothing to do with him.

They slept, and the next morning Francis went to work as usual at Louards Bank. Here, one might have thought, he would find consolation for the disappointments of his married life. He was a man, after all, who had seen his ambitions fulfilled, for though old Lord Louard was chairman, Francis was managing director of the bank. He had the finest office, after Lord Louard's, and could ask whom he liked to lunch in the director's dining-room. The other employees all deferred to him, as employees do to the managing director, and his fellow directors invariably agreed with whatever he put to the board. He was liked and trusted; he was still young; and his salary was large and secure.

Yet changes were taking place in the City of London and Louards had been obliged to change too. Financial markets abroad had begun to poach the business that had hitherto come to London. Alert and unscrupulous foreigners in Tokyo and New York had begun to lure away clients who had been served by banks like Louards since the days of the British Empire. The English gentleman as banker and broker had been forced by this competition to acknowledge that tradition alone would not sustain him; that if his business was to flourish in the future, he would have to abandon some of his gentlemanly ways and play the game according to a new set of rules.

The public manifestation of this awakening to a new realism in the City was the deregulation of the Stock Exchange. Banks like Louards had had to decide whether to grow or shrink – whether to buy or sell or merge to form a competitive conglomerate which offered financial services of every kind. Louards decided to expand. Partly thanks to Francis it had grown in the course of the late 1970s and early 1980s to be a leading merchant bank: it seemed inconceivable that it should step aside. It therefore bought the stockbroking partnership of Gates, Harmsworth and Scott, and then merged with the New York firm of security brokers, Grossman, Mittelschmidt and Klein.

The equity of this conglomerate was owned equally by Louards and their American partners, GMK, and it was understood by the board of the holding company, upon which Francis naturally had a seat, that Louards should be allowed to continue as before without any interference from GMK. GMK, however, sent its men to London to help prepare for the 'Big Bang'. Two of them – Katz and Greenbaum – had seats on the Louards board.

The first impact of this infusion of alien blood was a change in working practices. Katz, who as 'director of marketing planning' was to mastermind the company's preparation for deregulation, called meetings for eight in the morning. He himself arrived at seven, after half-an-hour's jogging on Wimbledon Common, and ate a breakfast at his desk of yoghurt, bran and molasses.

Francis, who when he had first started working at Louards had drifted in at half-past nine or ten in the morning, wrote a memo to the effect that no meetings were to be held before nine. This led to a flurry of telexes between London and New York which ended in compromise with meetings at half-past eight. Francis could as well have saved his reputation and capitulated at once by agreeing to the meetings at eight, because a competitive spirit entered into his English colleagues and suddenly they too were arriving at seven to study the opening prices in Tokyo; and it became incumbent upon him as managing director not just to follow their example but to set it by being in the office when they arrived.

A leisurely lunch fell victim to the same fanaticism. There had been a time when two or three times a week Francis would leave Louards at a quarter to one, take a taxi to White's or the Garrick, and there spend an hour and a half or even two hours over lunch with someone who had nothing to do with banking – getting back to the City perhaps as late as half-past three.

Now, with his partners in New York getting to their offices at seven, which was midday in London, and with the New York markets opening two hours later, Francis only had time for a ham sandwich and a cup of coffee at his desk. Even the lunches at Louards in the directors' dining-room – prepared by the jolly girl and served by the butler and the two middle-aged women – which had once enabled Francis and his friends to drink some exceptional wine at the bank's expense – even these were now subject to petty interruptions from the offices of everyone at table. Katz and Greenbaum rarely came, and when they did they sat glowering with moral distaste like Puritan pastors at a Mardi Gras.

There was no question but that these changes had to come; nor could Louards have effected them without the capital and experience of Grossman, Mittelschmidt and Klein. It was also undoubtedly true that if the venture succeeded – if Louards-GMK established itself after the Big Bang as one of the leading financial conglomerates in the City of London – then Francis, with his share of the equity, would emerge a very rich man. This prospect of wealth should have compensated for the changes: money, after all, was what had brought him into banking in the first place; but together with some of his older colleagues, Francis often felt he would exchange all the value added to his holding of Louards shares for a return to a more agreeable way of life.

There was also a possibility, which as the day of deregulation approached became less and less remote, that Louards-GMK would not flourish but would rather go under, beaten by the pitiless competition of larger and leaner corporations. The cost of adapting to the new conditions had been daunting, even for bankers who were used to dealing in large sums of money. It had already been agreed that the bank should move to a modern, air-conditioned building near the Thames – but since Francis knew little about the technical needs of the new market-making division, he was consulted on little more, once the decision had been made, than the décor of his office and the directors' dining-room. It was Katz who masterminded the transfer, and put through the purchasing orders for computer systems costing many millions of pounds. Francis and the old guard from Louards became mere spectators of this gigantic investment which might either make them rich or bankrupt.

It is one thing to take risks oneself; it is another to see others take them on one's behalf. Francis had backed expansion, and it was now too late to change his mind, but because he had no experience of market-making – because hitherto any purchase of stock on behalf of a client had been done through a jobber and broker – the thought that Louards was to trade in its own right quite terrified him. So did the vulgar, close-cropped young men whom Katz recruited to staff the market-making division. Gone were the days when a chat with an old friend from Eton or Oxford could secure the account of a life insurance company or a pension fund. Now it was the keenness of one's commission, and the sharpness of these barrow-boys in their pin-striped trousers and shirt-sleeves.

Because he did not control it, Francis did not believe in it. He half-hoped, indeed, that the whole thing would fail just to humble the coldly bumptious Katz, who treated his fellow directors with

182

increasing contempt. Yet it was just at this time that it became apparent that if Louards was now to go bankrupt it would not be because of Katz's extravagance on computers, or the salaries he was paying to the young men whom he tethered to their telephones and VDUs, but because of loans Francis himself had made in his early years in the bank.

These, as we know, had been the ingenious solution of many Western bankers to the problem posed by the surplus revenues of the oil-producing states. The sheikhs and the emirs had deposited their money with Louards and Louards had lent it, at a rather higher rate of interest, to the governments and municipalities of impoverished countries in the Third World. When the time had come for the loans to be repaid, and it had become apparent that the debtors had no money, the debts had simply been rescheduled: new larger loans had been made to repay the old ones, and the interest had rolled in as before.

This rescheduling of debts might have gone on for ever, since the Arabs did not need their money, if it had not now reached a point where many of the debtors – especially countries like Mexico and Brazil – could not afford to pay the interest, let alone repay the loan; or more accurately, would not pay the interest, because it took too large a slice of their foreign reserves. Indeed encouraged by their bishops and liberation theologians, one or two even declared that not just the interest but the debts themselves were a form of oppression and would not be repaid.

Thus just at the moment when Louards-GMK was committed to the awesome investment required by the deregulation of the London Stock Exchange, a large proportion of its notional assets suddenly disappeared. It was all announced, moreover, in a most public way with press conferences in Lima and Mexico City. Nothing was hidden from the markets and the markets reacted as markets do. The shares of Louards-GMK dropped forty-eight points in a day.

To Francis this did not matter in the short term: he could hold on to what he had and hope that in time the bank's profits would lead the shares to rise again. But his colleagues in New York reacted to these developments with a menacing rage. When the two firms had merged Louards had been valued on the basis that its Third

World debts were good. The Americans now spoke as if they had been swindled out of several hundred million dollars, and they blamed not the South American politicians or the liberation theologians but a scapegoat closer to home – Francis Morton.

Nor was it only the Americans who were angry. Lord Louard, it was said, had borrowed heavily on the security of his own shares and now avoided looking Francis in the eye. Some of his fellow directors on the London board had done the same – one to buy a stud farm in Sussex, another to invest in a marina on the coast of Asia Minor. They were now in the uncomfortable position of having liabilities in excess of assets, with only their salaries to protect them should things go wrong.

And even these were not secure. There was some talk in the financial press that the institutions were angry at the loss they had suffered from their Louards shares, and that Louards-GMK was therefore vulnerable to a bid by a stronger competitor before the Big Bang had even happened. It was only a trenchant article in the *Financial Times* which stopped this speculation. Louards' exposure to Third World debt, it pointed out, was less than many other banks. As first to write off these debts it was in fact entering the brave new world of deregulated markets without the encumbrance of uncertain assets. Francis Morton, far from being a fuddy-duddy from the previous era, was one of the shrewdest bankers on either side of the Atlantic, and the shares in Louards-GMK were therefore a bargain.

Since this piece appeared under the by-line of the respected financial journalist Charles Eldon the markets half believed what he said. The shares rose around thirty points and the sharpened knives in the board-room at Louards were returned to their scabbards for the time being. Even the angry *mafiosi* at Grossman, Mittelschmidt and Klein knew it would be disastrous to try and topple Francis on the eve of the Big Bang.

This gave time for Francis to consolidate his position, and if by nature he had been an office politician he would have found many ways in which to outmanoeuvre Katz and Greenbaum and convince Lord Louard that he could not do without him. But Francis was suddenly tired – not just because he had to get up so much earlier than before, but because he had done what he was doing for so long. If he had still enjoyed it, that would have been one thing; if he had been working for the good of others, that would be another. But all he had gained from his fifteen years' hard labour was the opprobrium of vicars and the ingratitude of his colleagues.

There was his family, of course, and at one time he would have said that he worked for them: but now, with Laura besotted with her Czech, Johnny and Belinda away at school, and when at home only passing by to throw their clothes into the laundry basket and get him to write a cheque, there remained only little Lucy to console him for the worry and drudgery of his working life.

And how fond would she remain if he was dismissed from Louards, or if Louards itself went under, and he could no longer afford her pretty clothes, private schools or holidays abroad? All he had came from Louards in the form of his salary, his shares and the bonuses paid at the end of each year. His pension fund was managed by Louards; so too was Laura's money; and while there was no necessary connection between the fortunes of the bank and the value of her portfolio, they could not sustain even a shadow of their present way of life on the income from her investments alone.

He kept his pessimism to himself. Again there had been a time when he had shared his worries with his wife, but now, if he even hinted that there might be hard times ahead, he saw a frown of petulant irritation appear on her brow and heard her say 'Oh surely not' or 'You always were a worrier' before changing the subject to some more pressing issue such as Johnny's chances of getting into Oxford or finding a publisher for Birek's book.

This too, on occasions, made Francis almost hope for some kind of financial disaster which would demonstrate to Laura what he had done for her over so many years. Certainly she had brought money to their marriage, but it was only a fraction of what they had jointly spent. She had never had to work; she had never had to worry; and he had never questioned her plundering of their joint account. He felt sure that he could manage better than she could if money ever got tight because he already had a thrifty instinct, buying wine in bulk or at auction, searching for bargains on the Portobello Road, and stocking up at the start of each year when so much was offered at a discount during the January sales.

SIXTEEN

Birek had yet to meet the Mortons' older children. Boarding schools of the kind they attended are there not just to provide a good education. They also enable parents to delegate all the vexatious problems which accompany adolescence to the curious men and women who teach in institutions of this kind. Fathers are then free to pursue their careers without the irritating distraction of raising their sons, and mothers to develop interests of their own away from the prying eyes of their daughters.

The only snag, of course, is that three times a year there come the school holidays – always sooner than expected and considerably longer than one would wish. For Laura Morton, that year, the summer holidays seemed particularly precipitate and exceptionally inconvenient. They had been worrying her for some time – ostensibly for the quite practical reason that Birek was sleeping in Johnny's room. The obvious solution to that problem was to move the household to Risley as soon as the holidays began. Birek could stay in Lansdowne Square and Laura could pop up to London every other day or so to discuss with him the last touches to her translation of his novel.

Unluckily there was not just an inconvenient week between the end of Johnny's term and the end of Lucy's, but also Johnny had made it quite clear, when speaking from Eton on the telephone, that he wanted to spend some time in London. He did not say exactly why, or what he wanted to do, but he had reached an age when he decided his movements for himself, and Laura – though she would not admit it – was rather more frightened of her son than she was of her husband. She had not dared tell him that Birek was using his room; indeed she had not dared tell him that Birek was staying at all; and although she knew that he was pleased that his mother should be associated with someone whose name was in the newspapers (she had sent him the piece in the *Telegraph*), she was not at all sure as to how he would react to giving up his room – even to a winner of the Nobel Prize.

Yet it would be absurd, or so she told herself, to move Josef out of Johnny's room simply for the week when Johnny would be in London. She therefore decided to move Lucy in with Belinda and put Johnny in Lucy's room. She suggested this plan to Lucy a day or two before Belinda was due back from North Foreland Lodge, presenting it as an extraordinary privilege, and then as a great adventure, but both ploys failed. Lucy refused point-blank to move from her room. She screamed when Laura insisted; stamped her foot; wailed at Gail; complained to Francis and even, to Laura's great embarrassment, ambushed Birek as he crept upstairs, saying that *he* should share with Belinda and let Johnny have his own room.

Birek, of course, was as embarrassed as Laura and told her at once that he would move out of the house; but Laura explained how absurd and expensive it would be to decamp to a hotel, just for a week; and that evening, after some hard bargaining, a deal was struck involving a camp-bed in the nursery on the one hand and a My Little Pony Grooming Parlour on the other.

Laura did not imagine that this solved the problem altogether, but as so often when a crisis approaches we cross our fingers and hope for the best. She got Fatima to clean out Lucy's room; she took down her Beatrix Potter calendar and hung up one of Francis's English water-colours instead; but when she looked at the My Little Pony stickers on the chest-of-drawers, and saw the narrow little bed with its pink duvet matching the pink valance and the pink curtains, she knew only too well what Johnny's reaction would be.

You reap as you sow, she thought to herself as she anticipated the anger of her eldest son. She was glad that he was not a neurotic but wished that he was perhaps a little less confident that he would always get his own way. It had been a mistake, perhaps, to provide him so comprehensively with the best of everything; but she could remember so well how pleased they both were that their first-born child had been a boy – Laura, perhaps, because she had always wanted to be a boy; Francis because he had old-fashioned notions about continuing the family name.

Yet with the joy had come the anxieties which all parents feel as they contemplate the responsibilities which parenthood involves. They had worried particularly about his education – for though they were not yet living in the high ground of Holland Park, but were still near the river in Chelsea, they already knew that while it only took money to buy a finer house, the best education took something more. Sometimes, when she was pregnant, Laura and Francis would both have nightmares that they had forgotten to enter the baby for a private school.

Such anxieties were not absurd. An ascendant class must be exclusive or lose its mystique and allure. Since the private schools in England are the portals through which the ascendant class is entered, they must be as narrow as the gates of Heaven to serve their purpose. The great colleges of secondary education like Eton or Winchester keep people out not just by demanding early registration or charging high fees, but also by setting high academic standards which in turn ensure good results which enhance the school's reputation. To reach the standard required to enter such a school, a child must therefore attend an equally good school beforehand – a school like the Manners Academy in Holland Park where every morning little boys and girls in pretty blue uniforms and velvet-collared coats clambered out of their fathers' company cars – Mercedes, BMWs and Volvo Estates with their mothers at the wheel.

To get into the Manners Academy, however, was no easier than getting into Eton. A year before Johnny was born, Laura had gone with her friend Mary Richardson to enter her daughter who was just two months old. The headmistress's secretary had laughed in their face: the list for that age-group was already five times over-subscribed.

'But when should I have entered her?' Mary had asked.

'At conception, Mrs Richardson, at conception!'

Laura had learned from her friend's mistake, and no sooner had she and Francis decided to have a child than she had crouched, as it were, at the starting line, ready to sprint to the school. Only a week after her period was overdue she went to the doctor and when, two days later, he confirmed that she was pregnant, she went straight from the surgery to the Manners Academy. The secretary could hardly refuse to enrol the foetus, but she did so with bad grace as if it gave her more pleasure to turn pupils down. Laura had returned triumphant but also uneasy: she was terrified, in those days, that her friend Madge might discover to what lengths she had gone to ensure a private education for her unborn child; but greater than her fear of Madge was her dread that the child once born might fall back into the educational abyss with the unwashed mass of the polyglot poor.

Was this snobbery and prejudice as Madge would have supposed? Madge, after all, had sent her son Zeno to a state school in Islington; and once, at dinner with Madge and Ben, Francis and Laura had met some luckless Americans who, posted to London before they knew what was what, had enrolled their little Randy in their local neighbourhood school where he had befriended the only other middle-class child, Zeno.

If the only foreigners to send their children to the London state schools had been Americans, that would have been one thing: but as Laura knew only too well from the long line of dailies who had come to clean her house on Lansdowne Square, there were also the Irish, Pakistanis, Indians and West Indians, who had come to find work in the dank capital of the empire to which they no longer belonged; and then the Lithuanians, Estonians, Poles and Czechs who had come to avoid Hitler and had stayed to avoid Stalin; and finally the Spaniards, Portuguese and Filipinos who worked so well for £3 an hour.

All of these immigrants had children and their children went to the state schools along with the sons and daughters of the fossilized remains of the English working classes, and even one or two other sub-categories of sub-cultures such as the *Guardian*-reading would-be Tribunes of the People like Ben who lived in Islington and worked in television; or the blouson-wearing lumpen-intelligentsia who lived around Notting Hill Gate and gave it its Bohemian reputation. Even celebrated left-wing playwrights had been known to send their children to muck in with the immigrants at the local schools until they had made enough money from their revolutionary writing to pay the fees at a private institution.

Some of these people, Laura supposed, would consider her snobbish and prejudiced to refuse even to consider sending her children to state schools; but Laura was confident in her own conscience that she had made her decision for honourable reasons. She had done her own research – always reading what was written in the *Times* or the *Telegraph* about the manic excesses of the ILEA. She had also, later, had her impressions confirmed by her own experience – going with Madge one afternoon to fetch Zeno from his primary school. Nothing she had seen there had made her feel that she had been wrong. A warm damp aroma of unwashed anoraks had hit her as she had walked through the double doors of the overheated school, and a crowd of multi-coloured, multi-ethnic children had milled around her like the crèche at the Tower of Babel.

The smell had grown stronger as she had walked down the corridors – of the unwashed bodies beneath the unwashed anoraks, of chilis and spices oozing out of the perspiring little bodies in the hot-house classrooms. The walls were decorated with toilet-roll collages and the notice-boards studded with fierce commands about racial equality and women's rights. Nothing, thought Laura, would ever have induced her to send a child of hers to a place like that. She did not, of course, share her thoughts with Madge although even Madge had looked unhappy.

What a contrast was the Manners Academy where first Johnny and then Belinda and finally Lucy had started their climb up the educational ladder. Here the children gave off the aroma of their mothers' scent and their fathers' cigars. The teachers, who were gentle and well-spoken, taught reading, writing and arithmetic rather than racial equality and women's rights. Yes, thought Laura, as she prepared Lucy's bedroom for Johnny to sleep in, she had done much for her children: they had no right to complain. She had suffered pain to bear them and, in Lucy's case, had had a needle stuck in her stomach for an amniocentesis test, that first examination a child must pass to enter life at all. And now the little wretch would only rent her room for a My Little Pony Grooming Parlour! And Johnny. Thirty-six hours of labour, and then all the worry and indecision about whether or not to have him circumcised.

She had never known Francis so worried as in those first days of his son's life. First he had had to rush down to Eton to put his name down on the closed list; then he had to decide with Laura what name they were to give him, and register him in good time; and finally the question of his circumcision. When Francis was born it had been the fashion to cut off the foreskin of new-born boys, and he had presumed that what had been done to him would be done to his son; but then he was told by the doctors at the hospital that it was nowadays regarded as an optional operation.

Laura's gynaecologist declined to come down on one side or the other. In America, he said, most boys were circumcised: in Scandinavia almost none at all. It was certainly not done on the National Health but in private clinics (and Laura was in a private clinic) it was more common because so many of the patients were either Muslims or Jews.

Upon Laura's instructions, Francis had canvassed their friends. Madge told him that it was completely unnecessary and that no reputable doctor would do it. Ben went further and said that male circumcision, like female circumcision, was the result of primitive superstition. Roly Roper, on the other hand, said that it was a matter of class. The upper classes were circumcised and the middle classes were not. As for the working classes, well, they did what they were told and at present no circumcision was done on the National Health but that was only to save money.

Both Laura and Francis were tormented by indecision. Was it worse to be thought a savage or a member of the middle classes? Laura had disliked the idea of taking a surgeon's knife or pair of scissors to her baby's diminutive prepuce; yet if this was what he must suffer for initiation into his class, then she would have to allow it. But was it necessary? Was it the form? Finally, in desperation, she telephoned a friend from her childhood days whose nanny had once worked for a member of the Royal Family. Her advice was that it must be done. Johnny was therefore circumcised.

The end result of this gilded upbringing was a youth ready to rule the British Empire. That the Empire was no longer there did not diminish the boy's confidence in his own right to command. It exasperated Laura that he took for granted all the advantages he had been given by his parents and, beneath the courteous manner which usually comes with a public school education, felt contempt for anyone beneath him on the social scale. He was dutiful enough towards his parents, and always polite to his parents' friends, but she was not sure how he would take to Birek – particularly if Birek was using his room.

She drove to fetch Johnny at Eton and realized, as he loaded not just his school trunk but also three large cardboard boxes containing the component parts of his stereo system, that only a fraction of it could be unpacked in Lucy's room. She said nothing as they set off for London. He was so patently delighted to have reached the end of term that she thought it might be prudent to let his good mood get established before testing it with bad news. She also loved him and was glad to see him, not just because he was her son and mothers must love their sons, but also because he had grown up into a handsome and agreeable young man with the figure and features of her father, the explorer, and so in some sense a male version of herself.

On the motorway she took a deep breath and plunged in. 'Darling,' she said. 'I hope you don't mind, but that Czech writer, Josef Birek, has been staying with us and we put him in your room.'

'He's not still there, is he?'

'I'm afraid he is.'

'Isn't that a little much?'

She could tell that he was annoyed. 'The thing is, you see, that it seemed silly to turn him out if you were coming down to Risley in a week's time.'

'So where am I meant to sleep?'

'In Lucy's room.'

'Christ. Thanks a lot!'

'Lucy's going to sleep in the nursery.'

'Couldn't the Czech sleep in the nursery?'

'Not really.'

'Where am I meant to put my hi-fi?'

'Couldn't you leave it in boxes and take it down to Risley?'

'I never take it to Risley. I leave it in London.'

'It might be safer if you took it to Risley,' said Laura.

'Why? Might the Czech flog it?'

Laura blushed. 'No. Of course not. But it's the first thing they'd take if the house was burgled.'

'I wasn't even planning to come down to Risley for a couple of weeks,' said Johnny.

'You must,' said Laura with a tone of uncertain authority.

'Why?'

'We'll all be down there. There'll be no one to cook for you in London.'

'Dad will be in London.'

'Yes, but he has supper at his club.'

'Who's going to cook for the Czech?'

'He looks after himself.'

'So can I.'

'You always make such a mess of the kitchen.'

'I'll eat out.'

Laura's mind was working fast to find a conclusive, definitive reason why Johnny could not stay in London, but the only one she could think of was that his presence in the house would stop her sleeping with Birek. She could hardly advance that argument to her son so she thrashed around giving a series of increasingly inconclusive explanations – that Belinda and Lucy would want him there, that he could learn to drive from Risley; but she sensed as she spoke that the more pretexts she invented, the closer she came to giving away her true reason for wanting him to come to the country. The risk she was running showed itself when, as they were passing Heathrow Airport, Johnny finally said: 'So what's so bloody special about this Czech, anyway?'

She paused – afraid to talk about Birek. 'Didn't I send you that bit out of the paper?'

'Yes. I know he's a dissident and all that, but why does he have to move in with us?'

Laura sighed. 'It is a bore,' she said, 'but there was nowhere else.'

'Couldn't he rent a flat or stay in a hotel?'

'He's got no money.'

'Did *you* ask him?'

'It was your father's idea.'

'He might have thought about me.'

'He assumed – we both assumed – that he would have gone by now.'

'Why doesn't he go?'

'As soon as he's got a publisher for his novel, he'll move out. And then he'll be famous and you'll be very proud that he once stayed in your room.'

It was a difficult week. The beginning of the school holidays always disrupted the well established routine of life during the term.

Johnny slept until eleven, then came down to the kitchen to make himself some breakfast just when Fatima had started to wash the kitchen floor. If he ran into Birek, he was scarcely civil – scowling as he grunted a cursory greeting: Belinda, on the other hand, who returned the day after her brother, tossed her head and blushed whenever she saw him.

This reflex flirting with Birek irritated Laura more than Johnny's scowls. She told herself that it was absurd for a fifteen-year-old girl to affect adult mannerisms in this way. She recognized, certainly, that though she took after Francis, Belinda was extremely pretty – her figure well advanced and her face fresh and clear. She had that bloom which nature often accords to even the most ordinary girls, but though Laura never said so – not even to Francis – she thought Belinda rather stupid because throughout her childhood she had shown no interest in anything but ponies and point-to-points.

She forgot, because it was inconvenient to remember, that she herself had been obsessed with the same things at the same age; and discounted the influence of the school to which she had sent her daughter, which impressed upon its pupils a mould of county gentility. A psychoanalyst might say that Laura was jealous of her daughter – not specifically, let alone consciously, afraid that she would lure away the lover who was near her own age; but generally and subliminally resentful that, while a mosaic of lines and wrinkles had started to appear on her own face, her daughter's skin was soft and pink, and her pretty blue eyes, which darted those secret and timid looks at the Czech lodger, were free of the bloodshot bleariness that is the mark of middle age.

Birek kept out of the way as much as he could, but sleeping in Johnny's bedroom – and using, of necessity, the nursery bathroom – he inevitably ran into the children. He had never felt obliged to talk to Gail, nor Gail to talk to him, but he tried hard to befriend Johnny and Belinda in an apologetic way which charmed the older daughter but disgusted the already antagonistic son. It created, all the same, a kind of camaraderie among those who slept on the third floor which somehow exasperated Laura. She did not want to muck in with them herself; and it would be impossible to suggest that Birek used her bathroom; but it irritated her all the same to hear Birek chatting with Belinda and Belinda giggling politely at one of his feeble jokes.

These unsatisfactory arrangements continued only until the Thursday when Lucy broke up and the family moved to Risley. Laura did not even wait until the Friday morning but transferred Lucy, still in her school uniform, straight from the Golf to the Mercedes. Then with Johnny in the front, still complaining at being exiled to the country when all his friends were in London and that there were half-a-dozen films that he had not seen, with Gail, Lucy and Belinda on the back seat and the luggage, including Johnny's hi-fi, piled high behind them, they set off for the M4 and Risley.

There everything was much easier. To Laura's great relief, the Diston cousins were in residence – children more or less the same age as the Mortons, among them Rupert Diston, who was one of Johnny's closest friends. Therefore Johnny's mood improved. He also ate with gusto the heavy country food which Mrs Jackson cooked for them, and laughed and teased and quarrelled with his two sisters in the same old way.

Francis came down for the weekend. Birek remained in London. Although Laura missed him, she was not so besotted that she did not realize that it was better if the cuckoo was absent from the nest. She had even to acknowledge that with the children there, and so much suddenly going on, she had not the time to think of Birek quite as much as she usually did, and not thinking about him, naturally, meant not missing him either quite as much as before. Indeed she began to wonder whether it had been wise to ask Mary Diston if she could bring Birek to her ball.

What was done was done. It was important, she told herself, that Birek should see aspects of English life exemplified by the ball at Diston. Nor did she want to go to all the bother of dressing up if it was not to dazzle her lover and in flaunting her lover, dazzle her friends. It would also be absurd, now that they had booked a bigger villa, not to take Birek to Corfu along with some of the children's friends; but as she thought about that, and breaking it to Johnny and Belinda, a frown came on to her face (she was cutting roses in the garden at Risley) because she remembered how Belinda had flirted with Birek and wondered . . . No. That would be absurd.

She was too young to aspire to a man of his age, and he much too intelligent to be interested in the mind of an overgrown child.

It was irritating, all the same, for a mother to have to worry about how she would look in a bikini lying beside her daughter; and to have the prospect of her holiday marred by the snobbishness and intolerance of her son. She had not yet told him that Birek was coming because she dreaded Johnny's reaction. He could be furious at first, as he had been about his room, but later, perhaps, he would come round to the idea, as he had to coming down to Risley – particularly if it meant that he could invite a friend to go with him – Rupert, perhaps, or better still some pleasant-looking contemporary from Eton who would amuse him and distract Belinda.

She looked up from the roses at Francis who, now that the part had been found for the garden tractor, was mowing the lawn. So far as Laura could judge, the lawn had been mown by Mr Jackson a day or two before, but she did not grudge her husband his weekend pleasures and wondered whether, if she was particularly tactful, she could get Francis to tell the children that he had asked Birek to come with them to Corfu.

It would be a challenge to her powers of persuasion because Francis had been angry at losing the deposit they had paid on the first villa of four hundred pounds. This had led, in fact, to one of the very few quarrels about money that they had ever had because Laura had said that she would pay out of her own income, whereupon Francis had countered that if she felt she had enough to squander on wasteful extravagances of that kind, then perhaps she would like to contribute to the everyday expenses of the household like the farm overdraft and the school fees.

She had sulked; he had sulked; but in time the anger of both of them had been dissipated not in the kind of dramatic reconciliation which is found in the early years of a marriage, but in a resigned return to the status quo. It left Laura, however, a little uncertain as to whether it would be wise to involve Francis in the row which would inevitably arise about Birek going with them abroad. She decided in the end that she would not, and waited until he had gone back to London on the Sunday night before saying to Johnny and Belinda at supper: 'You must think of who to ask to stay in Corfu.'

'I thought there wasn't room for friends,' said Belinda.

'We've changed the villa,' said Johnny. 'We've taken something bigger.'

'Can I ask Sarah?' asked Belinda.

'If you like,' said Laura. She looked at Johnny. 'Why don't you ask Rupert?'

'I'd rather ask Henry except I think he's going to France.'

'Are you asking anyone?' Belinda asked her mother.

'We were waiting to see who you children wanted to ask,' said Laura.

'Dad said that the Czech was coming,' said Johnny without looking up.

Laura felt that perhaps she blushed and was glad that her son's eyes were on his macaroni cheese. 'If there's a bed, certainly, he's a possibility . . .'

'He could do with a bit of sun,' said Belinda. 'He looks as if he's been living under a stone.'

'He probably has,' said Johnny, who then licked the finger with which he had been mopping up the cheese sauce and went to the fridge for another can of beer.

Laura went up to London the next morning, looked in at the offices of the Comenius Foundation for an hour or so, and when she could be sure that Fatima would have left, went back to Lansdowne Square. On the way, at the supermarket, she bought some French bread and taramasalata for lunch in the kitchen with her lover. They took a pot of coffee up to the library to work on the novel after they had eaten, but despite the fact that they had the whole afternoon at their disposal, they were quickly kissing on the sofa while the coffee grew cold in their cups.

Since it was possible that on the sofa they could be seen from the street, they climbed the two flights of stairs to Birek's room and there made love for the first time since the children had returned from school.

She was back at Risley by seven, and stayed there until the Wednesday when she made another trip to London and went through the same routine – the Foundation, French bread and taramasalata, coffee in the library and sex upstairs. There was a gap on Thursday, then the same on Friday: such is love. On the Friday, however, she came up on the train and went back with Francis on the 6.15 from Paddington. The car was waiting at the station and supper, cooked by Mrs Jackson, in the lower oven of the Aga.

That Saturday it was her birthday – she was forty. The children brought her breakfast in bed together with their presents. Lucy had made a huge multi-coloured greetings card with glue, sparkle dust and felt-tipped pens. Belinda had bought her a red and black check scarf which Laura had noticed being sold very cheaply at a stall on the Portobello Road. Johnny, less on top of things, had had to find what he could in Pewsey – a box of bath-sized Roger et Gallet soap. Finally Francis came in from his dressing-room with a parcel of similar proportions to the one he had carried down on the train the night before. It was loosely wrapped and soft to the touch. Laura guessed that it was clothes of some sort. She peeled off the Sellotape and carefully unfolded the pretty paper so that it could be used again, and at once recognized the bright blue taffeta of a dress designed by Caroline Charles.

She bit her lip and then burst into tears. Francis looked puzzled, and the children embarrassed, until Laura laughed and said that she was only crying because of the trouble they had all taken to get her such lovely presents. In a moment, indeed, the tears had gone and for the rest of the day Laura behaved just as one would expect a woman to behave surrounded by her family on her birthday.

The birthday treat she had promised herself was lunch on the Monday with Birek at Boulestin's in Covent Garden. Their excuse for meeting in that part of town was the need to go to Moss Bros to hire a dinner jacket and black tie for Birek to wear at the Diston ball. Laura realized that her lover was extremely reluctant to go to the dance at all. He kept protesting that he would really rather not come to Risley while the children were there, and that he would have no idea how to behave at a large party in the country. 'Just be yourself,' Laura had said; and 'You don't have to dance if you don't want to.' She was looking forward to it enormously herself: she had more ball gowns, necklaces, ear-rings and evening shoes than there were occasions to wear them. She also felt that she had only a year or two more of turning men's heads with her lovely shoulders flowing out of a dress like toffee icecream from a cornet.

For the very same reason she was determined that Birek should attend. She knew quite well that he was thought to be her lover, and a cynic might say that she wanted him that evening as the ultimate accoutrement to her attire. A kinder interpretation of the thoughts which were by no means precise in her own mind would be that she wanted Birek to join in the fun – that she did indeed see him now as part of the family and hated to think of him alone in London, eating in the evening at a McDonald's, Pizza Hut or Kentucky Fried Chicken while they sat in the kitchen or the dining-room at Risley.

She had also convinced herself that Birek ought to witness the ball at Diston, which like the Changing of the Guard or the Coronation was the sort of thing that the English did well. At one time she might have added that it was one of the last opportunities to witness the extravagance of the *ancien régime* because income tax and death duties would make parties of that kind impossible; but since the advent of a Conservative government and the rise in the values of stocks and shares, no one talked about parties in such apocalyptic terms.

It did not occur to Laura to relate the indignant descriptions of lavish living among the Communist elite in Birek's early stories to the unhappy look on his face as he stood before the mirror in Moss Bros trying on the jacket he was to wear for the ball. People like the Distons had been rich for so many generations that their parties had a style which raised them to the level of art. It was rather like going to the opera. Birek would never find it among the *parvenu* Americans, let alone among the Party leaders in Prague.

She paid for the suit; she paid for the lunch; she paid for the taxi back to Holland Park. The more she paid, the gloomier Birek became. By the time they got back to Lansdowne Square Birek was so gloomy that there was no question of going up to his room for what Laura had envisaged as the culmination of her birthday celebrations. Instead they sat in the library and went to work on the heavy manuscript of *The House of Culture* which because it had so frequently been abandoned on the floor had begun to look rather grubby.

The words on the paper, as well as the paper itself, had taken on a dog-eared look as if the prose had been prostituted too often as a pretext for other things. There is also an awful moment in the life of a manuscript when the vitality drains out of it as the prospects for its publication fade. The future best-seller or *succès d'estime* becomes tomorrow's clutter in a bottom drawer. Certainly a copy had gone to Orloff the day after the disastrous dinner, but both of them knew he would not take it on. Laura's line was now that they should perfect the translation before trying elsewhere, but since the children's holidays had started she had only managed to work on it during her trysts with Birek – and then for the few moments which preceded their embraces on the sofa.

That afternoon, since his mood excluded that sort of thing, she stubbornly continued to discuss the nuances of meaning, and suggest parts of the book which might be cut to make it more accessible to the Anglo-Saxon reader. Birek listened, and agreed to everything she proposed, but his mood did not improve until she came up with some tea on a tray and lighting the imitation log fire, since it was a cool afternoon, sat on the kelim rug with her elegant legs folded beneath her.

He then came and sat with her on the floor. For a while they drank their tea in silence. Then he smiled at her mournfully and said: 'I am sorry to be such a poor companion.'

'It doesn't matter.'

'You must say if ever you would like me to go away.'

She leaned forward and touched his hand. 'I will, but I don't. You make me very happy.'

He gave a little laugh and said: 'If I do, then I think that it is my only achievement.'

'You mustn't be depressed about your novel,' she said.

'No.'

'It's famously difficult to get a first novel published – particularly if it's in translation.'

'I know. It's not that, exactly. It's more that the book now seems remote, as if it was written by another person.'

'Yes.'

'It is difficult to rewrite it or make changes because I am no longer the person who wrote it.'

'Of course.' She shifted, hesitated, then said: 'You were sure to become another person in such a different world, and for your writing that may turn out to be a good thing. It may give a greater depth . . . an even greater depth to your perception.'

'Perhaps. But now, when you are in the country, I try to write, but nothing comes into my mind because I am no longer a Czech writing about Czechoslovakia but also I am not yet a new man – the émigré or whatever – with something to say about my new condition.'

'It will come,' she said softly.

'Do you think so?'

'Of course.'

'Sometimes I am afraid that my inspiration was there, and only there.'

'No,' she said, stroking his brow. 'It's in there, in your mind and your imagination.'

He smiled at her, and they might have kissed, but there was something so exquisite about the affectionate melancholy of his present mood that Laura did not want to rupture it with passion. They therefore sat quietly as the gas flames flickered through the artificial logs until in due course Laura returned to Risley.

SEVENTEEN

The Diston dance was on the Saturday and Birek came down by train in time for lunch. Four friends of Johnny and Belinda were also staying, as well as a couple called Blacket who had been sent to them by the Distons for the night. As a result Birek's presence was hardly noticed and he retreated after lunch to his attic room. Laura was too busy preparing the dinner they were to give before going to Diston: she saw Birek from the kitchen window go out for a walk on his own, and thought for a moment that she might join him, but was distracted by Mrs Jackson in a panic saying that the *gêlée* around the *oeufs* had not set.

In fact it turned out that it was perfectly all right – a little soft, perhaps, for Mrs Jackson who had advised her to use more gelatine. But Laura had too many other worries on her mind to follow Birek over the lawn into the fields – in particular the question of what she should wear for the dance. She knew that Francis would expect her to wear the dress that he had given her for her birthday. It would certainly not have occurred to him that she had been considering what she should wear for a good three months before her birthday, and had bought in May a sumptuous gown of yellow silk from Victor Edelstein.

The dress from Caroline Charles was pretty, as her dresses always are, but knowing that it had been bought in the January sale somehow took the gilt off the gingerbread. However often Laura told herself that she should be delighted to discover that her husband had not bought the dress for another woman, she could not suppress the feeling that she would really rather that he had – not just to even the balance so far as Birek was concerned, but to save her the dilemma about what to wear.

If she alone had known that the Caroline Charles dress had been bought at a discount, that would have been one thing, but Emma would be sure to recognize the dress, and knowing Emma would probably make a joke of it and call Francis a stingy old bugger in front of a group of their friends. And it was, when she thought about it, a bit calculating and tight for him to buy something cheap so far in advance of her birthday; and while he could not know that she knew – and she was far too kind to tell him – the knowing did diminish her sense of obligation and justify her decision to wear the Edelstein dress instead.

She was too preoccupied, when she came down to dinner, to notice whether Francis was disappointed: but when finally they arrived at Diston she felt sure that her choice had been right. Torches of pitch had been lit at the gateway, and were placed in the ground at regular intervals all the way up the mile-long drive. Retainers stood with lamps, guiding the cars to the front door of the floodlit house where healthy young peasants stepped forward like valets outside a restaurant in Los Angeles to park the cars in a field and save the drivers the damp walk back.

They were not really peasants, of course, because the species has been extinct in the south of England for two or three generations, but as the sons of the farm manager or the estate workers they were happy to give up an evening watching television, or revising for their finals at the Reading Polytechnic, to watch the glamorous guests of their parents' employees arrive for an evening's fun.

The Distons received their guests with just the right mixture of haughtiness and *bonhomie*. There was disdain in the feeble handshake of Lady Cynthia and friendliness in the clap on the back from Lord Diston, so their guests first felt humbled by the one and then ennobled by the other.

The spectacle which met them as they entered was impressive even by the extravagant standards of the day. Diston Park, as many know who have paid £1.50 to trudge round it during the day, is one of the finest country houses in the south of England – finer, some say, than either Longleat or Easton Neston. With the notices reading 'This Way', 'No Smoking', 'No Entry' and 'Toilets' now removed, as well as the low-slung ropes which during the day corralled the public like sheep, the hallway of Diston Park made a fine impression just in itself; but lit, as it was, by a thousand candles, with flowers burgeoning from the base of every column, and waiters and waitresses holding bottles of champagne in thick white napkins accosting every guest at every corner, the *tableau vivant* was quite enough to make most of the guests feel that they had been whisked into another era.

Almost as soon as it arrived, the party from Risley disintegrated – the young going off with the young and the old with the old. While Francis stopped to chat to some of the bankers and brokers he knew from the City and the 6.15, Laura took Birek into some of the state rooms, pointing out portraits of the Distons by Romney and Lawrence, and a villainous-looking ancestor by Holbein. She even penetrated into the library which was never open to the public to show him the small Rembrandt which was kept there for the Distons' private delectation.

Was Birek favourably impressed? He certainly should have been, for though there are more houses like Diston than many suppose,

Diston was among the best of its kind, thanks largely to the perspicacity of the fourth Lord Diston – the grandfather of the present baron – who had gone to America in the 1890s, supposedly to hunt bison, and had returned with a Miss Mellon or Carnegie or Rockefeller or Guggenheim – no one could quite remember which. Yet Birek, walking through this gallery of magnificent possessions, did not take on the look of someone favourably impressed, but rather of someone baffled and even, at times, depressed.

They returned to the throng in the great hall where Laura was whisked off by Emma's husband Jimmy for a whirl in the ballroom to the music of a five-piece band. Birek, knowing no one other than those with whom he had arrived, strolled back into the drawing-room where he sat down. Every now and then a waiter or a waitress came to fill his glass, and almost as soon as they had done so he emptied it, more for something to do than from a conscious relish in the taste or the effect of non-vintage champagne.

After a while he felt ostentatious sitting alone in this way: he therefore stood and prepared to return to the crowded hall, hoping that Laura might have come back from her dance, but as he approached the drawing-room door, Francis came in looking almost as dejected as Birek.

'Ah,' he said, seeing the Czech. 'You've found a bolthole.'

'Yes,' said Birek.

'Are you enjoying the party?'

'Yes, of course.'

'As much as can be expected,' said Francis, walking a little further into the room to let some other guests come in behind him.

'Obviously,' said Birek, following him back into the room, 'there are not many people I know.'

'Laura should introduce you to some of her friends.'

'She meant to, I think, but she was asked to dance.'

'Yes. She loves dancing.'

'I wish I knew how,' said Birek.

'You don't have to know how these days,' said Francis. 'You just jiggle and wiggle around. I'm sure they do the same sort of thing in Czechoslovakia.'

'Of course. But even that, in its way, is an art.'

'I certainly can't do it,' said Francis, 'not because it's difficult, but because it's absurd.'

'And undignified.'

'Undignified? Yes. I suppose it is. But for the old, not for the young, and you are still young.'

Birek looked towards the door as if he should go and find Laura. 'I am afraid I already feel old in that respect.'

'Don't you like the house?' asked Francis, waving towards the great space of the drawing-room.

'It is outstanding.'

'The only advantage of a long tradition is that it saves swanking like this from vulgarity.'

'Yes.'

'It remains conspicuous consumption all the same, of course.'

'It is difficult for me,' said Birek, 'not to see it all in terms of the class oppression that I was taught at school.'

'I thought you'd seen through all that Marxist propaganda?'

'Indeed I have. But certain involuntary prejudices remain from one's indoctrination.'

'You think that all this champagne should go to the poor?'

'Not the champagne, perhaps, but the money which bought it.'

'Then you would throw a lot of Frenchmen out of a job.'

'Of course.'

'Look at this,' said Francis, leading Birek towards the open doors which led from the drawing-room into the garden. They walked out into the warm evening air and stood for a moment on the gravel path laid between the house and the floodlit lawn. 'Do you see the church there, standing all alone in the field?'

'Yes.'

'That was once the centre of the village – a thriving community of peasant farmers. Then the Distons, as Lords of the Manor, began to enclose the peasants' plots and put sheep on the land where the peasants had grown their turnips and cabbage. In the end the peasants were driven away, their houses were pulled down and the village of Diston became Diston Park.'

'That was dreadful,' said Birek.

'It was, wasn't it? And all the moralists condemned it at the time. But consider this. If the peasants had not been turned off the land, there would have been no pool of labour to work in factories at the time of the Industrial Revolution; and if the land had not been enclosed, there would have been no agricultural surpluses to feed those workers; and if the Distons and their kind had not amassed fortunes from sheep farming, there would have been no capital to invest in the factories. Therefore the present prosperity of the Western world, with which it not only provides its own people with a standard of living that only princes could aspire to in the Middle Ages, but also furnishes much of the food and medicine to the rest of the world, has its roots in the injustice of an earlier era.'

'That is certainly a paradox,' said Birek, who had never before heard Francis speak earnestly in this way.

'It is more than a paradox . . .' Francis began, but then was interrupted by Laura, who came out of the house behind them.

'So there you are,' she said, taking Francis by one arm and Birek by the other. She turned to her husband. 'Won't you ask me to dance?'

'I'd rather not.'

'But you will, won't you?' she asked Birek.

'Of course. If you like.'

They left Francis in the garden, musing on the sources of wealth, and walked back through the drawing-room and the grand hall to the ballroom. There the floor was now crowded with other guests who were jumping and slithering around the floor to the 1950s rhythms of the old-fashioned band. Birek, by now, had drunk half-a-dozen glasses of champagne whose effect had not been to raise his spirits but rather to bring on that melancholy self-pity which sometimes comes to the surface of the Slav soul under the influence of drink. It was with a gloomy mien that he took to the floor and began imitating the gyrations of those he saw around him, for when Birek had said that he could not dance, he had not been guilty of any false modesty. Even to a tune where almost any kind of rhythmic movement would pass itself off as the twist or rock and roll, Birek's gauche cavorting looked absurd. Laura, who rather fancied herself as a stylish dancer, threw herself into the ecstatic paroxysms of a Haitian negress under a vodoo spell, but rather than encourage Birek to lose his own inhibitions and allow the rhythm of the music to enter his blood, this only brought on an intense embarrassment which showed all too clearly in the expression on his face.

Laura therefore decided to give it up as a bad job and, when a lull came in the music, she suggested returning to the hall for a drink. She was a little disappointed, not so much that Birek could not dance (she could not blame him for that), but that he appeared to be hating the party. Worse still, there was a danger that his mood might affect hers, but Laura, who had so looked forward to this ball, and who drew so many admiring glances to her lovely body in her Edelstein dress, was still determined to enjoy herself, whatever the mood of her lover.

It would be too harsh to say that she decided to dump him because that was certainly not so. The thoughts which flitted through her mind – affected, like Birek's, by several glasses of champagne – showed some awareness of his predicament: he knew no one, after all, and also fell between the two stools of the different generations. Yet she also argued that he would never meet anyone else if she was always beside him, and that when two lovers who were used to a delightful intimacy suddenly find themselves together in the company of others, there is inevitably a constraint which equally inevitably must seem disagreeable to them both.

There were tables covered with white table-cloths placed between the columns to one side of the grand hall. Seeing some of their party sitting there, including Johnny and Belinda and some of their friends, Laura led Birek to one of the empty chairs and herself sat down beside him. Her children greeted her but ignored Birek. Laura called a waiter to ask for champagne for herself and Birek. When it was brought she sipped a mouthful from her glass while Birek, still mournful, swallowed his down.

There was a bottle on the table from which he filled his glass again while Laura, in an attempt to raise his spirits, and for want of anything else to say, gave thumb-nail sketches of the men and women at different tables. Tommy was a diplomat who had been offered the embassy in Tokyo but had turned it down because his wife had heard that women never went to parties in Japan. Gerry had made several million pounds making horrible little houses with Georgian façades for aspiring bourgeois from the working classes. Eddie had worked for Louards but then had started his own merchant bank and had made several million in only a couple of years. Eddie was having an affair with Rosemary who was Tommy's second wife: that was another reason for her not wanting to go to Tokyo. Eddie had always loved Marietta Jones but Marietta was married to the man with the receding hair who had made ten times as much as Eddie in only five years in Hong Kong. When he came back he had bought Beckington Park from Hamish Hawthorn, who had lost a hundred thousand at Crockford's in the 1970s when gambling was still fashionable. Hamish's wife had left him – she had only stuck with him because she had loved Beckington – and had gone off with Sammy Durand who had then been caught selling cocaine and sent to prison.

So it went on – a ceaseless stream of anecdotes which would have furnished the material for a library of society novels had Laura been a society novelist or thought it acceptable behaviour to write novels about her friends. As it was she only wanted to entertain Birek, and perhaps arouse in him enough curiosity to talk to some other women. Her gossip, however, only compounded Birek's melancholy: not only was he affronted by the lavishness of the Distons' ball – the free-flowing champagne, the buffet which no one ate – but now by the picture of depravity which Laura painted before him. Cupidity, adultery, drugs – it all seemed as bad as his Marxist schoolteachers had described; and worst of all he himself had been sucked into this vortex of evil by loving another man's wife.

When Laura saw that Birek was not amused her anxiety on his behalf turned to exasperation. The eyes of others which she imagined envying her for her handsome young lover, she now felt pitying her for being stuck with this lugubrious Czech. Since a woman's appearance is affected by her morale, she felt her allure fading as her spirits sank. She therefore decided that the time had come to share Birek with others – to leave him free, at any rate, to be approached by others; but knowing how he might misinterpret any abrupt departure she used the old trick that every girl learns at her first dance and whispered in his ear that she had to go to the ladies' cloakroom.

Knowing everyone, and being among friends, Laura was inevitably waylaid before she reached her destination, and it was only out of deference to her self-respect that she actually climbed the stairs to Lady Cynthia's bathroom to empty a bladder that was not yet full. She also took the opportunity to check her face in the mirror for smudged eye-shadow and running mascara; and when reassured that all was well she went back down the grand staircase.

Once again she was waylaid before she could get back to the hall and was whisked once again into the ballroom – first by Hamish, then by Tommy, then by Billy, then by Fred, and finally by Charlie Eldon, her old and steadfast admirer.

'How is your Czech enjoying the party?' he shouted in her ear as they jived around the room.

'Shut up,' she said.

'He looks as if he wishes he was back in Prague,' sneered Charlie.

'Shut up,' she said again.

'He asked Belinda to dance but she refused him.'

'How mean of her.'

'She has to think of her reputation,' said Charlie.

Laura glared at him: he smiled back with the mockery that was part of his charm.

The moment had come – it was around two in the morning – when the caterers had started to serve breakfast at the several small tables set out in the Distons' dining-room. Since it was now five hours since she had dined, and she had been dancing strenuously in that time, Laura, when she sniffed the frying of bacon and sausages in the air, suddenly felt exceptionally hungry. She therefore turned to Charlie and said: 'Let's have some breakfast.' They went back into the bustle of the great hall. Laura caught a glimpse of Birek, still sitting at the same table. Johnny and Belinda had left: no one sat on either his left or his right and the bottle in front of him was empty. He had not seen her. She looked away and followed Charlie into the dining-room.

Many of the other guests had had the same idea as Laura and Charlie and the eight tables were mostly filled, but two places were found for them by Francis, who had been one of the first to sit down. Emma sat at the same table. Johnny, Belinda, Rupert Diston and a group of their friends happened to be sitting at the next table and Laura, as she sat down, was able to mutter angrily to Belinda that she really should have danced with Birek.

'Why don't *you*?' Belinda answered back.

'I *have*,' said Laura, 'and you must too.'

Belinda pouted and turned back to her table while Laura turned to the waiter to order orange juice, bacon, egg, sausages, toast and coffee. Charlie was on her left while to her right sat a fat and greedy friend of hers called Jumbo Apsley-Ruck. He had already finished one breakfast and was hoping to get hold of another. He looked up through his thick Billy Bunter spectacles and seeing a young man standing behind Laura handed him his empty plate saying: 'Waiter, if you don't mind, the same again!'

It was Birek who, since the plate was thrust at him, took it in his hands. Johnny saw this from the other table, gave a guffaw and shouted: 'Hey, waiter, yes, and another cup of coffee for me!' His Etonian friends, realizing that Birek was not in fact a waiter, but seeing a rag under way, joined in with the kind of callous gusto that always goes with bullying in a public school. 'Yes, and while you're at it . . .' said Rupert Diston, shoving his plate on top of the one which was already in Birek's hands; 'And where's my toast?' shouted Andy Grimston.

Birek stood there as if unable to comprehend what had happened. He had turned towards the young when they had shouted at him, but now faced back towards the grown-ups' table. Tears welled up in his mournful eyes and he looked beseechingly towards Laura but Laura, having seen that there was no room for him at their table, thought it best to carry on for as long as she could as if she had not noticed him standing behind her. She therefore pretended to be engrossed by what Charlie was saying, and was saved by having Birek brought to her attention by Jumbo Apsley-Ruck who, realizing that he had done something thought enormously funny though he did not know quite what it was, said to Birek in his best officer-in-the-Lifeguards tone of voice: 'And do hurry up. We're all dreadfully hungry.'

For a moment Birek stood there, swaying and undecided, waiting for Laura to save him: but she did not turn; he saw only the silent tresses of her streaked hair; so he turned instead and with as steady a pace as he could manage after drinking so much champagne, he took the plates towards the counter at the far end of the room. He saw it in a blur because of the tears in his eyes which now broke the dike of his lower lids and trickled down his cheeks.

He could not brush them away – his hands held the plates – and the concentration he required to reach the end of the room distracted his mind from the effect upon his stomach of the smell of frizzled fat. Therefore just as he reached the table from which the caterers were serving breakfast (it was the Distons' dining table pulled back against the wall) he retched, lurched forward, dropped the plates, and then was sick into one of the silver dishes half-filled with scrambled egg.

EIGHTEEN

Towards the end of July a telegram was received in the offices of the Comenius Foundation from Laura Morton in Corfu. It read: 'Please find Birek central inexpensive flat. Return August 15th. Laura.'

The tone of this telegram irritated everyone who read it. Who did she think she was, sending instructions in this way? Miroslav Maier, who had just returned from his own holiday in Cornwall, wanted to send a reply c/o the Soulandros Line (from where Laura had sent her wire) saying 'Do your own dirty work' or words to that effect. MacDonald, however, reminded him not just of Laura's value as a translator but of her husband's value as a patron of the Foundation. 'He pays your salary and mine,' he said to Miroslav, 'so don't take umbrage if every now and then his wife treats us as her servants.'

Finding flats in London that were central and inexpensive is no easier than in any other capital city, but MacDonald told his secretary to telephone estate agents, and then went himself to inspect what they had to offer. Since MacDonald was both absent-minded and ascetic, he was not as appalled as others might have been by what he was offered or asked to pay.

It soon became clear that if Birek wanted to remain within range of the West End of London, yet be able to pay rent from a modest income, he would have to settle for what is euphemistically called a 'garden flat' – a dwelling carved out of the former kitchen, scullery, cellar and coal-hole of a terraced London house. To MacDonald one seemed much like another: he himself lived in a basement, so he hardly noticed the absence of daylight and did not feel the damp. He therefore took on Birek's behalf a one-bedroomed garden flat in North Kensington where the garden was no more than a small yard behind the house with paving-stones at eye level. The bed-room was at the back and the living-room at the front: there was a galley kitchen beneath the steps leading up to the house above and a bathroom in the former coal-hole. The walls of these amenities were blistered with damp like the skin of a man with smallpox, and the view from the front window was obscured by a row of dust-bins.

The rent for this dungeon was one hundred and twenty-five pounds a week – the lowest of all the flats that MacDonald went to see. Had he been less naïf he might have bargained a little, because there were signs that it had been vacant for a considerable time. There was a pervasive smell of damp and escaping gas and a black patch on the new beige carpet where rainwater had leaked in through the window. MacDonald, however, asked no questions and to make sure of the flat for Birek's return, paid a month's rent in advance. He was uneasy about this because Birek was now supposed to be independent of the Foundation. He assumed that either Birek would pay him back or Laura would subsidize him further. He did not agree with Miroslav Maier and others at the office that the telegram itself suggested that Laura wanted to be rid of her lover. Quite the contrary, it seemed to him proof of the Mortons' continuing commitment.

He was therefore taken aback when on August 15th it was Birek himself who telephoned from Heathrow airport not to ask about the flat but for help with Immigration. He had apparently left

England and entered Greece with only the Czech identity card with which he had arrived in the spring. Then, of course, the Home Office had been told to expect him; now, it appeared, his name had been forgotten and his file could not be found. MacDonald had therefore to try to get hold of those sympathetic civil servants who had helped him six months before. The crucial official was still on holiday, and it was not until five in the afternoon that MacDonald reached someone who remembered Birek's case and was prepared to tell his colleagues at Heathrow that Birek should be let in.

MacDonald would have gone out to the airport to fetch him if his own car had not broken down. Everyone else at the Foundation had by then gone home. He therefore told Birek to take the airport bus to Queensway, where he would meet him and escort him to his flat. The bus, as always, took longer than expected: MacDonald had to wait for almost an hour. This put this usually phlegmatic Scotsman into an impatient and irritable mood, so when he saw the sun-burned Czech he greeted him in the gruffest way, gave him the address of the flat, handed him the keys and saw him into a taxi.

Later he felt ashamed. He should at least have made sure that Birek had the money to pay the cab and buy himself something for supper. But then again, he reassured himself, surely Birek, once he had dropped his suitcase, would dine with the Mortons at Lansdowne Square.

Birek did not dine with the Mortons at their house in Lansdowne Square but dined by himself in his new dwelling off deep-frozen lasagne from the Pakistani grocer's shop on the corner of Golborne Road. He wished, as he did so, that he was not eating anything at all. The electric oven, unused for so long, had given off malodorous fumes which, mingling with the smell of damp, gas and the rotting carpet, destroyed what appetite he had had after his journey.

To stop the fumes he had switched off the oven before the lasagne was properly heated. Though warm on the outside, it grew cooler as his teeth bit into it and had an icy centre. He ate it all the same, and drank a glass of homogenized milk that he had bought at the same time as the lasagne, while sitting at the small pine table in the living-room. It was a furnished flat, and the furniture was all new, but like the carpets and the crockery it was the cheapest that could be found. The knife was so meagre that its handle cut into the palm of his hand as he cut into the frozen centre of the lasagne, and the fork almost bent as he prodded his food and carried it mournfully to his mouth.

The flat, of course, was reason enough for Birek to be gloomy if Birek had taken it in, but since it was already dark when he arrived, and the landlord had only furnished two or three forty-watt bulbs, the details of the décor and the view from the windows front and back were for Birek to look forward to in the morning.

He was rather cast down, firstly because he was tired after a long day spent first in a tightly packed Boeing 737 and then in a detention room at Heathrow Airport; and secondly because he was sad to have parted from the Mortons for the first time in many months – to have parted from them, also, in such fraught circumstances at the immigration desk at the airport.

He did not blame the Mortons for abandoning him. Francis had remonstrated with the officials, but there was clearly nothing he could do. Lucy had been fractious while Johnny and Belinda had been not just impatient to get home, but also as anxious to get away from Birek as Birek had been to get away from them.

Never before had Birek suffered so much from another human being as he had suffered from Johnny Morton. He had thought back to the bullies of his school days, to the most odious teachers, to the drill sergeants during the early days of his national service, to the apparatchiks at the Union of Writers, but none of them had subjected him to the humiliations which he had known since the dreadful dance at Diston.

It was not just that the name 'waiter' had stuck, and despite Laura's and Francis's frequent intervention had persisted throughout the holiday in Corfu – used not only by Johnny but also by Belinda, Rupert Diston, Sarah Everard, then little Lucy and finally, to his horror, but not to his face, by Francis when discussing a second boat for an afternoon's expedition. 'Are you coming,' Birek had overheard him ask Laura. 'And what about the waiter?' There were also a dozen other minor ways in which Johnny had persecuted Birek. There had been a horrible shuffling before lunch to avoid sitting next to him; then none of the young would pass him the olives, the bread or the tomato salad. They had put him in coventry, as they used to put unfortunate scapegoats at their boarding schools, and played petty tricks on him like slipping a dead wasp into his glass of wine, then laughing raucously when he choked and spluttered – Johnny running to the kitchen shouting: 'Quick, a bowl, the waiter's chucking up again.'

All this might have been tolerable if Birek had felt that Laura loved him as before. Never having lived in a large family, however, he had not envisaged the way in which the attitude of one member alters the attitude of the others. Even parents can change their minds when they see someone through their children's eyes; and already, after the party, when Birek had so embarrassed the Mortons by vomiting into the dish of scrambled eggs, he had sensed a certain reserve in her manner.

She had come up to London on the Tuesday after the party, and they had made love in his bedroom as before; but while her words, her smiles and her gestures had all been as affectionate as before, he had sensed for the first time since he had become her lover a certain impatience to get on with it, as if she had not come up to London to see him but for what he could do for her body.

He had also suspected that once it was over she had asked herself whether it had been worth the journey. There was no mention of working on the novel, and when she made a pot of tea she did not bring it on a tray to the library but poured it into mugs and drank it standing in the kitchen.

She had not come up to London again that week, as she might have done, on the grounds that there was much to do before they left for Greece at the weekend. The whole family spent the Friday night in Lansdowne Square and Birek had hardly a moment to see Laura alone. When he did he had asked her whether she really wanted him to come with them to Corfu, to which she had answered: 'Yes, you might as well. It's too late to get a refund on the ticket.' Then perhaps because this had sounded unfriendly, she had smiled and squeezed his hand as they stood on the landing outside the children's bathroom.

The villa in Corfu was what you might expect for a thousand pounds a week – two bathrooms, a swimming-pool and a terrace looking down through pine trees to the sea. There had been four double bedrooms and that had immediately started a quarrel. Clearly Francis and Laura took one, Johnny and Rupert a second, Belinda and Sarah the third, leaving Birek and Lucy to share the fourth. This Lucy refused to do. There was a tantrum which led to a bed being dragged out into the living-room which at first was meant for Lucy but, since the living-room served as a thoroughfare between the kitchen and the terrace, meant that she could not be put to bed before the grown-ups retired. Birek had then offered to sleep in the living-room but Laura would not allow it; so every night Lucy went to sleep in her parents' bed and then was carried to the bed in the living-room when Laura and Francis retired.

Worse than this feeling of being the odd man out, and the hostility of the adolescent children, had been the torment felt by both Birek and Laura of their unsatisfied desire. For while Laura had continued to show that element of detachment which had crept into her behaviour towards him after the Diston dance, he still sensed her eyes on his body as he lay sunbathing on the beach; and he knew, when she frolicked with him in the sea and caressed him surreptitiously under the water, that her sexual appetite had been revived by two or three days in the hot sun.

But when and where could they do it? How could they contrive to be alone? Every afternoon, and every night, Laura went to her room with her husband, and at every other moment of the day the children hung on to her like zealous little chaperones. By the end of the first week they were both so desperate that when Francis proposed a day's expedition on the boats they had hired, Laura feigned sunstroke and said she would stay behind. Birek offered to stay with her; but then Lucy announced that she did not like going out on the boats 'for a long time' and so she too stayed behind with her mother.

After lunch the three went to their rooms for a siesta, denoting with looks and gestures that they might creep together once the little girl was asleep; but on that particular afternoon Lucy stayed awake, reading loudly to herself from *Samuel Whiskers*. There was nothing to be done: they had both, as it were, to tighten their belts and hope for another opportunity.

It arose quite by chance one evening when Francis and Lucy had walked down to the village to buy some more wine. Suddenly the four teenagers decided to climb along the rocks to the point. Laura and Birek thus found themselves alone, but fearing that they might be discovered if they stayed in the house, they went for a walk in the hills behind. After a twenty-minute climb they sat down among the pines and olive trees to watch the sun set over the sea. They kissed, embraced, then hid themselves behind an old stone shed where in great haste and great discomfort they made love. It was over in a moment, leaving Birek with bruised kneecaps and Laura with pine-needles embedded in her buttocks.

They did not try again but promised, as they walked down the hill, that they would make up for lost time when they got back to London. It was then that Laura decided that a flat must be found for Birek and sent the telegram to the Comenius Foundation.

The arrangement she made for their return seemed to Laura to be both just and convenient. Clearly Birek could not go on living at Lansdowne Square: the children would not stand for it and Francis had been patient for long enough. It was time, anyway, for Birek to stand on his own two feet. It would also be more convenient if he had a flat of his own where Laura could visit him from time to time. She had not yet worked out who would pay the rent, and the question was sufficiently awkward to be put at the back of her mind. In due course Birek would have to find a job because it now seemed quite clear that it would be harder to find a publisher for *The House of Culture* than she had supposed.

She came to visit Birek in his basement flat the day after their return from Corfu. It was a hurried visit because she had to take the children to Risley that afternoon, but there was time enough to make love on the narrow double bed in the gloomy bedroom. Only after that did she take in quite how horrible that flat was, but at that particular moment it had served its purpose so its nastiness hardly seemed to matter. 'Most young people start off in basements,' she told Birek as she put on her clothes. 'One can often make them quite cosy.' Then she was off, but with a promise to meet him for lunch in two days' time.

Thus a routine was established which suited Laura very well and – or so she told herself – left Birek plenty of time either to go on with his writing or look for some sort of job. Quite what sort of job he might do was a question for Andrew MacDonald and the Comenius Foundation, and it was to them, at her suggestion, that Birek turned for advice.

MacDonald took Birek to lunch at the same small restaurant to which he had taken him when he had first arrived. The manner he adopted was somewhat different – businesslike rather than euphoric, with an edge of impatience in his tone of voice as he recommended some of the cheaper dishes, There were, he told Birek, very few jobs which required a knowledge of Czech, and for those there were in, say, the various schools of Slavonic studies or the External Services of the BBC, there was already a long queue of applicants who had better contacts and better qualifications. The best he could suggest was that Birek apply to one or two of the provincial universities, or perhaps to some of the newspapers and television companies, to see if any of them could use him as a researcher or sub-editor on some project associated with Eastern Europe.

'But in the meantime,' said Birek, abject with embarrassment, 'I have no money whatsoever.'

'You needn't worry about the rent of the flat,' said MacDonald, who had been worried about it himself. 'That has been paid by Laura Morton and I'm sure she'll be in no hurry to get the money back.'

MacDonald meant no more by this than that Laura was a rich woman to whom five hundred pounds was neither here nor there; but Birek, imagining that it was a reference to their liaison, blushed black in the face and said in the kind of gasping whisper that people use when they are struggling to control their emotions: 'Of course I shall pay her back.'

'In due course, in due course,' said MacDonald.

'In the meantime, however, I should perhaps look for an ordinary job which I could start tomorrow.'

'What kind of job had you in mind?'

'In Prague I worked as a school janitor.'

'Here, I am afraid, those jobs are in the gift of the ILEA. They only give them to the Party faithful.'

'What else would you suggest?' asked Birek, a mask of dignity hiding his growing despair.

'It's tricky,' said MacDonald. 'You can't just go to the Job Centre or sign on for the dole because it might get back to the Home Office and spoil your chances of getting a permanent visa.'

'I see jobs offered every now and then in the windows of shops . . .'

'Yes. That's your best bet. Something casual where you're paid in cash with no questions asked. In fact although there is unemployment in the nation as a whole, there is a great shortage of unskilled labour in central London.'

The reason for this, as Birek discovered, was that the wages paid for those unskilled jobs were not enough to cover the rent of a flat in the part of London where the job was to be done. He took one, all the same, delivering wine from a warehouse. The driver of the van was a young Londoner called Gary who was friendly enough until Birek asked him why he embroidered everything he said with an obscene expletive.

'You'd fuckin' like to know, wouldn't yer, you toffee-nosed cunt? Well I fuckin' well aren't going to tell yer!' was the only explanation forthcoming – followed by a permanent sullen silence as they did their rounds.

In time Gary's antipathy got him down and he gave in his notice. The real work he would have liked was that of a milkman or a postman because that would leave his afternoons free for his writing and for Laura, but a job like that might come to the notice of the authorities, so he moved on to loading and unloading furniture at a repository near Shepherd's Bush.

The money he was paid for this casual labour was enough so long as someone else paid his rent. When it came to the end of September, however, and the next month's rent became due, Birek had saved only ninety pounds, which was four hundred and fifty less than he needed. He told Laura when he next saw her that he would have to move out to a rented room.

'Why?' she asked. 'This flat is so handy.'

'I can't afford the rent.'

'Don't worry,' she said, 'the Foundation will go on paying until you've got a proper job.'

Birek said nothing – he swallowed his pride – and continued to pretend that he did not know that it was Laura herself who was paying his rent. But that lie ate into his feelings. He felt ashamed that he still depended upon her money, and would happily have lived in a hovel had it not been for Laura; but he still adored her – indeed Laura was all he loved – and if he stayed in the flat, and let her pay the rent, it was not because he liked the dreary basement, or wanted her to subsidize him, but because he wanted to do what she wanted, even if it involved his own humiliation. And he did, inescapably, feel humiliated since in the course of that first month after their return from Corfu they only met for sex in his flat.

At first, before he had a job, they would sometimes have lunch beforehand, but once he spent his days from nine until five lifting crates of wine or chests-of-drawers, that became impossible He might make a pot of tea but there was no time to toast crumpets because Laura had to be back before Francis got home. They therefore got down to what she was there for and once it was over she left.

The crudity of these encounters corroded the bond between them. Birek often returned to find the Mercedes already parked in the street outside his flat. She had a key and would be waiting with the pot of tea already made, but he was never able to have a bath or take a shower, partly because there was not time and partly because Laura said that she liked his smell of sweat.

Since his task was to please her, he dared not insist upon washing it off; indeed he became increasingly worried that his love-making fell short of her expectations. He was often tired after his day's work, and even when not tired he was nervous. This enervation affected her: she too became tense and there were times when their bouts were unsatisfactory to them both. When she left he sometimes wept, terrified that she would decide that the game was not worth the candle.

Laura too began to feel that there was something sordid about her regular visits to Birek's basement flat. The squalor of the surroundings isolated too crudely her reason for going there. She now understood why people went to Paris for their illicit affairs: the sex could be sandwiched between visits to the Louvre or walks along the Seine. Here in North Kensington she felt conspicuous in the Mercedes and was embarrassed to be so well dressed.

If Birek had not had to work during the week, or if she had not been taken up by her duties to her family at weekends, then they might have gone to the Tate or walked along the Thames; as it was, however, they could only meet for an hour or so in the late afternoon. There was no reason, of course, why Laura could not ask Birek to dinner at her house in Lansdowne Square. He was, quite apart from anything else, a single man and once the autumn season had got under way there were all the same old spinsters to be matched at table; but for some reason which it took Laura a time to divine, she felt an odd reluctance to include him. As September wore on she told herself that it would be unfair to Francis to bring him back into the house so soon: but when Francis himself asked after Birek, she was obliged to acknowledge that this was not the reason. The truth she was forced to face was that for both social and personal reasons, Laura did not want him at her table.

The social reasons sprang largely from the lionizing that had gone on before. The novelty of a celebrity lasts longer in London than it does in New York, but it does not last for ever. She had presented Birek to London as a persecuted genius whose works, once published, would astonish the world. Now, it turned out, his work was unpublishable: the lion was not a lion at all.

It had also to be acknowledged – now that she had removed the spectacles tinted by her early infatuation – that though useful in his capacity as a spare man, Birek was not much good at a party. Unlike Charlie, for example, who could always be relied upon to entertain his companions at table, Birek seemed to care about the truth of what he said, not about whether it was tactful or amusing. She remembered only too well the gaffe with Stephanie Parr and the debate with Theodore Zorn; but even those might be risked or avoided if Birek had pulled his weight in other ways. On the one occasion in late September when she did finally ask him to dinner, in obedience to Francis's prompting and her own bad conscience, he sat silently at table with a melancholy look on his face.

There was a third factor which made Laura reluctant to have Birek to dinner. She no longer liked the idea that people thought of him as her lover. In the spring and the summer, when he had been a celebrity, it had obviously raised her morale to know that others knew that this young genius had succumbed to her attractions: now she could not help seeing him through the eyes of others as 'the waiter' – a nickname now used not just by her children but by Charlie Eldon and his circle of friends. He was still handsome, of course, and she still took pleasure in his slender body, but hidden, alone, in the obscurity of his basement, not openly, publicly, in the light of day.

She knew, by early October, that the affair had to end. When Francis went to New York she took Birek out to dinner and meant to tell him then that it would be 'better' if she stopped her visits to his flat. When it came to the point, however, she could not bear to do it. He was so happy to have her for an evening on his own; so eager to be cheerful despite the constant undertow of melancholy; so proud that he could pay the bill; that she felt obliged to make a similar effort – to smile and affect a caressing tone of voice, hold his hand under the table, drink too much wine, then go back to his flat and make love when she did not particularly want to.

Thus the affair dragged on. She longed for something to happen to solve her predicament – for Birek to be offered a post teaching Czech at a Scottish polytechnic, or to be lured to America by some Mid-Western college which had not yet heard that his talent had been downgraded. She even had fantasies of which she was horribly ashamed of his visa being rescinded and his being obliged to seek asylum elsewhere.

Too weak to act without some external impulse, Laura waited – she even prayed – for something to turn up. One evening, in mid-October, she went to his flat as usual. The evenings were now darker and this was a particularly dark and rainy day. She went down the steps from the street to the door of his flat and did not notice that the drain had blocked leaving two or three inches of water. She stepped straight into this pool in her Manolo Blahnik shoes, cursed horribly and jumped back on to the steps.

She could see from the unlit windows that Birek had not returned, and since she had forgotten her key she could do nothing but return to the Mercedes and wait for him – the heater blowing warm air on to her soaking feet. She looked down at her shoes, which she had only bought the day before: they were ruined. She tapped her fingernails on the plastic of the steering wheel, recalling how they had cost her more than a hundred pounds. Ten minutes later, she saw Birek approach, his head in the hood of his anorak to keep off the rain. Seeing him thus like a bedraggled monk, she felt for the first time that she loathed him.

She went in all the same and while Birek took a spoon to dig out the cigarette cartons, crisp packets, icecream wrappers and sodden leaves which had blocked his drain, Laura stood with her back to the electric fire, breathing in the aroma of drainwater which arose from her damp feet.

They made tea in the usual way. Birek apologized over and over again for her wet feet and ruined shoes. When she had removed her tights and had hung them to dry on the arm of a chair in front of the fire, he sat on the floor and warmed her feet between his hands. As her feet thawed her mood improved, and when his hands strayed from her feet to her legs she even felt the desire which a short time before she had imagined was extinguished for ever; and when they had made love, and she saw his poignant body lying beside her, she once again could not bring herself to tell him that everything was over.

The time came to go home and, since Birek was not dressed, she left him at his door when she departed. It had stopped raining and she hesitated by the Mercedes while looking for the keys in her bag. The orange light of the street lamp shone down to show her where the keys were caught between her powder compact and credit card holder; and to show her also, as she came to unlock the car, three jagged stripes in its paintwork.

She blanched, cursed, crouched and saw to her horror that someone had gouged three lines along the full length of the Mercedes Estate with a chisel or a tin-opener. She stood and went to the other side of the car. It was untouched, but as she walked back to the pavement she saw that both the emblem on the bonnet and the radio aerial above the windscreen had been snapped off at the root – the aerial left lying in the gutter, the emblem no doubt kept as a souvenir.

She cursed again, got into the car and drove away – regretting the day that she had ever set foot in this dreadful area of London. She also thought fast of what she should tell Francis – where she should say the damage had been done. It was a company car, and Louards would almost certainly claim on the insurance. Forms would have to be signed and statements made – perhaps to the police – yet if she told the truth about where she had been, then the question would arise as to why she had been there. In the kind of superstitious way that often comes over us under duress, she saw the damage to the Mercedes as some sort of punishment for her sins and began to worry that worse might follow.

They stayed in that night, which was just as well, not only because Francis might have noticed the scratch had they gone out, but also because the winds which had blown from the west during the day grew first into a gale and finally into a hurricane – something quite unprecedented in the temperate climate of England. Both Laura and Francis were kept awake all night by the rattling of the sash windows and the occasional crack and crash as trees came down in the communal garden. Laura was so frightened that one might fall on the house that she actually clung on to her husband, something as unusual as the hurricane itself.

The devastation the next morning was such that Francis paid little attention to the damage done to his Mercedes. He noticed the scratch, and thought at first that it had been made by the branches which had been blown all over the road. Even when he realized that it was the work of hooligans, it did not occur to him that it had not been done in Lansdowne Square during the night. He would report it to the insurers from his office if, that is, he could get to his office: the news on the radio was that few trains were running.

There followed what turned out to be the most dramatic days of his life. The damage done by the hurricane was far worse than could be imagined from the few trees that had fallen in the communal gardens of Holland Park, but it was trivial when compared to the devastation of the financial markets which began that same day. Francis reached Louards on the Central Line, but with power supplies spasmodic and the computer systems not working, the few market makers who had got to work could only watch in horror as prices began to tumble first in New York and then Tokyo. With the screens blank on their VDUs, they resorted to the telephone to make their deals; but the positions they took were almost immediately overrun and the new positions had to be abandoned as quickly as they were taken as prices fell through the floor.

The weekend was hard for the brokers and bankers who had to contemplate the depredation of both their plantations and their portfolios. Risley, being in Wiltshire had escaped relatively unscathed, but a pretty umbrella pine was down at the end of the garden and one or two other trees had fallen around the farm. Inspecting the damage at least distracted Francis from his worries about the financial markets; but when he got back to Louards on the Monday morning his very worst fears were fulfilled. As soon as trading started, prices fell. Once again the positions taken by the market makers were proved by events to be absurdly optimistic. The bargains snapped up at nine were sold at a loss by ten, then bought again at midday at what had to be the floor, only to be sold again in the afternoon at a further catastrophic loss. Katz's young Turks at their VDUs trembled and even wept as Louards lost millions by the hour. New York opened, the Dow Jones index sank and the haemorrhage continued. As the sun rose slowly around the world, so the panic spread to Singapore, Hong Kong and Tokyo. Huge fortunes amassed over the past months evaporated before their eyes on the flickering screens.

In all this turmoil at Louards, only Francis remained calm. While Katz and Greenbaum screeched frantically to buy and sell or sell and buy, no longer knowing which or why, and while Lord Louard himself sat crumpled in a corner of his office as if his blood was seeping out of his body, Francis Morton sauntered around the office telling the young men and women who had never known a bear market how this sort of thing had happened before; how bulls always chased bears just as bears chased bulls; how what went down would come up again in time; how prices were still higher than they had been two years before. By the end of a day in which Louards lost between twelve and fifteen million pounds, this insouciance paid off. The trembling stopped, and tears were wiped away on the starched shirt-sleeves. Some colour came back into the market makers' faces. They were all poorer, perhaps, but they were alive. Katz and Greenbaum began to feel foolish and Lord Louard opened bottles of champagne to try and erase the impression made by his cowardice under fire.

In this way Francis's position as managing director, which had been uncertain after the crisis over Third World debt, was secured by the name he made for himself on Black Monday. His courage became the talk of the City. 'A remarkable fellow,' Lord Louard later told his friends. 'Looked as if he rather enjoyed it, or even as if he didn't care.' Of course no one believed that Francis had been indifferent: how can one be indifferent about money? And certainly the Mortons, on paper, were a great deal poorer. Louards' shares had halved in value and Laura's portfolio had gone down by a third.

Francis broke this news to his wife on the Tuesday evening. There seemed almost a glint in his eye as he told her that while they were by no means poor, they were considerably less rich than they had been the week before.

'But what does it mean in practical terms?' asked Laura crossly, as if Francis was somehow to blame for what had happened.

'I am not sure. We shall have to wait and see.'

The next morning Laura went to work as usual at the Comenius Foundation. There Andrew MacDonald called her into his office to say that Birek's rent was overdue. Laura replied a little sharply that he would have to ask Birek to pay his own rent. 'It isn't really fair to Francis,' she said, 'when you think of how much he already contributes to the Foundation.'

MacDonald looked perplexed. 'Couldn't you, perhaps, mention it to Birek?' he asked.

'I'm afraid not,' said Laura. 'You see now that his novel has been abandoned, I don't see him so much any more.'

She went back to her own desk and at once wrote a note to Birek in the style in which she thought such notes were written:

'My darling. I can hardly bear to write this – I couldn't say it on Thursday – but I cannot come and see you like that any more. I still love and respect you as much as I always did, but I can no longer bear the thought that in loving you I am betraying others. Please forgive me and in time come to think of me as your very, very best friend. L.'

She read it over quickly, afraid that Miroslav Maier might come up behind her. She wondered whether it was prudent to admit in writing that he had been her lover, but could not be bothered to re-write the letter so she put it in an envelope and sealed it. She then took her purse from her bag to find a stamp — she could hardly trust it to the office franking machine — and dithered between a first–class and a second–class stamp. Then deciding that it must reach him before the day he was expecting to see her again, she licked a first–class stamp and stuck it on the envelope, thinking as she did so one of those ignoble little thoughts which she immediately regretted – that the 18p was the very last sum of money that she would ever spend on Josef Birek.

NINETEEN

Birek found Laura's letter when he returned from work three days later. He had hoped to find her waiting for him, and thought at first that she must have delivered the note herself, but then he looked at the envelope and saw from the postmark that it had been sent three days before.

Two other letters had been delivered at the same time, but taking off his anorak, and going to sit at the pine table, he opened Laura's first. As we know, it was not long. He read it once in a moment, then a second, then a third time. He grasped at once what it meant – that their affair was at an end – but he could not make out why from any of its phrases. Convinced from his lessons in logic that every effect has a cause, he tried to analyse, decipher or read between the lines of the letter what had led her to dismiss him in this abrupt way.

It was a bad moment for detached thought of this kind because there was a searing feeling in his stomach and his heartbeat thudded in his ears. He put his elbows on the table, propped his head up with his hands, and read through the letter once again, pondering certain phrases such as 'I still love and respect you' and 'I am betraying others' and 'in time come to think of me as your very, very best friend'. The others, he assumed, were her husband and children. Had Francis perhaps discovered what was going on? Yet she had told him on several occasions that she thought Francis knew and had known for some time but did not care enough to make a fuss. And if he had just discovered, would she not have said so?

Birek was baffled. Nothing she had written seemed convincing. Perhaps, quite simply, she no longer loved him. He could not blame her for that. But if that was true, then why did she not say so instead of insisting that she would love him always? And why, he wondered, did she feel it necessary to reassure him that he still inspired her not just with love but with respect? No, he decided, it was impossible to end things with so many unanswered questions. He looked around his dark flat and his train of thought went a stage further: it was impossible to end it at all. He could not imagine life in London without Laura because without her it would be both unbearable and absurd. Her visits to his flat had been the stepping-stones which had carried him across the bog of his despair. If she no longer came, he would have no reason for living in this damp and desolate city.

He thought back to their last meeting – trying to recall whether there was something he might have said or done to offend her. He remembered her shoes getting wet, but that could not be the reason; then his warming her toes and caressing her legs. They had made love. She had seemed content – more content, indeed, than on some other occasions.

He would ring her and ask her to meet him at once in a café or a pub. There was no telephone in his flat so he put on his anorak again, and went out into the street. It was one of those dark evenings when drizzle falls from the orange fog and prickles the skin with the acid that it has filtered from the air. Birek walked down to the closest telephone box on the corner of Golborne Road. It smelt of urine and the line was dead. With little cause in the past to use a telephone, he did not know where the next one was but walked off down the Portobello Road. On Westbourne

Park Road he found two telephones. In the first he dialled the Mortons' number and waited, reading the stickers saying 'Lulu – French massage' and 'Scandinavian gives strict lessons to naughty boys'. Then Gail's voice answered the telephone but when he tried to insert his 10p piece he found that the slot was jammed. Gail was interrupted by a bleeping. Birek was obliged to ring off.

The next box did not even have a telephone: a wire hung limply from the receiver. Birek walked on. It would have been easier, now, to go to Lansdowne Square and ring the bell by the door, but Birek did not dare do that. He trudged instead all the way to Notting Hill and there, in the Underground station, found a telephone that was working.

He was afraid that by now Francis might have returned but once again it was Gail who answered.

He asked to speak to Laura.

'I'm afraid she's away.'

'I see. When will she be back?'

'Not for a month or so.'

'Where has she gone?'

'To Burma.'

Birek put the telephone back on the receiver and went out of the station into the street. Burma! To Birek who did not know that almost all of the Mortons' friends had been to Burma the thought of this country on the other side of the world finally made him realize that he had lost Laura for ever. He walked past Spud-U-Like and the Wimpy Bar quite forgetting that he would have to buy some supper, and went down towards Ladbroke Grove. Instinctively he was walking in the direction of Lansdowne Square, and it was only when he reached Ladbroke Grove itself that he realized his mistake and set off up the hill, past St John's Church, then down again, under the double viaduct, towards the Golborne Road.

He got back to his flat and after his long walk felt hungry. He went to his fridge in which there was nothing but half a carton of apple juice, poured it into a mug and went back to the living-room where he sat once again at the table. Laura's letter lay where he had left it, but he did not pick it up to read it again. Burma had made everything clear. Instead he opened the two other letters which had been delivered at the same time. The first was from Godfrey and Co, Valuers and Estate Agents, asking for rent of £541.66. The second was from Andrew MacDonald explaining courteously that the Foundation could no longer subsidize his lodging. 'As I think you know,' he wrote, 'our resources are finite and there are many calls upon them. I trust you do not feel that we have treated you ungenerously: we are still actively pursuing every opportunity for finding you employment suited to your talents, and remain eager to help in any reasonable way.'

To say that Birek now disappeared would be to dramatize and exaggerate what occurred. He was obliged, of course, to leave his flat because he could not pay the rent from his wages, and after looking for some days at the cards offering rooms displayed in newsagents, and studying the classified advertisements in the *Evening Standard*, he found a room in Acton for £35 a week. There were other lodgers in the same house – one of them was a Nigerian student – but this did not deter Birek: he was no longer worried about catching AIDS.

The Comenius Foundation knew his address – they forwarded a series of increasingly threatening letters from the landlords of the flat off the Golborne Road who claimed that they had not received due notice of his departure; but Madge, for example, whom Laura had asked to be kind to Birek before she left for Burma, could claim with some justice that she did not know where to write to him to ask him to Sunday lunch.

Nor did Birek himself try to get in touch with any of Laura's friends. He held his job at the repository, and earned enough to pay his rent and buy the basic necessities of life. He never went out in the evening with either his work-mates or fellow lodgers – indeed days would pass when his only contact with others were the commands he received about loading and unloading pantechnicons. Some of those he came across made efforts to befriend him – he was nice-looking, after all – but their approaches were always rebuffed. Birek cherished and cultivated his sadness because it was the shadow of the woman he loved. He did not want to forget Laura and held her image in his mind from the moment he awoke to the moment he went to sleep. He relived in his memory the scenes from his life with the Mortons – not just the passionate encounters with Laura but also the everyday incidents with Francis, Gail and the children. He missed them as much as his mistress, and sometimes dreamed that he was lying on the lawn at Risley or back in his room in Lansdowne Square.

That these people actually existed, and were living only two or three miles from his room in Acton, and even closer to the repository at Shepherd's Bush, was discounted in his mind. Even when he took a bus up Holland Park Avenue, he never turned to look in the direction of the house where he had been so happy. Since Laura had gone to Burma, her home could as well have been moved to Mandalay. The day of her return passed unnoticed. He did not expect her to make contact with him and when, in December, he moved lodgings again he did not give his new address to the Comenius Foundation so that they could not forward the letters from Godfrey and Co.

He did not try to write any poems or stories but in the evenings watched a rented television. Occasionally he read a newspaper and saw articles by Bartle, Henriot or Charlie Eldon; but they too had become figures from another life in another city. Perhaps it was just as well. He often wept when he was alone and looked for consolation in the Czech Bible which he had brought from Prague. It was difficult, however, to ask God to console him since his misery, he recognized, was the result of sin; and whenever he fell on his knees to pray to Mary, the Mother of God, her image was supplanted by that of Laura who smiled at him in a profane way.

On the Saturday before Christmas Birek was mugged by two tall young men with black skin and flashing eyes. They tripped him up, kicked him, then ran away with his wallet. He was therefore penniless and friendless and the repository was closed for a week. The thought of Christmas, however, reminded him of the church he had gone to in happier times. There he might find some charity, forgiveness and consolation. On the Sunday morning he got up in good time and took a train to the centre of London.

He found the church, sat through the service, and as before was invited into the parish hall. Here the good people were serving not coffee but mulled wine which Birek, who had not had any breakfast, accepted gratefully and quickly swallowed down. The effect of the wine, and the soothing sentiments inspired by the ceremony in the church, made Birek almost cheerful. He was encouraged that he was remembered by the two young men he had met before, and after a second and then a third glass of mulled claret, he accepted their invitation to Sunday lunch. 'We're having a sort of pre-Christmas celebration,' said the one, 'before we all go back to our horrible Mums and Dads.'

They led the way back to their flat in Ebury Street which was large and elegantly furnished. A table was laid for nine and the first of the young men, who was called Simon, quickly added another place. Remembering Laura's anxieties about even numbers, Birek hoped that his presence would not upset the balance between the sexes but when at around two all the guests were assembled it turned out that in fact there were to be no women at all. Some of the men were older, some were younger; many wore cashmere jumpers and pastel-coloured shirts. They all widened their eyes and gave lingering hand shakes when they were introduced to Birek, but it was the curate from the church, whom they called Gerry, who was placed next to him at table.

The food was unusually delicious – or so it seemed to Birek, who since the summer had eaten only in cafés and out of tins. There were a few squeals of laughter when Simon carved the goose and jokes were made about the stuffing up its bum. There were many bottles of Rhône wine, and with the Christmas pudding some sweet champagne. Birek drank as much as the others: Gerry made sure that his glass was always filled. Indeed Gerry was exceptionally solicitous and being rather older than Birek, and trained in the seminary to be sympathetic towards sinners, coaxed out of him the whole sad story of his love affair with Laura.

'Just forget her, that's my advice,' he said with a toss of his head. 'Women really aren't worth it. From Eve onwards, they've just led to a lot of trouble.'

Birek laughed. 'That's true, but we could hardly have managed without them.'

'On the contrary,' said Gerry, 'we would have managed very well.'

Birek laughed again. Sitting rather drunk among such friendly fellows, he felt that perhaps Gerry was right.

And so lunch went on until it began to get dark, when with a groan some of the guests left and others stayed to help clear up the débris of coffee cups, ashtrays and paper hats. Birek did his bit, under Gerry's instructions, but then, when almost everything had been taken from the table, he was stopped by Gerry in the narrow corridor which led from the dining-room to the kitchen.

'Look,' said the curate, his eyes raised.

Birek looked up. A sprig of a green plant with white berries was pinned to the ceiling. 'What is it?' he asked.

'Mistletoe,' said Gerry.

'And why is it there?'

'Why indeed!' Gerry took hold of his hand. 'But rules are rules. We have to kiss if we meet under the mistletoe.' So saying he pressed his lips to Birek's.

Birek was so astonished that he staggered back against a door. Gerry's hand which was anyway at Birek's bottom turned the handle and, like an instructor teaching dancing cheek-to-cheek, the curate led Birek from the corridor into the room.

'But what are you doing?' Birek asked.

'Love,' murmured Gerry, 'the only command is to love . . .' Then shutting the door with his foot, and clutching Birek once again, he kissed him with an open mouth and busy tongue while one hand clasped his buttocks and the other fondled between his legs.

'No,' mumbled Birek trying to pull away.

'Come on,' panted the other. 'You must be desperate after so long.'

For a moment Birek remained paralysed in the curate's embrace as in horror he realized that his body was reacting as if what he had said was true. A part of him longed to succumb, but another – the greater part – was revolted, and despite the weakening of the will that came from drinking so much wine, he gripped the man's wrists, prised his arms open, pushed him back towards the bed, then left the room and fled from the flat.

He ran, then walked, then ran again through streets of pale classical façades – disgusted by what had been done to him and horrified at his own reaction. Beneath the froth of his self-disgust was the constant awareness that he was friendless and penniless in an

233

alien city. In his pocket was the last fifty pence he possessed, and feeling completely weary as the effects of the wine wore off, and longing to get back to the privacy of his room, he went into the station at Sloane Square and bought a fifty – pence ticket from the machine.

It was Sunday evening. There were very few trains, but eventually one came on the Circle Line which carried him around to Notting Hill Gate. There he got off, intending at first to change on to the Central Line which would take him to Acton, but then he remembered that his ticket was only valid for the inner zone. He might have tried to bluff his way through the barrier at Acton, but he dared not for fear of getting involved with the police; yet he hesitated after being robbed the night before to walk so many miles through the dark and empty streets. He therefore sat on a bench with his head in his hands, paralysed by his own exhaustion and despair.

Until that moment Birek had been sustained by self-pity. There was even a kind of heroism in his own perception of what he had suffered through love, and a consoling detachment in the thought that in time it could be used as the basis for a novel. But his response to the curate had changed self-pity into self-disgust. Birek the hero, the martyr, the tragic victim, now changed in his own mind into Birek the posturing catamite – open to offers from either sex. And this made Birek long not to be Birek and as the next train approached he saw his chance. He stood, staggered to the edge of the platform, swayed as the clattering of the wheels grew louder, then lurched forward on to the line.

A hand grabbed his arm and pulled him back. The train hit his shoulder and Birek felt a sudden atrocious pain which reminded him at once that he was still alive. He looked round at the man who had saved him and imagined that he heard him say something in Czech. The driver of the train ran back to see what had happened. Birek, half-fainting, heard him offer to call an ambulance, but the small thick-set man who held him said in very bad English that it was not necessary – that his friend was only drunk.

The driver returned to his cab. The train moved out of the station. Birek, propped against the other man, staggered up the steps and passed through the ticket barrier, then up a further flight of steps to the street.

'Courage, comrade,' said the man in Czech. 'The fresh air will make you feel better.'

'Who are you?' asked Birek, wincing with pain as he spoke.

'Pavel Svesda, at your service. Driver at the embassy of the Socialist Republic of Czechoslovakia.' He said this in a humorous tone of voice as if he was a modern reincarnation of the Good Soldier Schweik.

'Have you been following me?' Birek asked.

'Follow you? No. I've got better things to do with my time.'

'But you know who I am?'

'Of course I do, Comrade Birek. Your face was in all the English newspapers.'

'But where are you taking me?' asked Birek, suddenly alarmed.

'The embassy is just here,' said the Czech. 'Our doctor can look at your arm.'

'But the embassy . . .' murmured Birek, almost fainting from the pain in his shoulder.

'It's not paradise,' said his compatriot, 'but if you ask me, it's better than under a train.'

When Birek gave his press conference, his arm was still in a sling. He was returning to Czechoslovakia, he said in a lifeless voice, because he was disillusioned with life in the West. 'Our society may have its faults,' he said, 'but its shortcomings cannot be compared to the decadence and injustice which I have encountered here.'

There was a brief furore on television and in the press at this public repudiation of the British way of life. The Comenius Foundation issued a statement claiming that Birek had been kidnapped and beaten. This was proved by the sling, and his sullen reading of a prepared statement suggested that he had either been drugged or blackmailed into reviling the West before going home.

Some newspapers took this up and sent reporters to investigate the Czechs' claim that Birek's shoulder had been dislocated by an Underground train. The ticket collector at Notting Hill described how Birek had been frog-marched out of the station and the driver denied that anyone had been hit by his train. The Home Office therefore insisted that before allowing Birek to board the plane for

Prague he should talk to two officials without any embassy personnel being in the same room. This was agreed but Birek confirmed that he was going back of his own free will. He appeared pale and hardly happy but there was nothing to suggest that he was either drugged or afraid.

That, then, was that. The news of his departure was taken off the front page and became a minor item of home news. Within a week no one in London gave him another thought. Within a month his name was forgotten. Only the Comenius Foundation showed any curiosity about what had happened to him upon his return, and by the end of February some rumours reached the émigrés in London. 'It's typical of Birek's luck,' Miroslav Maier told MacDonald. 'He's got off with a suspended sentence thanks to the influence of his father.'

In the spring of 1988 Milos Jakes replaced Gustav Husak as Communist leader in Czechoslovakia. Some said that had it not been for the son's defection it might have been Jaroslav Birek, but the father was an ally of Jakes and so no one was surprised when that summer Josef Birek was employed as an editor at the publishing house of Mlada Fronta. As Maier said, with a certain satisfaction, it was always only a matter of time before he sold out. 'He never writes anything any more, either in samizdat or for the official publications. And from what I hear the other dissidents don't even stop to spit at him when they see him in the street.'

This was related by Andrew MacDonald to the Mortons one evening when he went to their house for dinner. He could not tell Laura at the office because Laura had stopped working for the Foundation shortly after her return from Burma. She had picked up a resilient form of amoebic dysentery from contaminated water in Rangoon which had made her both weak and depressed. She had decided that in the end it was too much to try to run a home and do a job.

She had recovered by Christmas but remained at Risley until the very last days of the school holidays. She was therefore there when the news broke about Birek's return to Prague and for a week or so she became a very hot property for the dinner parties of the Wiltshire set. Was he kidnapped? Was he drugged? How had he broken his arm? Laura, of course, said she knew no better than anyone else but she was very skilled at suggesting as she did so that there were things she could not say.

Back in London, in mid-January, she faced the old problem of how to fill her empty days. It was too cold and wet for tennis and her experience of Burma had put her off planning any further trips abroad. The round of dinner parties was slow to get going, as it always was after Christmas. She had lunch with Madge and talked about Birek: Madge said that Ben had been told that Birek had been a spy all along. She had lunch with Emma when she came to London, and lunch with Eva to discuss redecorating the drawing-room in Lansdowne Square; but somehow lunch with women was not the same as lunch with men, and while she never for a moment missed Birek, she sometimes missed certain things about him.

In early March she gave a dinner and Charlie Eldon was one of the guests. He was the last to leave, as he always was, and had his traditional last-minute chat with Laura. Francis, after shuffling around picking up the glasses, had said good-night and had gone to bed. Laura saw Charlie to the door and as he was putting on his coat said: 'You never ask me out to lunch any more.'

'Whenever you like. Where would you like to go?'

She mentioned, quite by chance, the restaurant near his flat and they made a date to meet there the following week. It did a lot for her morale to have something to put down in her diary, and an excuse to have her hair done and buy a new skirt. She looked her best when she sat down in the restaurant, and from the look Charlie gave as he greeted her she knew that he appreciated the trouble she had taken.

Their conversation, as a result, though only about this and that, had, or so she imagined, a particular tenderness in its tone. After coffee he paid the bill and they went out together into the street.

'Have you got your car?' he asked.

'Yes. Why? Do you want a lift?'

'No. I'll take a bus to Fleet Street.'

'If you want, I'll take you there.'

'Don't bother.'

'Or if you've forgotten your copy,' she said with a smile, 'I'll walk back with you to fetch it.'

He patted his coat over his inside pocket. 'This time I remembered. I've got it here.'

She thought he might not have understood what she was trying to convey. 'We could go there anyway and have another cup of coffee.'

'I wish I had time,' he said, glancing at his watch, 'but if it's late it won't make the early edition.'

She smiled again but a quite different smile – a grin to hide her humiliation. 'Well thanks for the lunch,' she said, kissing him on the cheek.

'I'll see you soon.'

'Yes. In fact if you're free on Thursday, come to dinner. The Grays and the Bonningtons are coming and so is Emma so we're short of a man.'

When Laura got back to Lansdowne Square Eva Burroughs was waiting with samples for the new curtains. 'I'm sorry I wasn't here,' said Laura. 'I was having lunch with Charlie.'

'With Charlie? How funny. Because I had lunch with Emma.'

'She seems to come up to London all the time these days.'

'Well of course she does. Haven't you heard?'

'Heard what?'

'Well, Charlie and Emma . . .'

'Oh that! Yes. But both of them told me to keep it a secret.'

When Francis returned that evening, he changed as usual into his slippers and a jersey and then went to chat to Laura in her bath.

'I can never understand,' she snapped at him, 'why you take off your jacket and put on a jersey when you're going to take it off again five minutes later.'

'It is a little silly,' he said, turning to go back to the bedroom since Laura was better avoided when she was in a mood of this kind. 'It's just a habit.'

'Then break it.'

He shuffled out of the bathroom and went upstairs to say goodnight to Lucy. She hugged him and kissed him and made him ponder that in a year or two's time, when she grew out of that sort of thing, he would have to learn to live without any such gestures of human affection.

238

About the Author

PIERS PAUL READ was born in 1941, brought up in Yorkshire and educated at Cambridge. In addition to two years spent in Germany and one in the United States, he traveled extensively behind the Iron Curtain, in the Far East and South America. He is married, has four children and lives in London. *A Season in the West* is his tenth novel.